DEADLY ECHO

A gripping British murder mystery

CHRISTINE GREEN

Kate Kinsella Mysteries Book 6

JOFFE
Ostara
CLASSICS

Revised edition 2024
Joffe Books, London
www.joffebooks.com

First published by Severn House Publishers Ltd
in Great Britain in 2002

This paperback edition was first published
in Great Britain in 2024

Cover art by Dee Dee Book Covers

ISBN: 978-1-83526-320-4

For my lovely grandchildren,
Jack and Rebecca.

CHAPTER ONE

The trouble with dogs is that they have irregular habits and require walking in rain or shine. They also affect your street cred. As a private investigator virtually unknown in Longborough I now have several admirers but only in the dog world. I'm not the object of their interest, however, it's Jasper. Hubert Humberstone, my landlord, having been dogless for all his fifty-odd years, acquired Jasper only last year. Jasper is a terrier with no pretensions and no claim to good looks, other than the ability to look pathetic on the right occasions. Unfortunately, either by nature or nurture, he seems attracted only to male dogs. But, like parents, Hubert and I both think Jasper can do no wrong and is far superior to other, flashier dogs.

Hubert does have trouble with his image, being tall and having a face which I think has grown to look like his profession — undertaker — he is self-conscious on dog walks. He'd prefer a racy Afghan hound or a Rottweiler to enhance his image. My image is more suited to a stout little terrier.

I'm single, slightly past the curvy stage but not yet past my sell-by date. I'm currently working on the theory that, if I only celebrate my birthday once every two years, my thirties will last two decades. I'll feel younger as a result and, by having two years' worth of birthday cards in one go, I would feel tremendously popular, which would make a change.

It's April now and I am, at the moment, *resting* until someone realizes they need my services and so I'm doing more than my share of dog walks. As Hubert points out, *he* cannot rest until he's called to his permanent lie-in. I, on the other hand, should be more *proactive*. Hubert is being swayed by the current trend towards a more American style of death, so he's started using the jargon, but how either of us can be *that* proactive, I don't know. I'm in *Yellow Pages* and I've got a web site, so all I can do is wait and walk Jasper.

This weekend Hubert has gone to the annual Funeral Directors' Conference in Frinton-on-Sea — *a good customer base*, according to Hubert. Hardly anyone lives there under fifty and, according to him, the slow pace, the sea air and the lack of a fish-and-chip shop still don't mean they live for ever. Away from his hotel he hands out his business cards to any likely looking customers. The fact that we're a long way from the sea doesn't bother him. 'How many people are actually *born* in Frinton-on-Sea?' he asked me. 'Don't even try to answer, Kate — I'll just say that the departed go back to their point of origin. They have to. Frinton's graveyards and crematoria couldn't cope.'

I try to keep cheerful in spite of living above an undertaker's, but, with time on my hands, it does get difficult. Especially as it's Friday night and it's Jasper and I on the sofa watching some buttock-clenchingly boring television, and now his last walk is due and it's bucketing with rain. Jasper, unlike other dogs, doesn't seem to mind the rain. The little swine won't pee until he's sniffed every bush, tree trunk and street light for what seems like miles. His favourite place is near the river, because nearly every dog in Longborough uses the riverside walk for physical or predatory purposes.

I rarely use the word *walk* in front of Jasper but, genius that he is, he can now recognize W–A–L–K, even said in a whisper.

I'd barely picked up my mac when he went into paroxysms of excitement and hurled himself down the stairs to the side door. I rarely use the front of the building for obvious reasons of mental comfort.

I'd pulled the hood of my mac over my head and the force of the rain sounded thunderous in my ears. Puddles had already formed all over the car park and I did think of driving to the river but Jasper's strong little body pulled me forward.

On the way to the river we didn't see a soul. Sensible people stayed indoors on such a night. Jasper sniffed unconcernedly whenever I gave him the chance. The insides of my shoes were wet and I began to recognize the *Showerproof* label on my mac was telling the truth. It was not deluge-proof.

By the time we arrived at the river, even Jasper, looking like a drowned gremlin, had lost his enthusiasm. I felt past caring — wet is wet and, as long as Jasper kept going and didn't spend valuable excretory time on sniffing, I resolved that we'd run back and then I'd have a hot bath followed by a hot toddy. Jasper could have a rub down and warm Weetabix and, if he was really good, he could settle down with me to watch the erotic film on Channel Five.

Although the night was dark and visibility down to only a few yards, there were old-fashioned lamps lining the river walk. Jasper had regular sniffs at these, followed by a little leg-cocking and an attempt at a crouch. Strange how fussy dogs can be. I rummaged in my mac pocket for a plastic bag, wondering if I'd even see his offering, if any, in the murky light.

Still he pulled me on and I felt tempted to let him off his lead. I looked around just to check that my eyes hadn't deceived me. They *had* stayed true. There were no other dog walkers mad enough to be out on such a night. I snapped his lead from his collar.

'Go on then, Jasper,' I said. 'Get on with it!'

He was off like a damp rocket along the path. I sheltered under some bushes and waited. And waited. 'Jasper!' I shouted, into the rainswept murk. 'I'm cold and wet and fed up — just do it!'

I'd just decided to leave the relative shelter of the bush when I heard him barking. To a non-dog-owner, I suppose, all barks sound the same, but I was attuned to Jasper's various woofs, yelps, whines, growls and yaps. He was in some sort of trouble. Please God, not in the river. I'd have to go in after him but I'm not a strong swimmer and the river was steadily rising. I began running towards the sound. Just as I thought I had a fix on it, he changed to a low fretful whine that I could hardly hear above the rain.

In the gloom I eventually found him, by a tree. He'd stopped whining and was sniffing a bundle of old rags. 'Come on, Jasper,' I said, slipping on his lead. 'You can't eat that. Let's go home.' He resisted, but I gave a little tug on his lead and he began to follow me, but his head turned and he whined again. Something was bothering him but there was no way I was going to actually touch a bundle of old rags, so I walked nearer to the sodden mound and flicked at it gingerly using the toe of my shoe. It felt solid and, when it moved slightly, I nearly fell over with shock. Jasper barked his yappy *I'm-really-ferocious-and-I'll-defend-you-to-the-death* bark. I'd already moved backwards ready to make a run for it. Corpse, tramp, vagrant, drug addict all sprang to mind.

Then, from beneath the dark covering, there was a twisting motion and the back of a head emerged, then the white face of a young woman. It was one of those moments when shock and surprise leave you speechless. *Are you all right?* sounded fatuous, because she was bedded down at night in a deluge under a bush. Eventually I asked, 'Is there anything I can do? Are you hurt?' She shook her head. I couldn't see her face in any detail but she looked plump and didn't have the waif-like appearance of a heroin addict. It was the end of April and even the dry nights were still cold. 'You'll die of hypothermia if you stay here,' I said. She stared back at me, dumbly. 'I could telephone someone,' I suggested. 'There are hostels.'

'No,' she said, her voice hoarse. 'I'll go now.' She began to get up, slowly and stiffly, and I guessed that the reason she wasn't shivering was that she was past that stage. I was shivering by now and Jasper, for some reason, began to whimper. 'Where will you go?' I asked.

'I don't know,' she said, sounding confused. She was wearing a navy padded jacket and she bent down to pick up a large shoulder bag. I noticed she wore sodden, black, terry-towelling bedroom slippers. My thought then was — either she was an escapee from a mental hospital or from a domestic fracas.

I rooted in my mac pocket but all I could find was a pound coin. That wouldn't help much. 'Come with me to my place. I've got some money. I'll find you a bed and breakfast place.' She didn't answer, but we began walking to the sound of belting rain and squelching feet. Her gait was slow and cumbersome and Jasper wanted to rush ahead. I slowed to her pace. I was perished and, as we neared stronger street lighting, I saw that my companion looked, not just cold and wet, but ill. She seemed near to collapse and I took her arm and offered to carry her bag. 'I can manage, thank you.'

Now that she'd said more than six words, I'd identified her accent. She was Welsh. 'What's your name?'

'Why do you want to know?'

'I don't particularly, but it's polite to call you something. My name's Kate.'

Once we were walking back along the main path, within sight of civilization, I half expected her to say she had changed her mind and that she would go back to her boyfriend, or her hospital, or wherever, but she didn't.

Eventually we reached the side entrance of Humberstone's. She seemed not to notice the sign on my doorway, which stated I was a *Private Investigator, RGN* and other abbreviations of a dubious nature, that Hubert thought added to my professional persona. As I opened the door, deciding to keep Jasper on the lead to stop him shaking himself all the way up the stairs, she said, 'I've got money. I don't need money. Don't leave me, will you? Please?' What could I do? In the light of the hall, although she was well covered, she was corpse-white, with huge black rings under her dark eyes. There was a pleading fearful expression in those eyes and she had the same effect on me as Jasper did.

'You can stay here the night. I'm on my own. But perhaps you should be in hospital.'

'No, please. I'll be no trouble. I'll go in the morning. I'm not ill.'

Upstairs, Jasper was beginning to shake himself and it was a toss-up between which one I looked after first. My mysterious guest was now sagging at the knees, so, holding on to her arm, I grabbed a towel and sat her down on the loo seat in the bathroom. Then I gave Jasper a brisk rub down and told him his Weetabix was on its way, which sent him scurrying to the kitchen.

I began running a bath for *herself*. 'You'd better get out of those wet clothes and give me a false name if you like.'

'Megan Thomas. That's my real name.'

'Right Megan. Have you got a change of clothes in your bag?'

'I've only got one tracksuit.'

'OK. Not to worry. I've got pyjamas somewhere and an old dressing gown.' I rummaged around in the bottom of my wardrobe and, when I went back to the bathroom, she'd taken off her jacket, slippers and trousers. Although the bathroom was warm, she'd now begun to shiver. All I'd taken off, so far, was my mac and my shoes and I hoped she wasn't an *hour-long-soak-in-the-bath* sort of person, because I wanted to get out of my damp clammy clothes.

Once the bath was full, I tested the temperature with my elbow — nurse training dies hard. It was hot but not too hot.

'I expect you're hungry,' I said.

'I like Weetabix too,' she said, in a low monotone that still had the faint Welsh upward inflexion on the word *too*.

I'd sussed by now that Megan was either in shock, hypothermic, depressed — and who wouldn't be after sleeping rough — or she was bordering on a level of intelligence often exhibited by those on 18–30 holidays. Either way, she was not sparky. 'OK, Megan,' I said. 'Hot Weetabix all round.'

I left her to take a bath and warmed up milk for Jasper. He finished the cereal in no time and took to his basket and was asleep in seconds.

Then, I have to admit, I listened outside the bathroom door. I didn't expect her to be singing in the bath. I just didn't want her to drown herself or faint as she got out.

After a while I knocked and she murmured, 'Come in.' Her voice sounded a little muffled. She was towel-drying her hair and her face had lost its ashen tinge. 'How are you feeling?' I asked.

'Much better, thank you,' she said, with the tightest of smiles. I had a strong feeling she was going to be hard work.

She ate in silence, drank a mug of cocoa, ate six chocolate biscuits and, although I tried to find out how she came to be sleeping rough, she simply stared at me, then fell asleep. I'd planned to let her sleep in the sofa bed in my office, but I didn't have the heart to wake her, so I covered her with a duvet, switched off the light and crept off to my bedroom.

As I lay in bed listening to the rain, I had a feeling Megan was going to be trouble. She wouldn't give me earache with incessant chatter but her reticence could be a problem. In the morning, I thought, all will get sorted. Surely someone would want to claim her. She seemed stodgy in both the looks and personality department but someone, somewhere, must know her and want her back. At least that was my theory.

Jasper crept into my room in the middle of the night and whimpered by my bed until, half-asleep, I threw the duvet back and lifted him in. He smelt slightly damp still but, as he nuzzled his cold nose into my neck, I felt quite content.

A night's sleep wrecked my memory. Still in the twilight zone, I walked into the lounge at eight thirty and was shocked to see her, fully dressed, standing at the window. The balm of sleep had made me forget that I had a dilemma named Megan on my hands. She wore a grey tracksuit. Her dark hair hung straight and lank. She turned in my direction. 'I've just seen a hearse drive up.'

'Yes. This flat is above an undertaker's. The director, Hubert, is my landlord.' Did she sound perturbed by that? I wasn't sure. Her voice and accent didn't give much away.

I hoped she'd decide to leave after breakfast — she was very much like a one-night stand that you couldn't wait to get rid of.

'I've got no knickers to wear,' she said, with a pathetic expression that Jasper would have been proud of. For someone who said so little, what she *did* say seemed to have a paralysing effect on my vocal chords. I should have been generous and told her she could have a pair of mine, but I was fairly attached to my new knicker selection, having finally thrown out those with trailing elastic and indistinct colour.

'You left in a hurry then?' I said.

'I just grabbed the tracksuit.'

'You were frightened?'

'Very frightened.'

'Where was this?'

'I'm not sure.'

'You're not sure?'

'It was dark. I got a lift in a lorry and he dropped me off. I saw the sign — Longborough — and wandered down to the river.'

'You weren't sleeping rough, were you?'

'No. I was waiting till the river rose high enough and then I was going to let myself be swept away.'

I felt guilty about the knickers then. 'I'll find you a pair of knickers and we'll have breakfast — do you fancy a fry-up?'

'Yes, please. I'm really hungry.'

Perhaps for the first time I noticed how young she was. 'How old are you, Megan?'

'I'm twenty,' she said, as if that was old.

In my bedroom I searched out my third-best knickers — lacy but stretchy. For once I knew someone whose bum was bigger than mine and, somehow, that softened the sacrifice.

'You're very kind,' she said.

In the kitchen, she watched my prowess with a frying pan. 'I can cook and clean,' she said. Was that meant to be a reference, I wondered? Jasper, hearing and scenting the sizzling concoction, was salivating at the doorway. 'Don't worry, Jasper,' I said. 'One sausage is earmarked for you.' He wagged his tail and grovelled at Megan's feet. 'Jasper, I'm the cook — you should do any kowtowing in front of me.'

Jasper, being highly intelligent and knowing I butter his bread, switched allegiance immediately.

After breakfast and a desultory chat about Megan's basic cookery skills, she went off to the bathroom and I went into the lounge to fold up the duvet. There, on the floor, was her shoulder bag. It was more of a holdall really. It looked fairly heavy and I couldn't resist a peek. With one eye on the door I unzipped the bag. But soon both eyes were riveted on the contents. Bundles and bundles of notes. Only in films had I seen so much money. I couldn't guess how much. Thousands and thousands. The innocent, knickerless Megan could afford to buy her own knicker shop. No wonder she was on the run. Her reticence and naivety were obviously just one big con. Bank robber or mere thief, her plain exterior obviously hid some secrets.

I zipped the bag up quickly. All my instincts told me to kick her out. She was definitely trouble.

As she appeared in the doorway, smiling her tight little smile, she seemed suddenly sinister. Had I already left it too late?

CHAPTER TWO

The brief smile on her face soon disappeared and, for a few moments, I forgot about the money because I was looking at something else. The grey sweatshirt she was wearing was wet at the front, on both breasts. She saw my expression and folded her arms across her chest. 'I'm very tired,' she said. 'Do you mind if I have a sleep?'

'Use my bed,' I said. 'I'm going to take Jasper out for his walk.' Jasper heard the word and his tail wagged and he began turning joyful circles. My mind was also turning circles but not the joyful kind. I needed to think and walking Jasper would give me time.

Outside, the sun shone weakly but everywhere there was still the damp residue from the night's downpour. Jasper trotted ahead, tail in the air, and I tried to think. How would I get rid of her? She was still pale and exhausted but she wasn't at death's door, so I couldn't call an ambulance. The leaking breasts and the money were an additional complication. One thought that had crossed my mind was that she'd sold her baby. Or, maybe — and this was a chilling thought — she'd given birth by the river and somewhere near there she'd abandoned it. That didn't explain the money though. Had she robbed a post office or a bank to fund care of the baby? Perhaps the baby had died . . . *Stop it*, I told myself. Conjecture and imagination were a waste of time. The only person who knew the full story was Megan and when we returned she'd either tell me or I'd ring the police and get her removed.

Jasper, pulling me enthusiastically, led me back along the riverbank. The dry weather had brought out more dogs and their owners. We exchanged pleasantries, if the dogs allowed it, and I tried to avoid those who looked likely to jump up and cover me in muddy paws.

Now, in daylight, I tried to find the place we'd discovered Megan. It was muddy underfoot and Jasper's paws and my boots were already covered in mud. I found the spot at the base of a tree, amongst bushes that had a crushed area, and I explored all around for anything that might suggest a baby had either been born there or left to die. There was nothing.

The river level had risen and my eyes scanned the water looking for anything unusual. I noticed a child's red and white ball wedged amongst the reeds along with the odd lager can bobbing up and down. Again, there was nothing unusual. 'Come on, Jasper,' I said. 'Home and bath.'

The homeward journey was marked by Jasper's tardiness. Perhaps it was the thought of the bath or merely the fact that his walk was coming to an end. Eventually, though, we arrived and I carried Jasper upstairs, closed the bathroom door so he couldn't escape and ran his three inches of water — any more than that and he seemed to fear drowning.

Once he was bathed and towel-dried he sloped off to his basket in the kitchen and I went to check on Megan. I half hoped she'd simply disappeared but she hadn't. She was fast asleep in my bed breathing so deeply it was a virtual snore. Long-distance travel did that to me. I noticed her holdall was beside the bed. I certainly didn't have the heart to wake her.

I washed up and vacuumed and put the washing machine on. It wasn't relaxing. It made me feel more on edge. Hubert was due back tomorrow and he might decide to forego the conference Sunday lunch and come home early. Although I had an office and a bedroom and bathroom, the lounge and the kitchen were his domain. I did have the freedom of the top floor, but there was no way Megan could still be around when he came home. Hubert liked order and routine and a pale depressed waif was unlikely to be a welcome guest. If she wore eight-inch heels and a short skirt, he might feel differently. Shoes and feet were Hubert's little peccadillo. Harmless enough, but it restricted his choice of women. He'd been married once and had shown a brief interest in my mother, who had all the right tarty credentials and, in a dim light, could pass for a mere forty-five, but her middle name is fickle and she'd recently decided to take a working holiday in Greece. No doubt in the hope she'd meet a toy boy. She'd told me she would find work as a waitress. Thank God she really was well past the pole dancing stage because, given half a chance, that's the sort of thing she would do.

It did mean that, for a while, my small terraced house in Farley Wood would be free. I hadn't been there since my mother had flown the coop but, knowing her, the place would be a complete tip and take me weeks to put right.

Saturday progressed and, by late afternoon, there was still no sign of Megan making an appearance. I checked on her at regular intervals, just in case she'd slipped into a coma or was quietly haemorrhaging to death, but she looked OK, whilst I became more of a nervous wreck. When the local paper arrived I scanned it for robberies, burglaries or abandoned babies and, although there was the usual amount of crime, there was nothing to indicate the involvement of a young woman, Welsh or otherwise.

Finally, as I was growing fraught at the thought of my having to face the awfulness of another round of either *Blind Date* or *Casualty* on TV, she appeared. Her face was pinker and creased, she was still wearing the tracksuit and her eyes seemed swollen, but she sat down on the sofa and asked, 'Is it Saturday?'

'All day. It's just after seven.'

'I like *Blind Date*,' she said.

'Well, in that case we'll watch it. Tea?' I said, flicking on the TV with the remote. She failed to notice the terseness of my tone or, what seemed more likely, chose to ignore it.

'Yes, please,' she said.

In the kitchen I kicked the cupboard and swore a few times. I was hungry by now but I was damned if I was going to cook for her. Watching *Blind Date* was sacrifice enough.

By the time I returned with a tray of tea, Megan was listlessly watching Cilia Black's OTT introductions. I poured the tea and tried not to lose the will to live. I'd already decided that once the programme was over it was showdown time. I may not be the world's greatest private investigator, but I don't like mysteries, especially ones that involve me, and I am, by nature, persistent. Not only did I want to know what was going on, I *needed* to know for my own sanity. I couldn't just throw her out until I knew what had happened to her.

During the commercial break Megan announced she was hungry. I didn't respond.

'Shall I cook something?' she asked.

I shrugged. 'Please yourself. I thought you liked this programme.'

'It doesn't seem the same now,' she said, with no further explanation.

I told her the fridge freezer was full of food and she could surprise me if she wanted to. So I wandered into the lounge, switched off the TV and picked up a book. I heard her clattering around in the kitchen for a while and then, suddenly, it went quiet. It was Jasper who alerted me with squeaky worried yelps. I rushed along to the kitchen just as Megan and a saucepan crashed to the floor. Luckily, the water in the saucepan was cold, but broccoli florets were dotted all over the floor and Megan. I took her pulse, which was rapid and a bit thready. Luckily, she'd fallen on her side and was showing signs of coming round.

'What happened?' she croaked, trying to sit up.

'I think you fainted. Don't try to move.'

'I felt dizzy,' she said. Then she added, 'I'm so sorry, Kate.'

Guilt nudged me as if it were as real as Jasper's nose. Whatever Megan had done, or not done, she was weak and exhausted and needed help.

When what little colour she had returned to her face, which took about five minutes, I suggested she sat up gradually. After another few minutes I helped her back to my bed. I tried to help her undress but she seemed nervous and defensive. 'I'll come back,' I said. 'And we can have a chat.'

I removed the broccoli from the kitchen floor and mopped up the water and noticed Jasper creeping off towards my bedroom. I thought he might be planning to merely investigate but, when I popped my head round the door, he'd slipped in beside Megan. I stood there feeling as betrayed as anyone would finding their male, supposedly faithful, companion in bed with another woman.

As for Megan, she was asleep again and I'd lost my appetite.

Jasper redeemed himself somewhat by joining me in the early hours, but he'd shown his true colours and, no doubt, he'd worked out that if he wanted an early walk he'd need to be in my good books.

* * *

Sunday began well enough. I was full of resolve to sort the situation before Hubert's return. On the way back from our walk I bought the Sunday papers and some bacon and breakfast was sizzling away when Megan appeared.

'Are you feeling better?'

'I feel really rested,' she said. 'Thank you.'

'Good. Because, after breakfast please don't slope off back to bed. We need to talk. Hubert comes back today and if you're still here he'll want an explanation.'

'I can't go outside,' she said. 'I'm scared, see.'

'Well, you'll just have to tell me *why* you're scared, won't you?'

She nodded, looking slightly more tearful and pathetic than previously.

She didn't say a word during breakfast, although, I must admit, I wasn't very encouraging, as I had my head in the Sunday papers. 'That was a lovely breakfast,' she said as she carried out the plates to the kitchen. 'I'll do the washing up.'

I was a little on edge whilst she was out of sight but, within a few minutes, she had returned and she sat in the armchair looking pensive.

'Do you want to start at the beginning?' I said, firmly.

There was no reply.

'Fine. Tell me where you were born.'

'I was born in North Wales, in Criccieth,' she said in her slow melodic way. 'It's near the sea — I loved it there. But my dad died when I was sixteen, so, because I had to look after my mother — she was an invalid — we moved to a bungalow outside Criccieth — all old people and a bit isolated.'

'Did you go to work?'

'No. I left school and just looked after my mother. She was poorly. I had to do everything for her.'

'What about friends?'

'I had a few friends at school but I couldn't leave my mother, so they stopped asking me to go out with them.'

'And no boyfriends?'

'No. I went to a girls' school. I didn't know any boys. Hywel Davies, the pharmacist, asked me out once. I used to go to the chemist quite often for my mother's prescriptions. He was always nice to me . . .'

She trailed off. 'I should have stayed where I was but I wanted to do things.'

'What happened?'

'I'd gone into Criccieth shopping and, when I came back, I thought at first she was asleep. She was still in bed, because she'd said she didn't feel well enough for me to get her up. She was dead, of course. I'd never seen a dead person before. My dad died in hospital. I watched her for hours and hours. I didn't move at all. We hadn't said proper goodbyes, see, and I was in shock, I suppose. I was all on my own. My auntie lived in South Wales but she wasn't well and she couldn't help me. I rang the doctor and she was very good to me and she came out and told me what to do.'

As I listened to her lilting Welsh accent and watched her eyes fill with tears, I thought how some teenagers have responsibility thrust upon them and no one gives a damn. If she had got herself pregnant, was it surprising? More to the point, I realized, I suddenly seemed to have acquired her as *my* responsibility. What the hell was I going to do?

'Tell me about the money in your bag,' I said.

She looked shocked. 'You looked in my bag?'

'I was trying to find out something about you — you didn't say much.'

'I felt very ill,' she said. 'That money . . .' she broke off as we both heard Jasper whimpering, quickly followed by knocking at the side door.

'It's Hubert. Quick — go to my office and stay there.'

Megan dashed off looking terrified. Perhaps I'd given her the wrong impression of Hubert. He was a real softie but I didn't want to take advantage of that or upset him in any way.

'It's good to be back,' he said as I opened the door. 'I thought I'd come and see you first, Kate. What have you been up to? I hope you've taken good care of my Jasper.'

By now, Jasper was tucked under Hubert's arm and I was left to carry up Hubert's overnight bag.

I made Hubert coffee and we drank it in the kitchen. Thankfully, Megan had left no sign that anyone was around. 'It looks tidier than usual in the kitchen,' he said.

'*You* look tidier than usual,' I said. 'In fact, that sweater looks . . . trendy.' It was navy with thin purple stripes.

'Perhaps I've got a new image,' he said.

'Well, it's not before time.'

He looked a little hurt at that. 'Image is important,' he said. 'You should bear that in mind, Kate. The Funeral Federation thinks sober is in, but sombre is just a tad passé in the funeral world. I've got so many new ideas, Kate — I'm quite excited . . .'

As *excited* was a strong word for Hubert, I interrupted him. His excitement is usually based on seeing a new and exceptional shoe. 'There's been a development.'

'You're on a new case?' he asked, sounding hopeful.

'No . . . Not exactly.'

'You've not met a new man?'

'Is that likely, Hubert? You haven't been away two full days.'

'Well, tell me then. I've got such a lot to tell you — Humberstone's is going to be the best.'

'You already are.' Then I blurted out, 'There's someone staying here.'

'A friend of yours?'

'No. We only met on Friday night.'

'Where did *you* go on Friday night?'

Already he sounded suspicious and I realized I'd mishandled the whole thing.

'What's going on?' he asked. 'It is a man. You've had a one-night stand and he's still here. He's not hiding in the cupboard, is he?'

'It's not a man — it's a woman.'

'I didn't know you were like that, Kate.'

'I'm not. She's not well.'

'Call a doctor.'

'It's not as simple as that.'

'You make nothing simple,' he said. 'Come on, tell Uncle Hubert the full story.'

I took a deep breath. 'On Friday night it was raining, a real deluge, but it wasn't going to stop, so I took Jasper for his late-night walk by the river.' Jasper wriggled excitedly at the sound of the magic word and I shook my finger and said, 'No!' which left him looking confused.

'You shouldn't go down there when the river's high.'

Hubert sees danger in most things, especially where Jasper is concerned. 'Well, I did,' I said, 'and Jasper made a discovery. At first, I thought it was a bundle of old clothes but it wasn't, it was a girl — well, she's just twenty.'

'I don't care how old she is. What was she doing there?'

'I'm not sure,' I said, weakly.

'You're not sure. She's still here and you don't know?' He sounded incredulous. I smiled and murmured, 'It's complicated.'

'I don't think so,' he said. 'She was sleeping rough and she's probably a drug addict, which is why she hasn't told you what she was doing there.'

'She's not a drug addict.'

'How do you know?'

'The pupils of her eyes are fine.' The moment I'd said it, I wondered if they were. Had I looked properly?

'You're an expert on pupils, are you?'

'When you meet her, you'll see she isn't the type.'

He laughed, one short burst. 'You read a newspaper — of sorts — every day, Kate, and you know there is no one type.'

Then he added, before I had a chance to say any more, 'When is she leaving?'

I shrugged, 'Well, it's . . .'

'Don't tell me — it's complicated. You've landed yourself with a down and out who has nowhere to go and no money.'

'She does have money,' I blurted out.

'How come she's sleeping rough?'

'She's in trouble, but I'm not sure what type of trouble.'

'Your detective skills haven't improved, then, while I've been away.'

'That's not fair. She isn't a client.'

'Not yet.'

'She just needs to get physically fit.'

'So, she's ill?'

I was getting in deep water here but sometimes Hubert could be relentless. 'No, it's more emotional, I think.'

Hubert frowned. 'What you're really saying is — she's a nutter and now she's living under my roof.'

'She's been bereaved recently.'

'Oh, I see.' His tone was a bit more conciliatory now. 'Well, I'd better meet her, I suppose. I know you're hiding something from me. Perhaps I can find out what it is. After all, I'm the expert on the bereaved.'

I couldn't argue with that and I left the kitchen and walked along the corridor to my office.

The sound of a muffled mobile phone was coming from Megan's money-filled bag. She was staring at the bag looking petrified. 'Do you want me to answer it?' I asked.

She nodded, mutely. I rummaged amongst the bundles of notes and eventually found the mobile. Whoever was calling remained persistent.

'Hello,' I said, trying to sound like Megan.

There was a long pause before the response. But I knew then why Megan was so scared.

CHAPTER THREE

The voice was male, deep and with an accent I couldn't place. 'You stupid bitch! Don't think you'll get away. You won't. If you go to the police, they won't believe you. You're a known nutter. You're dead. You might as well kill yourself now. Go on. Try again. We know where you are and we're coming for you.'

I switched off. Megan was crying. 'He's bluffing,' I said. 'You're safe here.' She came towards me and put her head on my shoulder. I'm five-four. She was shorter by at least a couple of inches. I hugged her but she carried on crying. 'Come on, let's go and see Hubert. He's very sensible.' Then I added, 'There's just one thing — your baby?'

'Dead,' she said. 'My baby's dead. Stillborn.'

'I'm sorry. How long ago?'

'A few days. It's all a blur in my mind.'

'A few days!' I echoed. 'Have you seen a doctor?'

'I'm all right now.'

'Are you still bleeding?'

'Yes, but not much.'

'Would you see a doctor if one came here? Hubert knows all the doctors. He even knows two women doctors.'

'She'd report it, wouldn't she? You'll look after me — I know you will.'

No one can be forced to see a doctor but I was very uneasy. I'd have to watch her like a hawk.

She was still tearful when we found Hubert in the lounge, reading the paper. She was clinging on to me but, when she glimpsed Hubert, she clung even harder. Hubert is tall and thin with deep brown eyes and a serious sort of face that was either moulded by the job or the generations of undertakers before him.

'Don't worry about me, love,' he said. 'You have a good cry. Kate will sort you out. She's the best private investigator for miles around and the best one I know. I'll make some tea, shall I?'

Once he'd left the room, she began to calm down. 'I didn't know you were a private investigator,' she said. 'I saw the nursing books. I guessed you were a nurse.'

'I used to be.'

'I thought private detectives were men in trilby hats.'

'You've watched too many black and white films,' I said. 'PIs come in all shapes and sizes.'

'I can stay here for a while, can't I?'

'It's up to Hubert, not me. If he says yes, then, in the short term . . .' I broke off, not wanting to upset her by having to spell it out that it was only temporary — very temporary. It was only natural that she was scared — I'd heard him and I was scared, and it was only natural that she'd want to stay where she felt safe until the danger was over. Her aggressor, whoever he was, needed to be stopped.

'We'll have to get the police involved,' I said, firmly.

Her face crumpled as fast as a deflating soufflé.

'Don't look like that,' I said. 'I'm not talking the Spanish Inquisition. The local cops are OK.'

'They won't believe me — they won't, I'm telling you.'

'I think that's what *he's* been telling you. When you're frightened, you don't think properly. He's making you a victim — we've got to fight back.'

Hubert came back with a tray of tea and Jasper at his heels. 'Jasper, sit!'

Jasper did sit, but not on the floor. He struggled on to Megan's lap and rested his head on her large bosom. She began stroking his head and, after a while, she looked more relaxed.

'Kate tells me you've had a sad loss,' said Hubert, by way of an opening gambit.

'My mam died just over a year ago.'

'She must have been young.'

'No. She was old. She was sixty.' Hubert cast a baleful glance at me. He thought ninety was old. I was undecided. 'She'd never been well. She had heart trouble and diabetes and arthritis.'

'Was she in hospital?'

'No, I looked after her. I'd always looked after her. She wouldn't have anyone else.'

'Did she die suddenly?'

'Yes, I told Kate about that . . .' She broke off. 'I don't want to talk about my mother anymore.'

'Well, I've got to unpack and check up on my business, then I'll walk Jasper . . .' Hubert never remembered that Jasper had a vocabulary of at least eight words and *walk* was guaranteed to get a major response. He left with Jasper's tail wagging for England.

Megan picked up the remote control and flicked on the TV. 'You can switch that off,' I said. 'Somewhere there's a man out there who means you harm and, if you're going to stay here and I'm going to help you, it's time you told me what's been going on.'

She looked surprised at my outburst. 'You're right. I have to tell. I'll do my best but some of it's fuzzy, like in a mist. Not at first, though. See, after I sold the house and got the money, I had these ambitions — I wanted to go to London and see the sights. I'd never been to London before. I'd been to Cardiff once but never London. My mother was old-fashioned, chapel-going. She thought London was a dangerous place. It made me want to see it even more.'

'Did you know anyone in London?'

'Not a soul. I wanted to stay in a posh hotel like the Ritz or the Dorchester. I'd read about those but, when I saw them, I thought they were too posh for me, so I booked into a small hotel near Euston.'

'Why Euston?'

'It was near the station. I was frightened of the tube trains and the crowds and I thought if I was near the station I could get home quickly. But then I remembered I hadn't got a home — I couldn't stay in the bungalow after Mam died — I just couldn't. I used to hear her calling for me. I knew she was gone but I could still hear her.'

'What was the name of the hotel?'

'Why do you want to know that?'

'Because we're trying to retrace your steps — a year or so ago you were in London. Then you turn up by a river in Longborough. So, you need to tell me all the details.'

'It was called the Georgiana,' she said. 'It was really comfortable. I had a lovely room and everyone was very kind. I could watch all the channels on the telly and I had a kettle and teapot in my room, so I could make my own tea. And I had biscuits and lovely meals. And there was a bar, but I don't drink, but sometimes in the evening I went down and talked to the barman.' She must have seen the expression on my face, because she added, 'I'd never stayed in a hotel before. My mother couldn't travel, so we didn't have holidays. I did go camping once with the guides but it's not the same, is it?'

'No, it's not the same,' I agreed. 'So, how long did you stay?'

'A month.'

'That's a long time in a hotel on your own.'

'I met someone in the second week.'

'The voice on the mobile?'

'Yes. I was in the bar one night and we got talking. He was quite a bit older than me, but he seemed very nice and he listened to me — you know what I mean?'

I nodded. 'I do — it's the best aphrodisiac in the world.'

'What does that mean?' she asked.

'It's a big turn-on.'

'Oh,' she said. But I didn't think *turn-on* meant much to her either.

'So, he was a good listener and you liked him. Then what happened?'

'He offered to show me the sights. I'd been there more than a week and I'd been too scared to go anywhere, except for a walk near the hotel.'

'What was his name?'

'Michael Whitby.'

'And what did he look like?'

For a moment she looked non-plussed.

'Was he tall or short? Fat or thin?'

She thought for a moment. 'He was about six foot, medium sort of build. He had crinkly brown hair and hazel eyes.'

'Good-looking?'

'I thought he was at first — not handsome — just sort of ordinary.'

'So where did he take you?'

Now she smiled. 'Oh, it was lovely. He took me to the Tower of London and the Planetarium and Buckingham Palace and the Science Museum and Madame Tussauds.' Her voice had become animated and there was no doubt that he'd found a grateful devotee.

'And you trusted him at this stage?'

'Oh yes, Kate. He was so kind to me. He paid for everything and he made me laugh and he explained things so well.'

'What sort of things did he explain?'

'About the tube trains and how to get tickets and how to order meals in restaurants. All sorts of things I didn't know.'

'And did he try it on?'

'You mean try to get me into bed? No. No. I told him I was a virgin and he said he respected that.'

'So far then, Megan, everything was fine. You saw London — what was in it for him?'

'What do you mean?'

'Come on — most men want some sort of payback.'

'I didn't know that then,' she said, miserably.

'Did you ask him if he was married?'

'I'm not stupid,' she said, sharply. 'Of course I did. He said he'd left his wife because she'd been unfaithful and he was staying at the hotel until he found a place of his own.'

'Did that bother you?'

'No. Why should it?'

'I thought you might object to going out with a married man.'

'Separated,' she corrected.

'OK. It didn't worry you.'

'No, why should it? I wasn't in love with him. He was far too old.'

That surprised me, I'd got that part all wrong. I'd been convinced she'd fallen head over heels in love with him. In fact, I'd suspected she'd have fallen for any man who showed her some attention. I'd underestimated her choosiness.

The noisy return of Hubert and Jasper ended our chat abruptly and she murmured that she'd like to lie down. I didn't mind, because I hadn't had a chance to talk to Hubert and she still had the pasty complexion of someone who hadn't seen daylight for some time. Was that due entirely to the pregnancy, I wondered? But until I knew the full story, I could jump to all the wrong conclusions and already had, in part.

'Well?' said Hubert. 'Cracked it yet, Sherlocka?'

'Very funny, Hubert. Your return made it necessary for her to lie down in a darkened room.'

Hubert pointed a warning finger at me. 'You just be careful. She seems innocent enough but looks can be deceptive where women are concerned.'

'Well, you'd know that, Hubert — you thought my mother was a Sister of Mercy.'

'I did not! I recognized your mother for a complete trollop and I was right.'

'You like the tarty type,' I said, only slightly aggrieved, because he was speaking the truth.

'I admit that,' he said, 'but she's as reliable as a pair of boots made of candyfloss.'

'Could we leave my mother out of this, please? We were talking about Megan.'

'Well, I'm starving, so go and ask Miss Wales if she wants to come out with us for Sunday lunch.'

Half-asleep, Megan muttered that she was too scared to go outside and I was hungry enough not to want to argue. 'Don't worry,' I said. 'We won't be long.' As I said the words, I realized my life was being redesigned. Responsibilities seemed to have been foisted upon me with no input at all from me. My mother's prodigal return, Jasper being acquired and now a needy live-in client. PIs are meant to be unencumbered free spirits, able to drop everything at a moment's notice for a new case. I'd seen the films, the cynical loner battling with crime and corruption, smoking cheroots and drinking neat whisky. Or skulking in cars with fancy cameras, catching errant husbands. It all seemed so simple. It's just that real life gets in the way.

And real life with Hubert was a pint, pasty and chips in the Saddlers' Arms. He'd decided to drive five miles out of Longborough *for a change* and because someone had told him the Saddlers' Arms had a good restaurant.

'Sorry, mate,' said the landlord. 'We're having the place refurbished. No Sunday roasts today. Can do pasty and chips, though.'

'Baked beans?' enquired Hubert.

'That's pushing it, mate. We're out of beans.'

I was all for trying another pub but Hubert thought pasty and chips sounded good, so there we stayed.

We sat at a corner table in a virtually empty pub with the smell of paint wafting from the restaurant area. Hubert was in optimistic mode. 'I've got a few new ideas for the business,' he said. 'And it could help yours, too.'

'Tell me all about it,' I said, knowing that Megan would have to wait.

'Firstly the catering suite is under-utilized. We can provide drinks and food, so we have an ideal venue for—'

'Don't tell — karaoke nights?'

'Don't be flippant. This is serious. We could provide a bereavement-counselling service.'

'Free?'

'You're being silly again, Kate. Free to those on low incomes. And we could provide a service for those caring for the terminally ill. Arrange talks from nurses and doctors and get a support group going. And then, when their loved one does die, they'll be among friends.'

'And with the right undertaker.'

'You know I'm the best in the county,' said Hubert, crisply.

'You told Megan I was the best PI you knew.'

'It's true. You're the only one I do know.'

I didn't want to burst Hubert's bubble. I'd been less than enthusiastic at his catering-suite idea. But many people had been grateful to have the burden of catering removed and, although tasteful, the suite was more bistro-style than funereal.

The arrival of our pasty and chips shut us up for a while. I swear the food tasted of paint and, after a few mouthfuls, I gave up. Hubert seemed to be enjoying his. 'You're not getting anorexic, are you, Kate?' he asked.

'That's about as likely as me being voted Private Investigator of the Twenty-First Century,' I snapped. Hubert looked a little downcast at my sharp reply, so I smiled and said, 'I think your idea for the counselling service will be a winner. It's a point of contact with their loved one, a sort of safe haven. They could meet other people and know that, at any time, they'd get a sympathetic ear. It's a great idea.'

Hubert beamed. 'There are times,' he said, 'when you surprise me.'

Wait for it, I thought.

'If you're not too busy, perhaps you could give me a hand setting it up.'

'Yes,' I said. 'If I get the Megan problem sorted.'

'What exactly *is* her problem?'

'I'm still getting to grips with it all.' I answered, trying to sound confident.

'You're taking your time.'

'She's traumatized. She needs rest and space.'

'Your time is valuable,' said Hubert, dabbing tomato sauce from the corner of his mouth.

'Yes, but I don't have a case at the moment, so that doesn't apply.'

'If she needs money to go back to Wales, that's not a problem.'

'Money isn't a problem. She has money. She needs protection.'

'There's something you haven't told me,' he said suspiciously. 'Come on, what's going on?'

'She had a phone call on her mobile. I took it. A man's voice making death threats, saying he knows where she is.'

'End of story — ring the police.'

'It's not as easy as that.'

'Only because you make things difficult.'

'I might go to the police, but not yet. I don't know the full story.'

'You never will at the rate you're going.'

'That's not fair. I've told you I can't rush her.'

He sipped his beer, thoughtfully. 'There's still something else, isn't there?'

The trouble with Hubert, I thought, is that he knows me too well. 'She's recently, very recently, had a baby — a stillborn baby.'

'That's a shame,' said Hubert. He'd had no children of his own and he regretted that. Babies definitely were a soft spot with him. A baby in the chapel of rest would upset him for days.

'Who was the father?'

'I'm presuming it was the man she met in London and the voice on the mobile phone.'

'Bastard,' he muttered.

On the way back we stopped off at McDonald's to buy a takeaway for Megan's lunch. Tomorrow I'd be more organized but a Big Mac and fries was an improvement on strange-tasting pub grub.

We crept up the stairs and, for once, Jasper didn't come bounding down the stairs to greet us.

I opened the door to my bedroom very quietly. If Megan was still asleep, I reasoned she must need it. She wasn't in my bed. I peered into the kitchen to find Hubert putting on the kettle. Jasper wasn't in his basket. I walked along the hallway to the lounge.

'Hubert, she's gone!' I yelled. 'And she's taken Jasper with her.'

CHAPTER FOUR

I rushed to the kitchen door, where Jasper's lead had been hanging. It was still there. I rushed along to my office but there was no sign of her or Jasper. Hubert and I were acting like headless chickens when we nearly collided between rooms. 'I'm ringing the police,' he said, really agitated. 'She can't be walking Jasper. She must have let that bloke in.'

'Let's take it calmly. I'll check if her bag is anywhere.'

'What's her bag got to do with it?'

'There's thousands in it,' I said, as I dashed back to my room. It wasn't under the bed or on the chair. I opened my wardrobe and Jasper shot out, leaving Megan sitting there in the crash position. 'For God's sake, what are you doing?'

She lowered her arms. Her eyes were red with crying. 'He rang again. He said he knew where I was.'

'He's just trying to scare you. Now come on out. We've got to stop Hubert ringing the police.'

I pulled her from my wardrobe, none too pleased that half my clothes were dragged out with her. Hubert, by now, was at the door clutching Jasper to his bosom. I could see he was so relieved Jasper hadn't been abducted, he was prepared to be forgiving. 'Come on, young Megan,' he said. 'I've bought you a Big Mac and chips. I'll warm it up in the oven for you.'

Megan followed him like a little lamb. I needed a breather. I was mad with her. So I decided to walk Jasper just to calm down.

The fresh air made me feel better. 'I'm mad with you too, Jasper. Why didn't you bark?'

He wagged his tail in answer as he paused in one of his umpteen sniffs. We walked and stopped, walked and stopped, with me resolving that, once I got back, Megan was going to tell me the whole story and nothing but the whole story and then I'd decide if I wanted her as a client. One thing was certain. I wanted my bed and my room back *and* she could hang my clothes back up properly.

* * *

She met me at the top of the stairs. 'I'm sorry I upset you, Kate. I was so scared. I heard you and Hubert come back but I couldn't move.'

I shrugged. 'It's OK. Have you eaten?'

She nodded. 'It was lovely. I'd never had a McDonald's before.'

'I think you've had a lot of experiences recently that you've never had before,' I said with a smile. 'You've led a very sheltered life. I'm surprised you've even got a mobile phone.'

'I had to have that. Mam insisted, you see, so that when I went shopping she could ring me if she needed me.'

'Why did you give *him* the number?'

'He asked me for it.'

'Has it crossed your mind, Megan, that he can't know where you are? Because, otherwise, he'd use the land line to prove it.'

She smiled. 'I didn't think of that.'

'Where's Hubert?'

'He's sitting in the kitchen. He's been ever so kind. He says if I tell you everything, then you and him will sort it out for me. But it's all jumbled up in my head, see, as if I've had an accident. Sometimes I see things in my mind.'

'You mean flashbacks?'

'Yes, flashbacks. They scare me because I don't always understand them.'

I waved to Hubert as we passed the kitchen. He was reading the Sunday newspaper. 'Go to it!' he mouthed.

In the lounge, Megan sat upright on the sofa. I sat directly beside her. She wasn't going to get away.

'This voice on the line is, of course, Michael?'

'Yes, it's him.'

'So, you went from being . . . friends . . . to him wanting to kill you. How did that happen?'

'We're weren't, you know, sleeping together. He was at the hotel for a week and then he said he'd found himself a little flat and he could still see me quite often. He took me out and we had some lovely walks around London. He even took me to see a musical. It was lovely. And a nightclub. He bought me champagne — I'd never drunk it before. I knew I was a bit tiddly. I wasn't drunk or anything. He brought me back to the hotel and took me to my room and then he left. Later on . . .'

She'd broken off suddenly, looking distressed and frightened. She opened her mouth then started biting her lip.

'Did you fall asleep? Was the room spinning?'

Finally she found her voice. 'I woke up later on. It was still dark but I could see the clock, only I couldn't see the numbers properly. It was all fuzzy. I was in bed, my clothes were off and I was so scared. But I didn't know why I was frightened. I just had this terrible feeling something had happened to me.'

'Was it a nightmare?'

'It was like a nightmare but there was only one part of it I could remember.'

'Which was?'

'There was someone in the room with me. I don't know who it was but I knew it was a man.'

'What did you do?'

'I lay in bed for ages, trying so hard to remember. I could remember Michael saying goodbye and would I be all right.

And I said I was fine and I'd go straight to bed. But I don't remember getting into bed or getting undressed.'

'It sounds like a blackout,' I said. 'How much champagne did you drink?'

'Only two glasses.'

It seemed unlikely that a mere two glasses of bubbly would cause her to black out, so I was mystified.

'Are you sure it was only two glasses?'

'I'm positive.'

'And you had nothing else to drink after that?'

'Michael gave me some orange juice.'

'You didn't say that before.'

'I've only just remembered.'

'Tell me about it. Was it *your* juice?'

'Yes, I have a glass every morning.'

'And did he stay with you while you drank it?'

'Yes, but why is that important?'

'Don't worry about it,' I said. 'Every little detail is important. Was the glass still there in the morning?'

She frowned. 'I don't know. I can't remember . . .' She broke off, tears threatening.

'We'll leave that,' I said, swiftly. 'We can go back to it later. You were in bed. What time did you get up, or did you go back to sleep?'

'I couldn't sleep. After a while I got up. I felt really shaky, as if I was going to fall over. I managed to get to the bathroom and then I noticed . . .'

'What?'

'I noticed a tiny trickle of blood down my legs and it wasn't my period because it was in the middle of my month. I knew then that something had happened in the night. I was a virgin before, but I guessed I wasn't one any more. I felt really sick and I started to vomit. The rest of the day I stayed in bed and the hotel manager called on me later in the evening to ask if I was OK. I said I was fine. When he'd gone I couldn't help wondering if *he'd* come into my room in the night. He had the master keys.'

She gazed at me then, like an imploring child, and I put my arm around her.

'What should I have done, Kate?'

'I think you should have gone straight to the police.'

'They wouldn't have believed me. A stupid Welsh girl — they'd think it served me right.'

'No, that isn't true. They have heard of incidents like this before, where the woman has no memory but thinks she might have been raped.'

'But how could I have been raped and not know it?'

'Have you heard of the date-rape drug — Rohypnol?'

She shook her head.

'It has no taste and can be added to drinks. It wipes out memory but leaves the victim very anxious and frightened.'

'But if it makes the woman semi-conscious, why do men do it?'

'I really don't know, Megan. In most rape cases a woman might put up a fight, might scratch and claw. This way the victim is docile and poses no threat. Who knows how many men have got away with rape using the drug? But some have been caught with forensic tests.'

'You think it was Michael, don't you?'

'He seems the likeliest, doesn't he?'

Megan fell silent. Then she began to tremble. 'I've been such a bloody fool. He tricked me right from the beginning. But what did he want from me?'

'That's what we're trying to find out. When did you next see him?'

'About two days later. He wasn't staying at the hotel then. I told him something awful had happened to me and he said I was still in shock about my mother and that it was only a nightmare. I didn't tell him about the bleeding — I don't know why. Two weeks later I'd missed a period. I'm as regular as clockwork, so I was worried sick.'

'Was he still taking you out?'

'Yes, but he said he was working. I didn't know if it was my imagination or not, but I felt different. My breasts tingled and I felt tired. I didn't want a baby, especially a stranger's. I was so sure it wasn't Michael who raped me and I didn't want to tell him I thought I was pregnant. I suppose I hoped it would just go away. It was then he suggested I move in with him. He said the flat was small but big enough for two. So I had to tell him then.'

'How did he react?'

'He was very concerned. He said I should have told him before. He went out and bought a pregnancy-testing kit and, when it was positive, I was really upset. I kept thinking what my mother would have said — it would have broken her heart. She was very old-fashioned, see. She even thought sex before marriage was a sin.'

'So, you moved in with him?'

'No. He said he had a better idea. He knew I'd looked after my mother, so he said he'd find me a job as a carer, where I could live in and earn money.'

'But you didn't need to work, did you?'

'No, but I didn't tell him I had money.'

I smiled. 'Megan, that's the most sensible thing you've ever done. Tell me why you didn't tell him.'

She shrugged and hugged her knees. 'I don't know really. My mother always told me to keep quiet about what we had, so I let him think I would be glad of a job. I was bored anyway.'

'So, you took the job?'

'Yes. I moved out of the hotel to this big house in Hampstead.'

'How did that work out?'

'It was a bit lonely. The old lady I looked after was in her nineties and she'd had a stroke. She couldn't speak but sometimes she'd laugh or cry. I'd feed her and change her and read to her. She liked that.'

'What about staff?'

'There was a cleaner who came in every day and a cook. The food was lovely.'

'And what about Michael?'

'He came sometimes in the evening but he didn't stay long.'

'And what about the pregnancy?'

'I tried to forget it but I got very big.'

'What did the doctor say?'

'I didn't see a doctor. Michael said it was best not to involve a doctor. He knew a midwife and if I wanted the baby adopted she could arrange things and no one need ever know.'

'So, you saw this midwife?'

'Yes. She was foreign but she spoke good English. I trusted her. She said I could either keep the baby or have it adopted. Then she said I could go back to Wales. I was very homesick anyway. When it was all over I planned to buy a little house in Criccieth overlooking the sea and, perhaps, go to college. But as the baby grew and I felt it move, I wasn't so sure about adoption. I mean, I had enough money to bring a child up on my own and my mother wasn't around to be upset, so I changed my mind, but I didn't say much to Michael.'

'He wanted you to have the baby adopted?'

'Oh yes. He said one day I'd want to get married and I was young enough and healthy enough to have ten children if I wanted them.'

'What did you say to that?'

'I kept quiet.'

'Were you frightened of him?'

'Not exactly. But I wondered why he was bothering with me. We weren't sleeping together and I convinced myself he was just a kind person.'

'But instinct told you otherwise.'

'Yes. I felt more wary as I grew bigger. When I only had a few weeks to go, I said I thought I should leave and find a proper flat.

'Michael said he'd find me somewhere. He kept looking but there was nothing suitable and the rents were so high. In the end he said it would be better if I stayed put and he'd help me nurse Alice.'

'Did he know Alice personally?' I asked.

Megan looked at me vaguely, as if somehow I should know the answer. 'Alice is his great-aunt.'

'Oh, I see.'

'Anyway, about a week before I was due, the cook and the cleaner stopped coming and Teresa, the midwife, and Michael moved in.'

'Were you worried by that?'

'I felt trapped. I wanted to leave. Alice didn't like either of them, I could tell. She had a frightened look in her eyes. Sometimes she tried to make sounds. Once, I thought she was trying to say *Go* but I was scared. I didn't want to give birth on my own. I asked Michael to take me to hospital, but he said they would ask too many questions and, if I said I'd been raped, they wouldn't believe me.'

As I listened to Megan I wondered what I would have done in the same circumstances. She, after all, was used to caring for an invalid, hardly going out, watching *Last of the Summer Wine* with her mother, shielded from the real world in a rural backwater with retired people for neighbours. I'd travelled, I was older, had had boyfriends, and I'd landed up feeling safe with Hubert as my friend and landlord. I also had a mother and, for all her faults, if I were in real trouble, she'd be there for me. There was no comparison. But if I'd been as alone as Megan I'd probably have reacted the same way.

'I went into labour three days early,' she continued. 'Teresa was really good. I felt quite safe with her. When the pain got worse she gave me an injection and that helped. I suppose I'd been having pains for about six hours and she examined me and said it wouldn't be long before I'd start to push . . .' She broke off, her voice choked. 'Then I blacked out. I don't remember pushing. I just don't remember . . .'

'Take your time,' I said. 'Just tell me what you do remember.'

She took a deep breath and tried to keep her hands still, so I held on to her hands and she managed to carry on. 'When I came round, Teresa was sitting by the bed. At first I didn't remember about being in labour . . . I felt just as I had that night. I wondered why she looked so miserable. She told me she was sorry but the baby had been born dead. Since I didn't remember the birth, I patted my stomach — it was fat and empty. I was fuzzy in the head. I asked to see the baby but she said best not, because he'd been dead for some time and he looked horrible. I didn't cry. I was numb. I stopped speaking and she gave me an injection and I went to sleep.'

'I'm so sorry,' I said. 'Where was Michael?'

'He was standing in the doorway. When I woke up I lay with eyes closed. I didn't want to move or think. I was like I was after Mam died. But then I heard a baby crying. It sounded far away. But it was like before — I could hear my mother calling even though I knew she was dead. I kept very still. I knew it would stop.

'Then I heard voices. It was Teresa and Michael. They thought I was still asleep but I have very acute hearing. She said, "What are we going to do about her?" and he said, "God knows. We could offer her a holiday in Spain and use her as a mule — she's stupid enough." I didn't know what a mule was but I put two and two together when they started talking about drugs. He said, "She can start with hash and move on to crack. She'll be the innocent, she'll get it through." Teresa said, "What if she doesn't?" They must have moved away from the door, because their voices got fainter. But I'd heard enough and I knew then that God was looking after me.'

'So you ran away?'

She nodded. 'I waited for a while. When I got out of bed I almost fainted. I put on my tracksuit, put a few things in my bag and crept down the stairs. I'd just opened the front door when I thought I heard that baby cry again, but it was a big house and the wind whistled down the chimneys. And I knew I wasn't in my right mind.'

'Was it night or day?'

'It was three o'clock in the morning. I wanted to get a taxi but there were none about. My mobile's battery was run down. So I waited for a lorry or a van and I thumbed a lift.' Megan swallowed hard. But then carried on in a rush. 'I stood there for ages and then a lorry driver picked me up. He said he was going to the midlands and he'd take me there. He stopped at a transport café about five thirty and he bought me breakfast. He was ever so kind. I don't think I looked very well and I slept in his cab for most of the way. We got to Longborough and I didn't know what to do then. I stayed for two nights in a bed and breakfast and I charged up the battery on my mobile. And then Michael rang. He said he knew where I was and he was coming to get me. I panicked, left the B&B and made my way to the river. I was going to kill myself. I felt so tired, like my life had been sucked out of me. But I couldn't do it. My mother said suicide was a sin and if you committed suicide you wouldn't go to heaven. I thought my baby might be in heaven and then I wouldn't be with him.'

I wanted to cry with her and for her but I couldn't let myself. I had to keep a cool head. Michael Whitby sounded a very dangerous man and the type who would stop at nothing.

'Tell me, Megan,' I said. 'What job did you say Michael had?'

'I didn't say,' she said. 'But he's a police inspector.'

CHAPTER FIVE

Later that evening, when Megan was in bed, Hubert and I sat sharing a box of chocolates he'd brought back from his weekend. It was getting to the squabbling stage — the best ones were gone. We were down to a marzipan and a strawberry cream.

'We could leave them for Megan,' he suggested.

'Two measly chockies!' I said. 'You have them. I don't like either of them, anyway.'

So Hubert ate them and the box was empty and we both felt disgusted with ourselves. 'Now,' said Hubert. 'What's all this about him being a police inspector?'

'She's convinced he's with the Met. Working near Tottenham.'

'You obviously don't believe her.'

'It seems unlikely. What are his motives?'

'There *are* bent coppers, Kate.'

'Yes, but this one isn't just bent, he's twisted up his own backside.'

'You have such a delicate way with words,' said Hubert as he poured us both a brandy. 'This great-aunt of his, I take it she's quite wealthy?'

I sipped at my brandy. 'The house alone must be worth a fortune, especially if it's as big as Megan suggested, and it seems that Whitby, being her nephew, would inherit that. So it wouldn't appear that he had any money problems.'

'The old girl isn't dead yet,' he said. 'And anyway, what was he planning to do with the baby?'

'The only thing I can think of is that he isn't separated, his wife is desperate for a baby and, for some reason, they can't adopt. He gets a nice healthy girl pregnant and they steal her baby, but when the baby's born dead, it all goes wrong.'

'What about the drug angle?' he asked.

'Who knows? Maybe he's corrupt and works for the drug squad.'

'There's only one way to find out, Kate.'

'What's that?'

'Investigate.'

'Thank you for that, Hubert. I do have to plan a strategy.'

'You never have before.'

'That is not true.'

Hubert shrugged. He was in one of his *I-know-best* moods, so I didn't argue.

'I thought I might start off in London,' I began.

Hubert was shaking his head. 'If I were you,' he said, 'I'd start off in North Wales. Find out as much as you can about Megan first. It might save you grief later on.'

I struggled to accept he might be right. 'I'll think about it,' I said, grudgingly.

I went to bed early, leaving Hubert nightcapping. I lay awake for some time wondering how Megan would react to being left behind at Humberstone's. I didn't think she was fit to travel and I knew Hubert would look after her, but he couldn't be with her every minute of the day. I was worried about her mental stability, because she gave me the impression something trivial could spark a major relapse. She'd proved herself to be amazingly resilient, but I didn't think I could spend more than one or two nights away from her. She also needed to lose that mobile phone. And I needed to learn more about Rohypnol, but Hubert could find me that information on the Internet. As Megan seemed to have blacked out during the actual birth, I suspected she'd been given more of the drug and I wondered if the baby had died in consequence. And was this Teresa a qualified midwife anyway? Was the birth itself totally botched?

I'd drifted off to sleep when something woke me. I peered at the clock on my office wall. It was two thirty. Then I heard it again, Megan's indistinct murmuring followed by the sound of sobbing. I jumped out of bed and walked the short distance to my room. The door was slightly ajar and, as I pushed it further open in the half-light, I could see Megan with her back towards me frantically searching the bed. She'd thrown the pillows and the duvet on the floor and now she scrabbled at the bottom sheet. I stood watching her; she was sobbing and talking in Welsh. I made out only one word of English — baby. She was looking for her baby. I called her name softly. 'Megan,' I repeated, a little louder. She seemed to freeze and then she looked slowly round the room as if seeing it for the first time. I went up to her and put my arms around her and she sobbed so hard that we collapsed together on the bed. 'What's happening to me?' she asked over and over. Then she said, 'I heard my baby — he's calling to me. I saw him. I did — I saw him.'

I didn't try to answer or contradict her and, gradually, she quietened. I retrieved the pillows and duvet from the floor, helped her to lie down and gave her a fist full of tissues.

'I'll stay till you fall asleep,' I said.

She sighed several times and, with the tissues in a ball held to her mouth, she fell asleep. I sat there for ages. I'd switched on the bedside light thinking the dark may have disturbed her and, when I left the room, I also left the door wide open.

Back on the sofa bed in my office I lay wide-awake until daylight.

In the morning she remembered nothing. Over breakfast I told her of my plans to start retracing her steps. I baulked at telling her I was going to Wales. She might have wanted to come with me and, if Michael Whitby really was after her, he might have suspected she'd return there. Megan was far safer in Longborough. I didn't see how he could trace her to Humberstone's, especially if she laid low. And, at the moment, she was in no condition to do anything else.

Whilst she was in the bathroom, I acquired her mobile phone. If Whitby was going to phone again he could talk to me. Jasper watched me taking her phone. 'It's all in a good cause,' I said, but I still imagined his baleful expression was tinged with suspicion.

I managed to brief Hubert on the night's events before he left for a rather grand funeral of an ex-Mayor. 'You will keep an eye on her, won't you?'

'Shame on you for saying that,' he said. 'I'll be back by lunch time. I'll make sure she eats something decent. She can help me plan my bereavement group.'

'Opportunist!'

'She'll feel useful,' he said, sounding only more convinced.

Unusually, I was in Humberstone's reception area. It was tastefully funereal, with large vases of arum lilies casting a rather sickly smell. It wasn't somewhere I wanted to linger. Just as I was leaving, Hubert said, 'Have you fixed up anywhere to stay?'

'I thought I'd find somewhere when I got there.'

From his pocket he produced a sheaf of papers and handed them to me. 'Info. on Rohypnol,' he said. 'Plus details of your hotel. It's the Vine Lodge in Criccieth. It's all paid for — two nights.'

'Hubert — you really shouldn't have . . .'

He didn't let me finish. 'You just enjoy a bit of luxury for a change.' He obviously expected me to be grateful and I was, for the drug information, but not for him booking the hotel. I'd wanted to make that choice myself, but he hadn't committed any sin and he'd only had good intentions, so I gave him a peck on the cheek and said I'd ring as soon as I found Vine Lodge.

Leaving Megan proved more difficult. She was pale and worried. 'You will come back, won't you?'

'Of course. I'll ring. Don't be frightened of the phone. If it's a business call, just say I'm out of town for a couple of days and take their number. The answer call service will deal with it if you're not around.'

'I won't be able to take Jasper out?'

'No — don't go out at the moment. Hubert will get one of the pall-bearers to walk Jasper if he's not around. But he'll be back at lunch time.'

Jasper, on cue, having heard the magic word, bounded towards me, but as I picked up my overnight bag his tail stopped wagging. I bent down to nuzzle him and he licked me like a lolly, but I still felt his disapproval.

Megan waved goodbye to me from the window. Her round face looked ghostly white and there was no trace of a smile.

* * *

Criccieth was smaller than I imagined but, having driven through heavy mists, it was a relief to find the town bathed in bright spring sunshine. I stopped the car to gaze out at the sea. There was hardly a ripple and, from my high vantage point, I got that feeling of excitement that I'd had as a child when, after miles and miles, suddenly the sea was there in your line of vision — vast and shining like a foreign country in its own right.

I would have stayed longer looking at the sea but hunger drove me on. I found the Vine Lodge Hotel easily enough. It had a mock-castle appearance and steep steps to the reception area and it overlooked the sea. Inside, it had a continental feel with marble floors, rattan chairs and a huge variety of potted plants.

Having signed in, I was shown up to my room by an elderly porter. 'One of the best rooms, this,' he said. 'I reckon it's better than the bridal suite. How long are you staying, madam?'

'Only a couple of nights.'

'Well, you make the most of the sunshine. We get a lot of rain.'

'You're local, are you?'

'Lived here all my life, madam.'

I gave him a large tip and asked him the way to Megan's old address, somewhere between Criccieth and Penrhyndeudraeth. He laughed at my pronunciation but gave me simple directions and told me to have a good day.

The room was spacious but the main feature was the glorious view. The windows were so large I seemed to be part of the sea. Good old Hubert. Since coming back from New Zealand, I'd missed the sea. This felt like home.

The holiday feeling lasted until after lunch, then I drove towards the village with the unpronounceable name. The bungalow that Megan and her mother had lived in was indeed isolated. It seemed to have been tacked on to the village as an afterthought and I was surprised Megan hadn't needed a car. It was something neither of us had mentioned. The bungalow was long and low with picture windows facing a huge green field full of sheep. There were no visible neighbours, so I drove back into the village.

I stopped at the chemist's. Inside, there were two elderly women customers talking in Welsh, who glowered at the sight of me. Across the other side of the world, I'd felt more at home. Wales suddenly seemed alien territory and I had become an instant foreigner.

I ambled to the make-up section and began looking and testing. Eventually the two women left, casting me venomous looks as they passed me by, and I took my mascara and lipstick to the counter. The assistant, who was about twenty and appeared to have sculpted her face with make-up, did manage to smile at me. When I asked to see the pharmacist, the smile faded. 'What do you want him for?' she asked, suspiciously.

'It's a personal matter.'

'Mr Davies,' she called through the hatch. 'A woman here wants to talk to you. She's English.'

A stocky man of about thirty, dark-haired with brown eyes and long lashes, appeared behind the counter. Not bad-looking if you liked that type. 'Thanks, Bethany,' he said, smiling pleasantly at her. 'Can I help you?' he asked me.

'Could we talk privately?'

'Is it a medical matter?'

'No, it's personal.'

Meanwhile, Bethany was still looking daggers at me.

'Come round,' he said, signalling to the inner sanctum.

There, amongst shelves filled with box upon box of pills, capsules, medicines and lotions, he said, 'Now then, what can I do for you?'

'It's about Megan Thomas.'

'Where is she? Is she all right?'

'Yes. She will be. I'm here to get some background on her. I'm a private investigator.'

'What's she done?'

'She hasn't done anything. She just needs help.'

The shop bell sounded and at least two sets of footsteps followed. 'Look, I can't talk now, it's getting busy,' he said. 'I close at six. I'll meet you outside. We could go for a drink and have a proper chat. I liked Megan — if I can help, I will.'

Bethany was busy speaking in Welsh to the next brace of customers and I had a feeling she'd overheard our conversation. I could almost feel their eyes boring into my back. It reminded me of one of those Westerns where all the locals are practically spitting poison at some innocent stranger.

I spent the afternoon wandering around Criccieth's small shops and having numerous cups of tea. I limited myself to a mere slice of Bara Brith. After all, I didn't want to spoil my appetite for dinner at the hotel.

* * *

At five to six it began to rain, dark clouds loomed and the wind whipped up. It had seemed a never-ending afternoon and now I felt the effects of the long drive. I wanted a bath, a meal and bed. I looked forward to watching a ferocious night at sea from the comfort of my bed.

At six there was still a customer in the chemist's so I hung about outside. At two minutes past I was getting soaked so I walked in and gave Bethany a cheery wave. She ignored me totally and I wondered if she saw me as some sort of threat. Or, more likely, she'd heard Megan mentioned and perhaps Megan was considered in some way an obstacle to pharmaceutical romance. I had to admit, even with the make-up overload, Bethany was the more attractive.

At six fifteen Hywel appeared, wearing an anorak, with the shop keys at the ready. Bethany managed a tight smile at me as the door was opened for her. She disappeared with her head down against the rain into the gloomy evening.

'There's a wine bar a few doors up,' said Hywel. 'I don't drink but you're welcome to have one. I'll drink coffee.'

Inside, it was warm and smelt of cheap wine and damp clothes. A few men in suits collected in groups near the bar, but Hywel suggested a corner table and strode off to order red wine and coffee. Once he sat down he leant forward and said, earnestly, 'Now, tell me about Megan. I've been very worried about her.' Something in his voice told me he was really fond of her. I decided to tread warily. 'Megan is OK . . .' I paused. 'She's staying with me at the moment.'

'Is it her old trouble?' he asked.

'What do you mean?'

'She was very poorly after her mother died, very poorly indeed.'

'I'm sorry. What do you mean by *poorly*?'

'Reactive depression,' he said. 'She should have been on antidepressants a long time before her mother died. I blame myself. I was in a position to help.'

'So why didn't you?'

He shrugged. 'Megan never complained, but everyone knew Gwyneth Thomas was a very demanding, difficult woman. That's why Megan had no help. She did everything — the cooking, shopping, housework, gardening — and looked after her mother. She got out once a week to do the shopping and once on Sunday to go to chapel.'

'I would have thought her mother's death would have been a relief.'

He sipped at his coffee and stared at me with slight suspicion. 'She hasn't told you the full story then?'

'Obviously not. What is the full story?'

'It seems that the day Gwyneth died Megan had been out shopping. She came back to find her dead in her bed.'

'She told me that.'

'It seems that the paper boy collected their paper money every Saturday morning. When he got no reply he told the newsagent and, as it had never happened before, on the Sunday morning he went to investigate. He walked in through the back door, as it wasn't locked, and there sat Megan by her mother's bed. Her mother had been dead since Wednesday. The shopping bags were still at Megan's feet.'

I'd listened in horror. Now I tried to think back to what Megan had told me. 'So, she didn't ring the doctor?'

'No,' said Hywel. 'She was like a zombie. The newsagent rang the doctor and the police. Megan was shipped off to a mental hospital in Rhyl and there she stayed for six weeks.'

'So, she didn't go to the funeral.'

'She wasn't well enough,' he said. 'I went to see her once a week when she was in hospital. At first she hardly moved a muscle but, when the medication kicked in, she improved during the day, but at night she would say her mother was calling her and she'd get out of bed to look for her.'

'Poor Megan,' I murmured.

'Yes, indeed,' he said. 'When she came out she was subdued, but she put the house on the market and it sold very quickly. Then one day she came to the shop to tell me she was going to London for a few days. I tried to dissuade her, I really did. She was a girl who'd never been out of Wales before but she'd made up her mind and there was nothing I could do.'

'And she didn't contact you?'

'Not a word. I know she has a mobile phone but I didn't know the number, so there was nothing I could do.'

I sat contemplating my empty wine glass. I wasn't driving and I needed another one.

Hywel began zipping up his jacket. 'Megan was different,' he said. 'Pure. Innocent and unselfish. I would have married her, you know.'

'What do you mean — would have?'

'Going away to London like that. More than a year now. She won't be the same Megan, will she?'

I was getting mad now. 'You mean she won't be the docile little slave anymore?' I'd started now, so I thought I might as well go on. 'You think London has tainted her in some way or that she might have given up pious chapel-going for streetwalking . . .'

'I don't know why you're having a go at me,' he blustered. 'She could have written or phoned. I was her best friend, after all.'

'As long as you didn't have to put yourself out,' I snapped. 'And where were all those good chapel-going folks when Megan needed a break from her mother?'

'I told you — Gwyneth was a harridan. No one wanted to get involved.'

'Megan couldn't opt out though, could she? Even when her mother was dead, she still stayed at her post.'

'I know we let Megan down,' he said, sounding like the feeble little worm he was. 'But what can we do about it now?'

'I just have a feeling,' I said. 'If ever Megan did come back here, there wouldn't be much of a welcome in the green, green grass of home.'

I stood up. I'd said my piece and, perhaps it was unfair to blame Hywel, but if her baby had lived, I could imagine the little tuts of disapproval. *If only she'd stayed in Wales*, they would have said. And if she *had* stayed, Hywel would have married her, bought another shop with her money and Megan would have resumed her slave role, only this time she'd have been a sales assistant from nine a.m. to six p.m. and then chief cook and bottle washer after that. On Sundays she would have gone to chapel and in the summer he'd have suggested Tenby for two weeks in a medium-cost guest house.

'I don't suppose I'll see you again,' I said. 'I'll tell Megan I've met you.'

He looked slightly ashamed. I guessed he was bonking Bethany and that Megan was a mere blip on his conscience. It made me more determined than ever to help Megan in whatever way I could.

As we got to the door of the wine bar, he took me by the arm and almost whispered in my ear. 'There were rumours going round that Megan had given her mother an overdose. That she went mad after doing it. The doctor signed the death certificate. Death was said to be by myocardial infarction — a heart attack. Gwyneth was cremated and, knowing that the doctor had a soft spot for Megan, some people thought it was a cover-up.'

'Where do I find the doctor?'

He gave me the address and I walked into the rain thinking that some frogs never become princes. In his own snide little way he was more poisonous toad than harmless frog. Megan was well out of small-town gossip and innuendo and, if nothing else, going to London had saved her from a life of selling suppositories, sanitary towels and cough syrup.

It was only as I approached Vine Lodge, with the walk and the soaking rain to calm me down, that I did wonder if maybe Megan *had* reached the end of reason with her mother. She hadn't told me the whole truth. Was she unstable enough to be spinning me a web of lies that was sucking me in to some strange fantasy of hers? Was her naivety real? Had she murdered her baby and her loss of memory was a carefully constructed tale to cover the fact? The money in her bag that she said she got from selling the house. Was that instant cash too big a temptation for her?

As I collected my key, the receptionist said there'd been a phone call for me. I felt in my pocket and examined my mobile. It was switched off. Just as I was about to ask who from, she said, 'A local call — there was no message.'

'You're sure it was local?'

'Oh, yes.'

'Male or female?'

'It was a woman.'

CHAPTER SIX

Before dinner I rang Hubert. He sounded cagey. 'Are you sure Megan's OK?'

'I've told you once, Kate,' he said. 'She's doing a bit of spring cleaning at the moment. There's no problem.'

I was still suspicious. *If* there had been something wrong, he wouldn't have told me, knowing there was nothing I could do. I wanted to get back to Longborough as quickly as possible. Wales in sunshine was a great place to be — wasting time in Wales in the rain was a depressing prospect.

Dinner at a round table with an elderly couple from Barnsley and two equally elderly sisters from Doncaster was fairly excruciating. For some reason they seemed to think I was interested in how rain affected their arthritis, how long the batteries to a pacemaker lasted and how lavender on their pillow helped them sleep. I did toy with the idea of telling them I was a Soho lap dancer but I don't think it would have made any difference. I managed to escape before coffee was served by saying I'd left my Rennies in my room. *That* they could understand.

I spent the rest of a long evening with one eye on the TV and the other watching a restless sea. This was followed by an equally restless night, where I dreamed I was back working in

A&E and I was in charge of the overflow corridor. More and more patients crowded in. I could hardly move between the trolleys and beds. The patients insisted on vomiting, bleeding and needing oxygen, plus they needed fluids and sustenance, which, of course, meant bottles and bedpans and, when I wasn't quite quick enough, they needed washing and changing too. Finally, having screamed, *I can't go on*, and heard someone answering, *You must go on*, I woke up in a hot, twisted duvet very relieved that, for me, it hadn't been real.

I went down to breakfast and sat alone. The other residents were mostly genteel, retired people on a bargain spring break. It was no place for sun-worshippers. Outside, the rain poured down and they all seemed fully equipped with hooded anoraks and boots. I wasn't so well equipped, but I didn't intend to be out of my car long enough to get really wet.

I had to make a decision about seeing Dr Lewis — should I go early to catch her before morning surgery or creep in just as she was finishing? No doubt, either way, I'd have to run the gauntlet of ferocious Welsh receptionists. I decided on Plan B, so that, after I'd seen her, I could go directly back to Longborough. My uneasy feeling wouldn't go away.

In reality the receptionist was a pleasant, motherly type, who disappeared into the inner sanctum to ask Dr Lewis if she would see me at the end of surgery on a personal matter. 'She's got two more patients to see and then it'll be your turn, dear,' she said. 'Just you take a seat.'

I flicked through a magazine and watched as the last but one patient made a tortuous trip down the corridor with the aid of two walking sticks. The remaining patient, a young girl, was hacking and coughing and I was relieved I'd sat well away from her. Like hospitals, doctor's surgeries can damage your health. The weak don't emerge unscathed.

Dr Lewis was in her late thirties with fair, bobbed hair and tired eyes. The desk in front of her was covered with medical files and letters, which she pushed to one side as she leant forward to shake my hand. Her welcoming smile lit up her face and, when I said I'd come to talk to her about Megan Thomas, she seemed pleased but not surprised. 'I tried to ring you at your hotel,' she said. 'I heard you had news of Megan.'

'How did you hear so soon?' I asked.

'Bethany Evans isn't called Beth the Voice because she can sing. Nothing passes her by and discretion is not part of her vocabulary. But, in this instance, I'm glad she gossiped. How is Megan?'

I paused, not wanting to say too much; after all, I was the one seeking information. 'She's staying with me at the moment.'

'Where's that — in London?'

'No. The midlands — Longborough.'

'What's she doing there?'

'Escaping from a bad situation.'

'I see. I knew she wanted to go to London desperately. The poor kid had had a rotten life.'

'Yes, I talked to Hywel, the chemist.'

'He's not my favourite person,' said Dr Lewis. 'He's a lay preacher — he gives the word *lay* it's modern meaning.'

'I thought he was keen on Megan.'

'He was,' she agreed. 'He thought she was very marriageable but only when he'd sown his wild oats.'

'Megan told me a little about her life,' I said. 'But she didn't tell me she'd had a breakdown when she found her mother dead.'

Dr Lewis sat back in her chair. 'I used to visit once a week on the pretext of seeing Gwyneth, but really my concern was for Megan. I offered respite care but Gwyneth always refused. She was one of the most selfish women I've ever met — a sanctimonious Bible-thumper. I think she used religion, as it's always been used in my opinion, to control. She wanted to keep Megan by her side, so she warned her of hellfire and the evil that lurked outside the safety of North Wales. London was simply a cesspit of vice and degeneration. And now, I suppose, you've come to tell me Megan is pregnant.'

'Why do you think she's pregnant?'

'Experience,' she sighed. 'The naive girls sheltered from reality seem to be the first to succumb to the call of testosterone.'

'She was raped,' I said, bluntly.

'Oh dear,' she said, frowning. 'Poor Megan — how's she coping?'

'Fairly well, actually. The baby was stillborn.'

'I'm so sorry,' she murmured. 'I had hoped things would turn out better for her once she was away from here.'

I decided not to go into any real detail. It was Megan's business, after all, and there was nothing the doctor could do about the situation. There was one more thing I wanted to discuss and, now I'd met her, I found it quite hard to broach the subject. After all, if there was any truth in Hywel's allegation that Megan had been involved in her mother's death, then it involved the doctor herself.

'I don't quite know how to say this, but Hywel Davies gave me the impression there had been rumours that Megan had somehow had a hand in her mother's death.'

'It's rubbish!' she snapped. 'Gwyneth Thomas would have been dead years before if it hadn't been for Megan's devoted care. She was a heart attack merely waiting to happen. Years of steroids, inactivity and painkillers finally take their toll. She'd also been taking drugs for angina for years. I was amazed, given her general condition, that she remained as well as she did and for as long as she did. I'd been seeing her every week and, that week, I'd started her on antibiotics for a slight chest infection. She was on a downward spiral and Megan had nothing to do with it.'

'Is that why there was no post-mortem?'

Dr Lewis fixed me with a steady gaze. 'If every old lady who died after years of illness had a post-mortem the country would have to have at least treble the number of pathologists.'

'But there is no doubt in your mind that Megan had anything to do with her mother's death?'

'No doubt at all,' she said. 'I think it's shameful that, after all her years of devoted care, rumours should be spread simply because the poor kid cracked up.'

'Three days she sat by the body, didn't she?'

'She was catatonic. Luckily she got better. And now she's still in a mess. What does she plan to do?'

'She's just going to rest up at the moment.'

'Do the police have any idea who the rapist is?'

I shook my head, deciding that nothing further could be gained by saying any more.

'When you see Megan, give her my regards, won't you?'

'I certainly will. I'll keep in touch to let you know what happens.'

'I'd appreciate that.'

As I left she shook my hand and I handed her my business card, which Hubert insisted no self-respecting PI could do without. She looked at it in surprise and, for a moment, I thought she was going to question me, but she changed her mind and murmured, 'Good luck.'

Megan had had some good luck in her life, finding such a concerned doctor, and at least we had one ally in Wales. I had a feeling that I might need Dr Lewis's help in the future but, for now, I just wanted to get back and find out what was happening at Humberstone's.

* * *

I arrived back late in the afternoon. There was no sign of Hubert in his office, so I went round to the side door and, as I walked up the stairs, I felt a slight shiver down my back. It was the quiet that disturbed me — no radio or television on, no sound of any kitchen activity. Worse, no Jasper yapping excitedly. Perhaps she's asleep, I thought, or maybe she's out somewhere with Hubert.

My office and bedroom were empty and I peered into Hubert's lounge to find all three of them asleep. Jasper opened one eye, wagged his tail in a half-hearted fashion and then closed his eye. I wasn't going to disturb them but I felt disappointed, as if my return didn't merit consciousness.

I sloped off into the kitchen, made tea and, considering I felt this to be a crisis, ate four biscuits. Then I unpacked and read the paper and finally Jasper trotted in to see me. Hubert followed a few minutes later, his face creased with sleep. With a croaky voice, he said, 'I'm glad you're back.'

'Why? What's been going on?'

'Is that tea in the pot?'

I gave him tea and waited for him to explain. 'The moment you left, she started cleaning,' he said. 'Nothing wrong with that,' he said. 'The place needed a bit of sprucing up. I know you don't do any—'

'That is not true. I do, occasionally, get the Hoover out.'

'Only once in a bluey,' he said. 'This was different. She didn't stop. All the furniture had to be moved. She even cleaned the skirting boards.'

'It sounds like good news to me.'

'It would be. But she blanked off. She wouldn't answer when I spoke to her. She seemed demented.'

'Cleaning has that effect on me too.'

'Don't start being flippant, Kate. You weren't here overnight. She was crying out, walking from room to room — neither of us slept.'

'Did she say anything?'

'Oh, yes. It gave me the shivers. She said her baby was crying and she had to find him.'

'It's a grief reaction, Hubert. After her mother died she said she could hear *her* calling.'

'You don't have to tell me about grief reactions,' said Hubert, obviously peeved that I'd ignored his professional experience. He *did know* about grief. It was his job to know.

'I'd suggest she saw a doctor,' I said, 'but she's opposed to that and they'd only medicate her, when all she needs is time and space.'

'How much time?' he asked, gloomily. 'Some people grieve for years. How long do you plan to give her?'

'I don't know. At least until Whitby is found and charged.'

'Come off it,' he said. 'The police will need evidence. Young Megan isn't going to be a star witness, is she? She could well get scared and do a runner.'

'That's why I'm on the case.'

Hubert had the cheek to laugh. 'You mean well,' he said, when he'd finished laughing. 'But you do blunder in and try to wing it.'

I was niggled but I tried not to show it. 'I've managed in the past and I'll succeed this time, too — even if I do have to *wing it,* as you put it.'

A slight noise at the kitchen door made us turn. Megan rushed towards me saying, 'Thank God you're safe, Kate,' as she gave me a crushing hug. Since I hadn't thought I was in any danger, I was a little taken aback. 'Hang on, Megan,' I said. 'Criccieth is not Moss Side, Manchester. My most hazardous encounter was with heavy mist and rain.'

She stood back from me and said, earnestly, 'It won't be just me in danger. You're in danger too.'

Hubert intervened then. 'You two stop being dramatic. You need some fresh air, Megan. Why not take Jasper for a walk?'

That was the cue for mild hysterics from Jasper. Megan looked worried but said, 'I'll go out if you come too, Kate.'

'Yeah, fine,' I agreed. I noticed she was still wearing the same old tracksuit, so I suggested she look through my wardrobe for something else to wear. As she went off to look, I thought — please don't let anything fit! Not because I begrudged her my clothes, but I was sure she was more rounded than me. She came back within minutes wearing my favourite purple long skirt and top. It was a little tight but it made me make two resolutions — one, she could spend some of her money, and two, I was foregoing biscuits, cream cakes and chips until I could fit into the smallest size in my wardrobe.

On our walk I mentioned the shopping trip. 'I think,' I said, 'it might help if you changed your appearance. If Michael Whitby does come after you, then you won't be so easy to spot.'

'I've only ever been clothes shopping on my own,' she said. 'I used catalogues mostly. It would be nice to go shopping with a girlfriend.'

I felt a bit uneasy about being a *girlfriend*. She was already clingy and, since that one phone call, nothing else had happened. Maybe Whitby had decided there was nothing to be gained by hounding a quiet Welsh girl who was unlikely to be a threat. Even so, I had no plans to let him get away with rape, threatening behaviour and charges that related to the failure to disclose a stillbirth.

'Where did you say Whitby was stationed in London?' I asked, trying to sound casual.

'North London — Horsefields Police Station.'

'And he's an inspector there?'

'Yes.'

'And you believed him? Why?'

'He seemed like a policeman.'

I laughed. 'Did he have big feet?'

She didn't laugh back. 'Fairly big, I think. Why?'

'Never mind, I'll try and trace him. It's always better to go on the offensive. Flush out the enemy and he might get careless.'

'I'm not used to this sort of thing,' she said. 'You do what you think is best.'

There were times when I wanted to yell at her, *You're so bloody trusting!* But that would have been as bad as kicking Jasper. They were both innocents but Jasper didn't have to make his own way in the world and Megan did. Megan needed more than a physical makeover; she needed a mental makeover, and how would I achieve that?

Later that evening, while Megan watched television, I went along to my office and rang Directory Enquiries for the phone number of Horsefields Police Station. I was sure I was wasting my time but, at least if I checked it out, I could reassure Megan.

'Inspector Michael Whitby, please.'

'Who's calling?'

'The Secretary, Tottenham Hotspur Football Club.'

I hadn't intended to say that, but football was the only thing I connected with the area.

'Just one moment,' said the cheerful human operator, 'while I try to connect you.' I continued to hang on. A metaphor for life itself, I thought. As I waited, I wondered if the operator knew what she was doing. Was she new? Did she actually know who worked there? The phone continued to ring. Then a moment's pause before a voice said, crisply, 'Whitby, Vice.'

CHAPTER SEVEN

I slammed the phone down instantly. The hairs on the back of my neck were busy dancing a tango and I felt slightly sick. If my reaction was even a *slight* reflection of how Megan felt when she heard his voice, then I had some idea of how she felt. I was scared and I'd never met him and, if I felt scared, then she must be terrified.

She looked up as I came into the lounge. 'Are you all right?' she asked.

'Fine,' I said. 'Never better.' She didn't look totally convinced. I sat down and watched her surreptitiously. Jasper was curled up on her lap and she was gently stroking his head. One thing I had learned was that Jasper was as fickle as most male creatures I'd met. As long as his needs were satisfied, he was anyone's for a walk, a tickle and a bowl of food.

The word *vice* still echoed in my head. Was it true about looking after the old lady? Or had she been doing something altogether less noble? I dismissed that thought. I was convinced that Megan had told me the truth. She was naive and gullible but she was no liar. And it wasn't surprising she didn't want to go to the police. Why, though, did Michael Whitby want to silence her one way or the other? I had the impression that he'd hoped to drive her to suicide. He'd raped her but was the pregnancy by design or accident? Once she was pregnant, had he found someone capable but cheap to care for his great-aunt?

'As a matter of interest,' I asked Megan, casually, 'how much did Whitby pay you for caring for Alice?'

'Nothing really. I had bed and board and he told me to ask if I needed money.'

'Did you think that was a good deal?'

She shrugged. 'I'm not used to earning money and I had my own money anyway.'

I resumed staring at the TV screen. I'd read the info Hubert had found me on Rohypnol, the brand name of Flunitrazepam. It has various street names such as Rope, Rib and Roofies and supplies originate in Mexico and Colombia and, from there, are smuggled to Miami. A combination of alcohol and Rohypnol, it seems, could cause blackouts lasting from eight to twenty-four hours. Withdrawal symptoms range from headache, muscle pain and confusion to hallucinations and convulsions. I wondered if Megan had had more than a couple of doses and if her blackout at the time of birth been caused by yet another dose? If she had been far advanced in labour, had the Rohypnol crossed into the placenta and affected the baby? Could that have been the cause of the stillbirth and, if so, was it planned? Had Whitby decided to recruit Megan as a drug runner for Rohypnol, perhaps getting her dependent? The pregnancy was a mere blip in his plans? Speculation alone wasn't going to solve anything. I needed to know far more about Michael Whitby. What, for instance, was he doing at the Georgiana Hotel?

'Megan, how would you feel about a trip to London?' I asked.

Her expression was a mixture of surprise and fear. 'I'd be so scared,' she said.

'I know, but if we give you a makeover, no one will recognize you. We'll change your name, your hair colour, your style.'

'I haven't got a style,' she said.

'You can decide on that tonight. Look through some magazines. Choose some expensive clothes. Expensive is the best style of all.'

She managed a tight little smile.

'We won't say anything to Hubert,' I said. 'We'll see if we can surprise him.'

Later that evening I did tell Hubert we were going to London. He was not best pleased. 'I think you two should stay put,' he said. 'If this Whitby bloke is a cop—'

'He is, Hubert. He's in the vice squad.'

Hubert went very quiet. 'Why don't you get in touch with David Todman at Longborough nick before you go blundering into something.'

'I do not blunder!'

'Yes you do. Check this bloke out with David.'

I didn't want to do that. I'd had a minor dalliance with David a few months back, but he'd taken the view that I was more trouble than I was worth and we hadn't spoken since. He was bound to ask questions and I thought the fewer people who knew, the better.

'I will talk to him but I'll fabricate a reason. I don't want to involve Megan at this stage.'

'Only you could say something like that.'

'What did I say?'

'Think about it . . .'

I did, but I was none the wiser.

There wasn't any point in ringing David on a Sunday evening and I'm a great believer in putting off awkward phone calls of an even slightly personal nature. I have to psych myself up for it.

Megan was a having a major love affair with the TV. She'd obviously just discovered Channel Five's late-night erotic thrillers. I left her still watching at midnight.

At two thirty I heard her calling out. I staggered half asleep into my bedroom, now temporarily hers, to hear her saying, 'I'm coming, I'm coming.' Her anxious tone of voice told me the erotic film hadn't affected her. She was responding to an inner voice. I stood watching her for a while, but she fell quiet and seemed to dip back into a deep sleep. I wasn't so lucky and, in the depressing early hours of morning, I lay awake wondering how I could speed up the investigation and make Megan's safe departure equally speedy.

* * *

For once Megan looked refreshed and less pale in the morning. I looked as if I'd been late-night clubbing on *grab-a-granny* night. She was excited about going shopping and to the hairdressers. At least that's what she told me. I hadn't noticed it for myself, so it was obviously a muted excitement, but then Megan had probably had to quell every girlish emotion to please her mother.

The main question for me though, was where to start with the makeover. Hair or clothes? I guessed we should start with underwear. I'd noticed there was no Marks and Spencer's in Criccieth and, judging by Megan's reaction to the underwear, she'd never even been in M&S before. She wanted to buy up most of the knickers. In the end I had to set a limit of ten pairs, plus three bras and five pairs of tights, pleading lack of drawer space as an excuse.

I'd managed to fix her up with a hair appointment, thanks to a cancellation, for two p.m. At this rate one day would not be long enough.

I was surprised by how good Megan looked in a skirt. She bought three expensive skirts, several bright tops and a denim jacket and jeans. Finally she chose a pair of black leather boots, high-heeled sandals, Nike trainers and a pair of classy medium-heeled courts. 'You'll have to practise your walking with a higher heel,' I warned.

'I'll do it,' she said, grabbing my arm. 'I've never had such a good time.' Almost as soon as she'd said the words, her face lost its animated expression. 'If it wasn't for . . .'

'I understand.' I checked my watch. We had three quarters of an hour to buy her all the cosmetics a face could need. The assistant was very helpful and I suggested one of everything. Megan was awe-struck at the selection and, since she hadn't worn make-up before, couldn't really make appropriate choices.

We made the final dash to the hairdressers and arrived with a minute to spare. Since the colouring process and restyling would take three hours, I left Megan and walked back to Humberstone's.

There was no sign of Hubert or Jasper, so I sat down to read the paper and woke up an hour and a half later feeling very groggy, but resolved to phone Inspector Todman with a cock-and-bull story which, I thought, would take me a while to concoct. In reality, it didn't take that long. I'd use the imaginary friend ploy. I just hoped he was a man who didn't hold a grudge for too long. I took a deep breath and picked up the phone, half hoping he wouldn't be there, but he was. 'Hello, Kate,' he said, warmly. 'It's been a long time. What can I do for you?'

'It's not work,' I said, hurriedly. 'It's a friend of mine. She's got involved with a police inspector in London and I'm a bit concerned. He's a little unreliable and he's in the vice squad.'

'And you don't approve of the vice squad?'

'It's not that. She's not the world's best judge of men and I don't want to see her hurt again.'

There was a fairly long pause before he said, 'It's you, isn't it, Kate?'

'It is not!'

'OK. Prove it. You give me the name and the nick and I'll find out what I can and meet you for a drink this evening, about eight.'

I didn't have much choice, so I told him who and where and said, 'Great. Thanks. See you then.'

When the three hours were up, I went back to the hair-dresser's. Even without the benefit of make-up Megan looked so different. The now soft, blonde hair had a feathery fringe and, although short, it made her face look thinner and suited her pale complexion. She was smiling with delight. 'I feel like a new person.'

'Just wait till the clothes and make-up are in place,' I said. 'You *will* be a new person.'

I was getting excited now but I did wonder if I was developing megalomania. It was necessary that she changed her appearance but did I want to create a whole new person? A new chassis and a coat of paint wouldn't necessarily heal her wounds. And after all, however glamorous, Megan would still be Megan.

When I'd made up her face and she was dressed in expensive jeans and a smart white top, she stared at herself in the mirror for a long time. 'This is the new me,' she said, 'and it feels lovely.' It was worth the effort to see Megan's confidence develop, because I had a feeling that in the days, maybe weeks, to come she'd need all the confidence she could acquire.

* * *

When Hubert saw her he did a double-take. Even Jasper looked a little confused.

'Well, Megan,' he said, grinning. 'What a difference! You're a real swan, grown up from a cygnet. The Longborough lads will think a film star's in town.'

Megan giggled. 'You're teasing me.'

'Would I? Seriously. You look terrific.'

Hubert had never told me I looked *terrific* and, I have to admit, I felt a tinge of jealousy. Megan was a good ten years younger than me and now she looked it.

Rather childishly I wanted to be in Hubert's good books, so I told him I was seeing David Todman for a drink. 'I've always thought you two were suited,' he said.

'You don't know everything — if the chemistry isn't there, it isn't there.'

'You've never given him a chance.'

I didn't bother to argue. I disappeared into the bathroom and emerged half an hour later looking for compliments. 'You've scrubbed up well,' said Hubert.

'You look very nice,' said Megan.

I supposed *terrific* was on hold for some future time. I'd obviously have to try a bit harder.

* * *

David was on time for a change and he wanted to drive out of Longborough to a country pub. At least I could drink. David didn't. Perhaps that was a reason I could never get involved with him. In my experience, a man who has had too much to drink shows himself in his true colours. Alcohol peels away a layer, causing loss of inhibition. So, the shy man reveals himself as gregarious, the meek man as aggressive, the Jack-the-Lad shows his morose side and the hard man reveals a softer side. The man who doesn't drink may be frightened of exposing his true self, losing control. So, for me, David would always be a mystery and who wants to get entangled in a mystery that might not get solved or might give you a very nasty surprise? There was one consolation though. I could drink his share and not worry too much about my inner self. He could like it or lump it.

On the way to the pub I told him business was not brisk. He didn't sympathize. He was working hours of unpaid overtime on a long-standing murder case. He didn't go into any details and certainly didn't ask for any advice from me. In his opinion, PIs should deal only with errant husbands and wives or lost dogs.

Once we were in the Rose and Crown — a pub as unoriginal as its name and with four customers, all men over fifty — he told me he'd thought the place might be quiet. Quiet? There was more bustle and life in Hubert's front office. The place grew on me though, after two gin and tonics, and I was no longer happy to pussyfoot about over the reason for our meeting. 'What did you find out about Michael Whitby?' I asked bluntly.

'You've got it bad, haven't you?'

'It isn't me. I told you that, David. It's a friend of mine.'

'What's her name?'

'Why do you want her name? It's Ann. She lives in London.'

He knew I was uncomfortable and he sipped at his Coke and took his time. Just to annoy me, he even crunched his ice. 'I checked him out,' he said finally, post crunch. 'He's been in the Met for fifteen years, not a high-flyer, but two commendations when he worked undercover for the drug squad. No real details on that. Divorced twice, once recently. No kids. Will that do you?'

'Nothing else?'

He looked puzzled. 'What else did you want? You sound disappointed.' Then he added, 'If your friend Ann is worried about two divorces — it's fairly common these days, especially in drugs and vice.'

'Why's that?'

'The irregular hours, working undercover, suspicions about the women they meet. It's not surprising marriages don't last.'

'There was nothing . . . shady . . . then?'

'You mean corrupt?'

'Yeah. Or any disciplinary actions taken against him.'

'Not that I found out. What do you suspect him of?'

'Nothing — nothing at all.'

I had two more gins then and got a little maudlin about New Zealand. David confessed he'd love to take a year off and was hoping to do a detective exchange with the NYPD because he was interested in their zero-tolerance policy, which, it appeared, had drastically reduced the murder rate.

I was home by eleven but, of course, I didn't invite him in. At the door, he took hold of my arm. 'Look, Kate, if you have any doubts about this guy Whitby, follow your instincts. If you don't trust him, why bother? Now, I am someone you *can* trust . . .'

I didn't let him finish. I gave him a quick smacker on the lips, murmured 'Thanks a million', and pushed him gently towards his car. As he opened his car door he turned. 'Ring me,' he said. 'Any time.'

Hubert was still up watching television, but when he saw me he switched it off. He looked grim. 'What's the matter?' I asked.

'Megan had a call on her mobile.'

'What did he say?'

'She wouldn't tell me but she was trembling and crying. Nothing I could say comforted her.'

I swore to myself. I'd left her mobile phone on the desk in my office. So, in a way it was my fault.

'Do you think she's asleep?'

Hubert shook his head. 'He's only just rung. Before you talk to her, what are you going to do?'

'We're going to London to retrace her steps and try to find out what really happened.'

'I think you'd be safer staying here.'

'Perhaps, but a man like Whitby can't be allowed to get away with rape.'

'And did David find out anything about him?'

'Yes . . .' I hesitated. 'At the moment he looks whiter than white.'

'If you go stumbling about asking questions, don't you think he might get to you first?'

'Some risks you have to take.'

'This time you're risking Megan's life.'

When Hubert was this serious it was best not to say too much, so I looked thoughtful and offered to pour us a nightcap, adding, 'I'll take one in to Megan.'

'She had one. She needed it.'

I poured us a brandy and Hubert stared into the amber liquid as if it held mystic qualities. After a few seconds of contemplation he asked, 'Have you thought that maybe this man is simply using the name Michael Whitby?'

'Yes,' I said, 'but the voice making threats and the voice saying, "Whitby, Vice" sounded the same to me.'

'You could tell in two words?'

Of course, now that he'd asked the question, I was unsure. 'I think so.'

'Think about this, Kate. Megan will have to identify the right man. Just make sure he doesn't see her.'

'That's a good point,' I conceded.

'And,' said Hubert, pausing to give me his special warning look. 'If Whitby is the man, he'll have a story lined up and the police always stick together. He'll say she was a poor little Welsh girl drawn into a life of vice and he was her knight in shining armour. Everything she says will be put down to a woman scorned. After all, there isn't any proof that she was raped, is there? She didn't report it. We've only her word that's she's even had a baby. She doesn't mention it much, does she?'

'She was still producing milk,' I said.

Hubert looked a little pained at the thought. 'Are you absolutely sure of that?'

'Her tee shirt was wet.'

'So is water.'

I sighed. 'You should have been a barrister, Hubert — prosecuting. Whatever you say, I think she's telling the truth.'

'As she sees it.'

Hubert was winning, so I downed my brandy and told him I'd talk to Megan and get back to him. 'I'll still be here.'

Megan was lying in bed staring at the ceiling. 'Hubert's told me all about it. What exactly did he say?'

Her eyes didn't leave the ceiling and, as my eyes grew accustomed to the dim light of the bedside lamp, I could see her newly applied mascara had formed black rivulets down her cheeks. She didn't answer. 'Come on, Megan,' I said sharply. 'What did he say?'

CHAPTER EIGHT

I'd asked her three more times and I was beginning to lose patience. 'I can't stay here pleading with you, Megan. If I'm going to help you I need your cooperation.'

Finally, she shifted her eyes from the ceiling to look at me. 'He said I should kill myself because only death will reunite me with my baby. And he said, as long as I live my baby will haunt me.'

'Oh God, I'm so sorry,' was my first reaction. Then I got mad. 'The bastard! We have to catch him. Don't you see what he's doing? He wants you out of the way so you can't finger him. He's trying to turn you into the ultimate victim. He's trying to murder you by proxy.'

'My baby does haunt me,' she murmured. 'Every night I hear him crying. I try to imagine he's in heaven with Jesus but I can't. He cries and it's me he wants. I think Whitby is right. I should be with my baby.'

'Stop it!' I snapped. 'If you hadn't heard his voice tonight you'd be OK. There's only one way to sort this.'

I left the room and went straight to Hubert. 'Where do you keep your hammer?' I asked.

'Hang on a minute,' he said. 'Calm down. She's not that irritating.'

I took a deep breath. 'It's not to clobber Megan with. You can watch if you like.'

'It's not really my bag,' he said, with a half smile. 'There's one in my tool box. But I'd better supervise you — it's a good hammer.'

Moments later we advanced on Megan's room. I carried the hammer and a breadboard.

Megan, wide-eyed, sat up immediately. 'Now then,' I said. 'I'm going to show you how we start fighting back.' I placed the breadboard on the floor, laid Megan's mobile phone in the middle of it and knelt on the floor. Then I raised the hammer high above my head and smashed it down, shouting, 'Die! Die!' I got quite carried away. Bits of the phone scattered across the floor. 'There,' I said, triumphantly, after four or five whacks had obliterated it. 'That's silenced him. He won't bother you on that again.'

Whilst I was well satisfied, Megan lay back against her pillows and muttered, 'I do hope you're right. He's a clever man, he's very cunning.'

'We can be cunning. Hubert will help us too — he's got a GCSE in cunning. We *can* win. Sometimes the underdog has to win.'

She didn't look convinced. 'Who says?' she murmured. 'I'm very tired now.'

'I'll sit here until you fall asleep, if you like,' I said. I thought that was a sensible thing to do. Hubert meanwhile was picking up the numerous body parts of the mobile phone.

'It's a suicide watch, isn't it?' she said. 'I had that in hospital.'

I hadn't thought of it as such, but it put the idea in my head that I should keep a very close eye on her. 'I'll go, then,' I said. 'If you need me for anything in the night — you know where I am.'

* * *

Hubert, having disposed of the well-hammered phone, seemed to be in the process of getting well hammered himself. His refilled brandy glass contained at least a treble.

'You don't believe she'll try to do a runner, do you?' I asked, simply for his reassurance that she wouldn't. He didn't give me any such reassurance.

'In my anxious mental state,' he said, 'I believe in fairies at the bottom of the garden, that New Labour has reformed the NHS and that our rail service is very soon going to be the best in Europe. Not forgetting a new-found belief in the afterlife . . .' He paused to sip his brandy. 'But since you asked the question — I think *believe* is the wrong word.'

'Thanks for that, Hubert. Being pedantic really helps. OK then — should I put Jasper in his basket at the bottom of the stairs or should I bed down outside my room?'

'I am not the oracle,' he said. 'Once, I just had professional worries, now I have two women causing me grief, three counting your mother. I'm going to bed. Come, Jasper.'

Clutching his brandy glass, he left the room followed by a sleepy Jasper. I followed them out and crept along to my room to check on Megan. She was fast asleep. I felt a little resentful because I knew I wouldn't sleep.

Twice in the night she cried out. I rushed along but her mumbling was unintelligible. I thought she was probably talking in Welsh and answering her mother. All in, the entire whole episode was beginning to give me the creeps. To while away the night, I packed a suitcase and tried to view going to London as a little holiday. I hadn't been to London for a couple of years at least.

At eight a.m. I booked two single rooms at the Georgiana Hotel. Ironically Megan didn't wake until nine, saying it was the best night's sleep she'd had in ages.

I'd already decided to risk the train. I wasn't used to driving in London and, since parking is not my strong point, I thought the train should definitely take the strain.

Hubert, in a better mood, insisted on driving us to Birmingham for the Euston connection. 'Don't forget, you two,' he said as his parting shot, 'this isn't a holiday. Stay alert and don't take any risks.'

I dozed as far as Coventry. Megan read the six magazines she'd bought in Birmingham. I didn't think the strait-laced Gwyneth could have approved of women's magazines, because Megan seemed unusually enraptured.

We'd stopped for a few minutes at Coventry when a young woman with a small baby in a pushchair clambered on board. I'd opened both my eyes by now but Megan carried on reading until the baby began to cry. The cry itself was high-pitched, the sound indicating a baby only a few weeks old. Megan was suddenly totally alert, startled. She half rose from her seat, then, realizing, sat down quickly. 'I thought it was my baby,' she said as she picked up one of the magazines and started reading again.

The rest of the journey I was deep in thought, while the baby had quietened and made not another sound. A nagging suspicion grew in my mind but I didn't want to say anything to Megan. Any thoughts I had, I wasn't ready to share with her until I was sure.

The Georgiana Hotel smelt of thick carpets and airlessness. Even in daylight the lights needed to be on and it had the atmosphere of perpetual evening.

In reception I asked Megan if she recognized anyone. She did not. When we'd talked previously she'd mentioned chatting to the barman, who she said was called Ben, so maybe the evening would be more productive.

Our rooms were adjoining but at the back of the hotel, where the view of brick walls and office windows would not have inspired a poet. I couldn't open my window more than an inch and wondered if that was because depressed guests, having lost the will to live, might decide the view was just one more depressing factor in their lives and take a final leap. I closed the inch after a few minutes because there was no fresh air coming in and the traffic noise irritated me.

We unpacked and I suggested we made our way to Covent Garden. I thought she might enjoy the buskers and the general atmosphere. We both did. We had lunch in an Italian restaurant and Megan mildly flirted with one of the young waiters. 'He's nice, isn't he?' she said, still watching his retreating back. 'Do you think he liked me?'

'I think he likes all his female customers,' I said.

'Can we come again?'

'If you want to but tomorrow we need to check out Great-Aunt Alice's house. You do remember the address?'

'Oh, yes. It's in Belsize Avenue, number . . .' She hesitated and looked embarrassed. 'My memory's terrible but I'll know the house when I see it.'

It was the house in which she'd given birth and I did wonder what sort of effect seeing it again would have on her. In the hotel she'd hardly spoken and, when I'd asked her if it brought back memories of the *incident*, she shrugged and failed to answer me. I hadn't used the word rape too often in her presence, because she couldn't remember it as such, which was perhaps a blessing. I hadn't mentioned the possibility of HIV infection either, but at some time in the future I'd have to broach that subject too.

After our evening meal in a near-empty dining room with two miserable waitresses in attendance, I asked Megan if she recognized anyone but she didn't. I supposed the hotel trade had a quick turnover of staff, the pay being so poor that going to another hotel for a few pence more per hour seemed worthwhile.

As we made our way to the lounge bar, I wondered if Ben the barman would be on duty. Megan took one look at the young man behind the bar and shook her head. I bought the drinks and asked, 'Does Ben still work here?'

'Sorry, never heard of him.'

If Megan hadn't shown such familiarity with the layout of the hotel, I would have begun to doubt that she'd ever been there before.

The next morning's events, however, took a different turn. I heard the rattle of the chambermaid's trolley outside my door and then Megan opening her door. I heard her say, 'Hello, Rosa.'

'Megan, is that you?' enquired a heavily accented voice. 'You have come back.'

'I'm here with a friend.'

'A boyfriend?'

I opened my door instead of earwigging. Rosa was young, pale-complexioned, with dark sad eyes and thick black hair in a single plait. When Megan saw me she smiled. 'Kate, this is Rosa. She remembers me.'

'Hello, Rosa,' I said. 'We're doing some more sightseeing and Megan hopes to catch up with her old boyfriend.'

'I heard about him from Megan,' she said, 'but I never saw him.'

'Is Ben the barman still working here?' I asked.

Rosa shrugged. 'I only work until two p.m. I work in another hotel in the afternoon. I'll try to find out for Megan. She must be in love.'

Megan had a fixed smile on her face, which I hoped proved she could keep up the pretence. 'It's lovely to see you again, Rosa,' she said.

Once Rosa had gone, I said, 'You two seemed quite friendly.'

'She was nice to me. She comes from Bosnia and she sends back money to her elderly parents. She does three jobs, so I gave her a very big tip.'

I left Megan to get dressed and practise the art of make-up and went in search of Rosa. I found her stripping a bed in an empty room. 'Rosa, I have a favour to ask you.'

She looked a little surprised.

'I know your time is precious, so I would like to pay you.'

'There is no need,' she said.

'I think there is,' I said firmly, as I pressed two twenty-pound notes into her hand. 'Megan is very keen on meeting up with Michael Whitby again. Could you ask around the hotel very discreetly to see if anyone remembers seeing him?'

'I do my best.'

Was it my imagination that she looked uncomfortable? Maybe the money had embarrassed her? 'I'll see you tomorrow morning,' I said. 'We're staying for a few days.'

She nodded and gave me a questioning look, or was it a suspicious one? Either way, I felt I had to explain my involvement. 'Megan's in love with him. She's making herself ill wanting to see him again. I'm a good friend and I just want to see her happy.'

'I understand,' she said. 'I'll find out for you.'

Later on that morning, when Megan was eventually ready and looking sporty in her jeans and trainers, we went to the tube station and found the Northern Line. While we were on the move in London, I could see Megan was stressed by the crowds and she clung to my arm like an elderly dowager.

Once in Belsize Park, we walked the short distance to Belsize Avenue. 'Top or bottom?' I asked.

'Middle,' said Megan. She looked anxious now, her hand on my arm seeming to be heavier, more insistent. The houses were large, many of them converted into flats for rent, with attic rooms that once housed servants and now housed young professionals unable to buy.

The early morning blue sky had now changed to a mottled grey, like the skin of a corpse, and the clouds held more than a promise of rain.

Megan stopped walking after about two hundred yards, saying she felt sick. 'I don't know if I can do this,' she said.

'Of course you can,' I said, briskly, in nurse mode. 'Take some deep breaths — you'll be fine.'

She wasn't. She vomited into the gutter. There were only one or two passers-by, who studiously ignored us. After a few moments she straightened up and said, 'I feel better now.' I felt decidedly queasy myself but we walked on. 'Kate, I can't remember the number and all these big houses look the same to me.' That wasn't true, of course, so I suggested she tried to remember just one feature of the house or the front garden.

'A monkey-puzzle tree!' she said. 'I remember that.'

Some way ahead I could see such a tree, so we crossed the road and there the house stood. A rather splendid white-painted Edwardian residence with a front door featuring a window of stained glass embossed with birds and flowers. 'That wasn't there before,' said Megan.

A bald man in paint-spattered overalls opened the door to us. 'Yes, ladies, what can I do for you?' he asked, cheerfully.

'Are you the owner of the house?' I asked, fairly sure that he wasn't.

'No love, but it's on the market.'

I smiled what I hoped was my most winning smile. 'We thought it might be. Is there any chance we could have a look round? Our parents are looking for a family house and this is just the sort of place they'd love.'

I thought lying was my best bet, because I guessed the two of us didn't look as if we were in the half-a-million-or-so mortgage market.

'No problem, love — come on in.' We followed him into the dusty hall. The floorboards were bare and the walls had obviously been replastered. 'We're working on the kitchen at the moment and doing a bloody good job, I can tell you. Upstairs we haven't started on yet. Old girl lived here. She snuffed it, so it's in a bit of a state. It'll be smashing when it's finished — real class.'

At least, I thought, we had come to the right house, although what a trip around the house would gain us, I wasn't sure.

In the open door of the kitchen one man, naked to the waist, was fixing tiles with artistic intensity and another man, showing no flesh, was using a steel rule. The radio blared out Tom Jones singing 'Sex Bomb' and they both winked at us as if by arrangement. 'You two go and have a look round,' said the bald man I took to be the gaffer. 'Take your time. There's no hurry.'

Megan stood at the bottom of the wide stairs looking upward. The walls on both sides had been replastered, the stair carpet had been removed and the stairs were covered with an orange dust. But I could see at the top that the old flowered wallpaper remained, faded blue, and one single naked light bulb hung there like a miniature corpse.

I pushed a reluctant Megan up the stairs. The men were talking or singing amongst themselves. They'd probably forget we were even in the building.

'This was Alice's bedroom,' she said, pushing open the door but hesitating to look inside. I peered into a large virtually empty room, empty, that is, save for an elderly bedstead with a striped mattress. 'There's just a bed left,' I said to Megan, whose complexion now matched the white plaster downstairs. She grabbed my arm again and we walked from empty room to empty room. 'My room was in the attic,' she said.

The dim stairs that led to the attic obviously frightened Megan even more but I pushed and she didn't resist too much. The walls of the attic room were plain nicotine-coloured. A roll of old carpet had been placed by the window and there was an all-pervading smell of mustiness. A divan bed sat in the middle of the room. Megan simply stared at the bed. 'It must have been awful living here all those months,' I said. She didn't answer but continued to stare at the bed. 'Was that where—' She didn't let me finish. 'Yes,' she said, sharply. Then, almost defensively, she added. 'It looked better when I was here. I used to buy fresh flowers from a shop near the station. Flowers always make a difference, don't they?'

I smiled in agreement but I would have needed more than a bunch of daffs for the room to have been acceptable to me.

I couldn't let the fact that she had given birth on that divan bed pass by. It could contain forensic evidence and by that I meant blood. I knew that certain chemicals could reveal blood invisible to the naked eye. I told her what I was thinking. 'You're mad,' she said. 'We can't take the whole mattress.'

Throwing it out of the window had briefly crossed my mind. 'You're sure this is the same bed, the same mattress?' She took a deep breath before walking to the bed and looking carefully. 'Yes,' she said, slowly. 'I know because one of the bobble things was missing on the left-hand side.'

'Good. Can you remember if that midwife put any protection on the bed?'

'I'm not sure,' she answered, miserably. 'But I don't think so. She may have put a towel under me.'

'It's still worth a try.'

'Yes, but how?'

'You'll have to lie on the bed, Megan.'

'I don't want to.'

'Tough! You have to. I have to see where I could expect to find any blood.'

For the first time she looked angry, which I thought was a very good sign. But, angry or not, she did lie down on the mattress. I placed my bag where her bum would have been and then began searching for a pair of scissors. I ferreted in every compartment of my shoulder bag. I didn't have a pair of scissors. I had practically everything else, including emery boards and a nail file, but no sodding scissors.

Megan slipped a hand into her bag and produced a little velvet pouch, tied with a gold thread. 'One thing my mother taught me was always to wear clean knickers and bra, in case of accidents, and to always carry a needle and thread and scissors.'

I laughed, partly out of relief, partly out of surprise. 'I'm surprised she didn't suggest knicker elastic too.'

'No need,' said Megan, with the slightest hint of a smile. 'She always told me to carry a spare pair.'

The scissors were small but sharp, but they were an alien object to me. I'd never been able to cut in a straight line, not that I needed to now, and I'd also never properly mastered sewing on buttons. I was as dexterous with scissors as the average five-year-old. Struggling to cut the material, I swore and cursed as I worked. 'Let me do it,' said Megan, sounding exasperated.

From below, the gaffer's voice boomed up the stairs. 'You all right, girls?'

'Fine,' I shouted back and rushed down the attic stairs to the top of the landing. 'Could I borrow your steel measure?' I said. 'We love the house and if we give them the room measurements they'll be round here like a shot.'

'Yeah,' he called back to me. Then I heard him call out, 'You 'ave finished measuring up, Stu, haven't you?'

I heard Stu's muffled voice above the radio. 'Yeah, I'm finished with it.'

I walked downstairs, smiled at all three of them and took the steel measure.

'You got a pencil and paper, love?'

'Yes, thanks.'

Back in the attic Megan was really making progress. 'While you're doing that I'll go back to the other rooms for a better look round. We're supposed to be measuring anyway.'

'You've got a nerve,' she said. I hoped I heard a touch of admiration in her voice. She was even more impressed when I produced a plastic bag for our *evidence*. 'I didn't expect to use it for this,' I explained. 'My mother always told me when eating out to take a doggy bag. She resented paying for food and leaving it behind.'

Megan resumed cutting the mattress cover but, as I got to the door, she said, 'I still don't want to go to the police — I'm frightened.'

'I know,' I said. 'But he has to be stopped. We need hard evidence.'

She looked at me sadly and sighed.

There were four bedrooms on the floor below. I'd had more of a look round in Alice's room than the other rooms, so now I had a good look round the room next to hers. I thought it strange that Megan hadn't been given that one. Had Michael Whitby been staying there? Had she, in fact, been sleeping with him *after* the rape? She had no memory of actually being raped and, being so vulnerable, he may have offered her *comfort* which, she had later realized, was less than appropriate. Megan, being so strait-laced, would not want to admit to anyone that she'd been sleeping with the enemy — who would?

I was in the last room at the end of the corridor when I found it. I'd accidentally kicked a few clothes hangers that lay in a pile by the window. And there it lay. One small plastic tab. I recognized what it was immediately. From my coat pocket I took an unused paper handkerchief that was still neatly folded and very carefully, using the tissue, I picked up the tab and enfolded it. Then I slipped it into my pocket.

This was a find I was not going to share with Megan. This was my niggle of doubt confirmed. Such a small item and yet it could change everything. And now I was totally convinced that Megan's life really was in peril and, by association, mine too. Once Whitby realized that Megan wouldn't top herself, he would *have* to do the job himself.

Had we, by turning up at the Georgiana and asking questions, exposed ourselves? And how much time had we got?

CHAPTER NINE

Megan had just finished cutting out the circle of mattress cover and was rubbing her sore fingers. 'Come on, quickly,' I urged her. 'Let's turn the mattress.'

'What's the matter, Kate?'

'Nothing,' I snapped. 'Let's just get out of here.'

I tucked the circle of fabric into the plastic bag and buried it in the dark cavern of my shoulder bag. Then we turned the mattress and, this time, I took Megan's arm and bundled her out. Thankfully I'd remembered the steel rule. The workmen were having a tea break. 'It's a great house,' I said. 'Mum and Dad will love it.'

'You haven't seen the ground floor yet,' said the bald gaffer. 'I'll show you what we've done so far.'

I was longing to get away but we had to endure twenty minutes of oohing and aahing about smooth plasterwork, new doors, ceramic floor tiles and the splendid light fittings. I did manage to ask him who the owner was and the answer came as no surprise. I also asked about the agents. That was Foster and Son, which meant nothing to me. Luckily Megan didn't say much. She may have changed her appearance but her Welsh accent remained as pronounced as ever.

Eventually we made our escape and I felt, as shoplifters must do, a mixture of adrenaline hype and sheer terror at the thought of being caught. We caught the tube straight away and, by the time we got to Camden Town, I was beginning to feel slightly more relaxed. I wasn't relaxed enough, though, to decide when to tell Megan we had to leave the hotel. After food, I decided, might be the best time for us both.

It took some time to find a pub that served food near Euston. I didn't know the area and it seemed to consist mostly of office buildings. After walking some distance we came across a small pub. Inside, it was gloomy and scruffy and that described the customers too. But I needed a drink and there was a corner table vacant and the food, judging by a quick glance at what others were eating, was substantial and had chips with everything.

In certain circumstances food has a calming effect, especially big, fat, hot chips with a gin and tonic. 'Megan . . .' I began slowly, intending not to be too blunt, but the rest came out in a rush. 'We have to leave the hotel immediately. Just pack, pay and go.'

'Why?' she asked.

'That's a fair question,' I said. 'I think we've been too blatant. If the builders mention us to Whitby, he may make the connection with the Georgiana. Let's face it . . . What the hell was he doing there in the first place? He couldn't be undercover, because he was using his own name. So, what exactly was he doing?'

'Just staying for a few days because he'd separated from his wife,' said Megan, guilelessly.

I tried to keep the irritation from my voice. 'Just consider *everything* he told you to be a pack of lies.'

Megan looked crestfallen and I was sorry I'd been snappy with her. 'He may be a cop,' I said, 'but he's a bad apple. In fact, that's putting it mildly. He's not separated, he's twice divorced . . .' I paused. There's an idea, I thought. Who would know him better than his two ex-wives? If we could find them. I didn't know if David Todman could or would swing that one for me. Being on the move, there was no way I could find out myself, but he was worth a try and perhaps I could be flirtatious enough to allow him to hope.

I looked across at Megan. She'd regained a little colour in her cheeks and her brown eyes had a luminous quality. All in all, she was looking quite attractive. And she was a sweet soul. Not a drinker or a smoker, religious but not pious. Maybe he'd fall for her with a little push from me. That might be worth a try.

Back at the hotel, I insisted we hurried. 'Are we going back to Longborough?' Megan asked.

'No. We're just changing hotels. We'll go to Palmer's Green. It's in North London and it's fairly near Tottenham. He'll find out we've left here but he won't expect us to stay in London.'

I rang Hubert on my mobile to tell him we were on the move. 'You've blown it already, haven't you?'

'I have not. Changing hotels is purely a sensible move.'

'First time you've been sensible. By the way, did you sign in?'

'You mean the hotel register?'

'Yes.'

'It's the law,' I said.

'I know it is,' he said. 'And what did you give as your home address?'

It took me a moment to remember. 'I gave my Farley Wood address.'

The little terraced house in Farley Wood was technically my home. My name was on the deeds. The fact that I spent so much time at Humberstone's was part laziness, part convenience and part liking Hubert's company.

'For once you've shown some sense,' said Hubert. 'Pity you didn't give an imaginary address.'

'I didn't think . . .' I began.

'Thinking is vital in your game, Kate. Get into gear!'

I was getting irritated but I took a deep breath. 'Do me a favour, oh best undertaker in the UK,' I began, but he didn't let me finish.

'I'm not taken in by flattery,' he said.

Liar! I thought. An atom of flattery where a woman was concerned turned Hubert's psyche to mush.

'Anyway, Hubert, would you ask David Todman if he'd ring me on my mobile? There's something he might be able to help me with.'

'What?' he asked, sharply.

I knew that tone, so I explained about the two ex-wives and I told him that I'd lied to David about a friend of mine being involved with Whitby and it was probably for the best if he thought it was me.

'I think that makes sense,' he said, sounding as if it didn't. 'Now, if you have any problems, get back to me.'

I promised I would. 'We're leaving here now and going to Palmer's Green.'

'I won't ask why Palmer's Green. Just let me know where you're staying.'

Hubert sounded anxious but he was a worrier. And there was nothing to worry about, was there?

In Palmer's Green we found a guest house called The Gables but without a gable in sight, which catered for businessmen from Monday to Thursday. It was clean and cosy, with only one drawback — we had to share a double room. But at least we didn't have to share a bed.

Once we'd unpacked, we were at a loss and, when it began to rain, we sat alone in the lounge watching an ancient Western on the TV. Out of the blue, Megan said, 'What am I going to do with the rest of my life?'

She'd taken me by surprise, but it was a question I'd once asked myself and then decided I was not a long-term planner. A day at a time had become my motto.

'What would you like to do?' I asked.

'When I was pregnant I realized I could cope with a baby on my own,' she said, wistfully. 'I've got money. I could have bought a little house and made it cosy. I would have made friends with other mums. When the baby was older, I could have gone to college and got a qualification.'

'You could still go to college or travel.'

She shrugged. 'There's no incentive when you're completely alone, is there? No one to share the highs and the lows.'

I sat watching her and listening and I so wanted to tell her what I suspected, but I couldn't until I was sure.

When the film ended, a quiz show began and since I rarely know the answers I picked up a newspaper and began flicking through it without much interest until my eye caught a small piece at the bottom of page six.

> *The body of a local GP, Dr Angela Lewis, aged thirty-nine, mother of two, was found at her surgery in Criccieth, North Wales, late last night. She had been shot. It is believed she disturbed a burglar. Local police are making house-to-house enquiries.*

I told Megan there and then as gently as I could, because she'd find out eventually and it was best she found out while I was with her. She burst into tears and began to shake uncontrollably. I sat open-mouthed for several seconds, feeling my stomach tying itself in knots. Very slowly, I dragged my leaden feet over to Megan's chair and put my arm around her.

'In cases like this . . .' I stopped. I had been about to say that it was likely to be someone she knew but, suddenly, I didn't believe it myself and it wasn't the right thing to say at that moment. 'I'm really sorry,' I said. 'I know she was very good to you.'

'She was my friend,' wept Megan. 'Who could do such a thing? I don't understand. She didn't do any harm to anyone. She only did good.'

'I know,' I murmured. 'I know.' I patted her back and hugged her but she couldn't be comforted.

Her misery began peeling like an onion, layer upon layer. Her mother's tyranny, her parents' unhappy marriage, her lonely childhood, the sheer drudgery of her life and then the terrible shock of finding herself pregnant and after that having to come to terms with the final, dreadful blow of the stillbirth. 'I didn't see him,' she mumbled tearfully, over and over again. Then abruptly she stopped and, looking straight at me, said, in a clear calm voice, 'But I did hear my baby — I did! I didn't imagine it. I did hear him. I know my eyes were closed. I couldn't open them but I did hear my baby cry.'

Very quietly I said, 'I'm sure you did.'

She wiped the tears from her face with the back of her hand whilst I rummaged for a tissue. 'What did you say, Kate?'

'I think you did hear your baby cry.'

'Do you know what you're saying?'

'I think so.' From my shoulder bag I produced an envelope and opened it up to show her the contents. 'What is it?' she asked.

'It's the sticky tab from a disposable nappy.'

'Where did you get it from?'

'One of the rooms at the house in Belsize Avenue.'

Wide-eyed, she stared at me.

'I don't think,' I said, gently, 'that if your baby had been dead, he would have needed a nappy. I think he was stolen. I don't know why he was taken but I do know we're going to find out.'

It took a while for the full implication to sink in. She began to rock backwards and forwards, at first in silence, then, after a few minutes, saying, 'Oh God! Oh God! Oh God!'

'Stop it!' I said, seeing hysteria looming like some tidal wave that would engulf us both. 'Take a deep breath.'

She took a deep breath and then another. I held her hands. 'Megan, we're going to do whatever it takes. If your baby is alive — we'll find him, I promise you.'

* * *

A whole day was set up for doing nothing but eating and watching TV, simply because I didn't know what to do next. Outside, it rained and the sky was like one grey mottled slab of marble pressing down, particularly on us. Megan refused to get up for breakfast, so I went down alone and tried to work out a strategy over a huge English breakfast. The dining room looked out on to the main road and I watched as the convoys of cars moved slowly through the wet gloom, their lights accentuating the dullness of the morning. Company cars, minicabs, private cars, hired cars . . . Suddenly it was so obvious. How could I be a PI without a car? Too chicken to drive in London, I'd put myself first and the case in jeopardy. Now, seeing how slow the traffic was, I realized I could cope easily, especially as we had no need to visit central London again.

In the lounge, I watched the news. There was nothing about Dr Lewis. Even in the two newspapers I scanned, it only merited a few lines. But seeing it in black and white unnerved me. I wondered if Whitby was licensed to carry a gun, although I doubted he would have been stupid enough to use a police-issue firearm. Deciding to hire a car wasn't exactly a plan of action but, maybe, we could sit outside the police station until he appeared.

With enough cash, hiring a car was easy enough. By lunch time, Megan was just about surfacing and she announced she didn't want lunch either. 'I've hired a car,' I said. 'We'll use it to find Whitby. You'll have to identify him, of course.'

'And then what?'

I thought that was a good question in the circumstances but it was one to which I had no real answer.

'We follow him,' I suggested.

'And where will that lead us?' she asked.

I shrugged. 'Well, he could lead us to your midwife, I suppose.'

'I've been thinking,' she said, as she slipped on her denim jacket. 'Do you think Michael had anything to do with Dr Lewis's murder?'

'No,' I lied stoutly. 'It's just a horrible coincidence.'

Her answering look showed me she thought I was talking a lot of old cobblers.

'He really is after us — isn't he?'

I couldn't allow myself to show I was scared. One scared person was quite enough in a duo. 'No,' I said, firmly. 'We are after *him*. I told you before, we are on the offensive. And we're going to get him.'

'How?'

'Trust me,' I said, smiling. 'I'm a PI.'

'Have you dealt with crooked policemen before?'

'Not exactly,' I said, still trying to sound confident and in control. 'But I do have a police contact and, at any moment, he could ring me with information.' To be honest, I was disappointed not to have heard a word from DI Todman. Longborough had its rough estates but its general crime rate was below average. Not because of any zero-tolerance policy but because, for the most part, the inhabitants were a little too comfortable to riot in the streets and their homes a little too well protected for any but the most determined of burglars. So David couldn't say that he was so overworked he didn't have time.

Megan dropped her interrogation and a little later we went out to the car park to admire my hired silver Toyota Yaris. 'Let's go,' I said, opening the passenger door. The brakes were a little fierce because it was new and I was used to various clapped-out models that lasted only a few months and had brakes that needed a damned good pumping. The accelerator needed a touch as soft as a ballerina's empty shoe, but even in the rain it was good to get away from The Gables and to feel we were actually doing something.

To find a vantage point from which to view the police station, I had to drive around several times. Too near and we were likely to be in a camera's eye. Too far away and we'd miss him.

We sat watching the front entrance, watching the comings and goings of every shape and size, every ethnic group. Megan commented, 'I've never seen so many foreigners in my life.'

'They were probably born here,' I said. 'It's not like Criccieth.'

'Very true,' she said, dryly and a touch wistfully. I guessed run-down Tottenham was not the London of her dreams.

After two hours or so, our vigilance grew boring and tiring. We sucked mints and lost concentration. 'Have you ever had a serious relationship?' she asked.

'I did live with someone once. He was a police inspector, nice guy, but hardly ever sober. He was killed in a freak accident, falling masonry. Luckily he was drunk as usual at the time. His death was instantaneous.'

'I'm very sorry.'

'I'm over it now but it has made me wary. It took me months to get over the shock alone. I was like a zombie going through the motions for a couple of years and then I came out of it. One day the daffodils bloomed again for me.'

'Do you think I'll ever get over this?'

'You're a survivor,' I said. 'Tell yourself that over and over again. One day you'll see that it's true.'

She stared out of the car window but visibility was getting worse not better and the day was beginning to take on the aura of a lost cause.

The trill of my mobile phone made me jump. As usual it was not to hand but in the depths of my shoulder bag. It had been ringing for ages when I finally retrieved it. I was convinced it was David. 'Hi,' I said, cheerfully. The pause was so long that I thought the caller had rung off. 'We know where you are,' said the voice. 'You two will soon be as dead as poor Dr Lewis.'

The phone in my hand shook. My heart was trying to leap out of my chest. Megan had paled and she clutched my hand, saying, 'Was it him?'

In all honesty I had to say, 'No. It wasn't him. It was someone else.'

CHAPTER TEN

Once I'd taken a deep breath I stared around. Tottenham carried on busily just as before. I couldn't see anyone watching us and I tried to convince myself that whoever had called was only bluffing. Even so, our nerves were shredded and the thought of sitting in the car, worried, watching the rain and hearing our stomachs rumble, was far less appealing than just driving away. Megan hadn't heard what was said; she only knew that it wasn't Whitby on the phone. And now, as the initial shock receded a little, I knew that Whitby and the other guy had not only killed Dr Lewis, they had killed her for a reason and we were that reason. I'd given her my card, so they knew my address, office number, mobile, e-mail address — and, of course, I'd signed the register with my Farley Wood address.

I resolved that I wouldn't panic; that we would sit for another hour. Megan had become mute and I had nothing to say. It had got to the point where I'd decided what the hell did it matter what Whitby looked like. Whoever was going to come after us, we'd know they weren't kosher if we were looking down the barrel of a gun.

After a further long half-hour, I said, trying to sound light-hearted, 'Right, Megan. Wagons roll. We're off. We're going back to the hotel and getting out fast. It's time we talked to the police.'

Surprisingly she didn't argue. Perhaps even she realized there is only so much individuals can do against what now seemed like organized crime.

'Couldn't we go to the police here?' asked Megan, looking towards Horsefields Police Station.

'The trouble is,' I said, 'that, on my information, he's a well-respected cop with a good track record; he's even been commended. We go in there making accusations of unreported rape nearly ten months ago, threatening phone calls and a suggestion that he murdered Dr Lewis. I can't see them taking much notice. He's bound to have an alibi anyway.'

'No one will believe us, then,' she said, as she traced her name in the condensation of the passenger window.

'Someone will. If I can convince David Todman, he'll try to find out something from within the police force.'

'So, it's back to Longborough, then.'

I didn't want to tell her that I wanted to be back there because I thought Hubert might be in danger. Three against two and perhaps a bit of police protection and we might just catch Whitby. The other phone voice remained a mystery but he could have been asked to call just for effect. Well, it had worked. I was very worried but, as I drove back to Palmers Green, I knew that if we stayed in Longborough, he'd come looking and we had to be ready.

* * *

The rain and heavy traffic slowed us and we arrived after dark at Humberstone's. Jasper raced down the stairs and, by the number of paroxysms and slavering, seemed more than pleased we had returned. Hubert, waiting in the hall for us, in contrast, looked glum, managing only, 'I'm glad you're back safely.'

'Of course,' I said with false brightness. 'Why shouldn't we be?'

'Your place has been done over, Kate . . .'

'My house?'

'Yes. Last night, sometime. That neighbour who keeps a key for you peeped in the front window. She'd heard a car draw up late at night but she hadn't looked out.'

'Is there much damage?'

'I'm afraid so. It's not so much been burgled as smashed up.'

'I'm ever so sorry,' said Megan. 'I can't help feeling this is all my fault.'

'No. It's not your fault — it's that bastard's fault. Bastard! Bastard! Bastard!'

'Feel better now?' asked Hubert.

I managed a weak smile. I did feel better, but only slightly.

We all shuffled along to the kitchen, leaving our bags in the hall. There was something roasting in the oven, which cheered me slightly. 'I'm cooking,' said Hubert, 'and I've invited David Todman. He doesn't get many home-cooked meals.' I played a little air violin. 'Don't be silly, Kate,' said Hubert. 'He knows there's no such thing as a free meal. He wants to hear the whole story. And if you want him to work on your behalf, I'd glam yourself up a bit.'

'Get stuffed, Hubert.'

'I've done that,' he said. 'The chicken's stuffed.'

'I'm not interested in him. I think Megan's more his type.'

Hubert put on his serious expression and low voice. 'Just play the game. You desperately need his help. He might be able to get you some protection if you convince him you have a good case.'

'So, my looking glam will help our case?'

'Just don't rub him up the wrong way.'

I could have managed a rude retort but I didn't bother. This wasn't about Todman and me. It was about Megan and I had to be her advocate any way I knew how.

'Come on then, Megan. Let's change for dinner. We'll slap on the slap and play helpless females.'

'You won't have to act too hard, then,' said Hubert, as he put on his pinny.

'You big Jessie!' I said, pointing in the obvious direction.

DI Todman, due at seven thirty, was already a half-hour late and had missed two aperitifs. Megan was still in the bath and I drank her share of dry sherry. Hubert opened the red wine to let it breathe but I preferred it asphyxiated and drank a glass as soon as he'd de-corked it and turned his back.

'Don't drink too much,' warned Hubert. 'You want to convince him not repel him.'

At ten past eight he turned up with no apology but with a bunch of carnations and a bottle of wine. David was the sort of guy who should have passed for attractive. He was slim with dark hair and hazel eyes. He was always well dressed. His image and his being a teetotaller made him a bit too squeaky clean for me. But he was just the type of cop to rebuild Megan's faith in the police. Even Jasper trusted him, judging by the way that he sat at his feet wagging his tail and waiting for a fuss.

Although there was no apology, he did say he was sorry about the damage to my cottage. 'I'll help you get it sorted,' said David. 'I know of two blokes doing community service who will do a good job for you.' He ruffled Jasper's coat and the dog responded by shamelessly lying on his back with his legs in the air. I was about to say that I'd sort it myself when I caught Hubert's warning glance. Tonight was a night for crawling and I could crawl with the best. 'Thanks, David,' I said. 'You're an angel. I appreciate it.' I flashed him a well-lipsticked smile and observed Hubert mouthing 'Well done.' I responded with a rude gesture that Hubert didn't see.

Megan appeared looking young and fresh. She was wearing one of her new tops, a sparkly little number in pink, and she was so well endowed that I could tell David didn't know where to look. I made the introductions and offered Megan some wine. She refused and David shot me a glance, somehow suggesting she was an unlikely friend of mine.

Hubert was by now fretting about the state of his vegetables, so he began serving up and we sat down to eat. To say that it was awkward at first would be an understatement. David, I'd now realized, had two topics of conversation — crime and the politics of crime. He began talking about the recent increase in the number of burglaries in Farley Wood and there I interrupted him.

'But this wasn't a burglary, was it? According to Hubert, everything has been smashed up.'

David chewed his food well before answering. 'So, you have a suspect?'

'Yes, but it's a long story.' I turned to Megan. 'Do you want to tell David what happened to you or shall I tell him?' Her face changed as though a cloud had settled on her and I realized that, in these circumstances, she felt both shamed and embarrassed. She was a victim of abuse and felt that somehow she was to blame. It was Hubert who came to the rescue. 'Let the poor girl eat in peace,' he said. 'I haven't worn a pinny and handled giblets for you to harass Megan while she eats.'

So, we finished our meal and Hubert waxed lyrical about his new ideas and we listened as though undertaking was as normal as sport or holidays, which, if you think about it — it is.

Post Hubert's delicious apple and apricot crumble, I'd drunk enough wine to make me very talkative. Megan excused herself, saying she was tired and Hubert insisted on doing the washing up alone. He did have a dishwasher, so I felt no guilt.

David and I sat in the lounge with silly little coffee cups and saucers that Hubert insisted on if we had guests. 'She seems a nice girl,' said David. 'What's she doing here?'

'I'll start at the beginning — do you want to take notes?'

He looked a little put out by that suggestion but he took out his notebook and pen.

'This isn't off the record,' I said. 'This is a formal complaint. And I want you to go through all the right channels.'

'I knew there had to be a catch — two lovely women, a great meal and then I pay the price.'

I smiled, mellow with food and wine. Everyone was my friend now and he looked more appealing by the minute. 'You chose the wrong career.'

'That thought does cross my mind occasionally,' he said. 'Now being one of those occasions.'

I started at the beginning and told him how I'd found Megan and then a little of her history. 'So, you're telling me she thinks she was raped but she can't recall it.'

'She knew something had happened. She was a virgin prior to this. She was bleeding. And at that point she didn't think Whitby was responsible.'

'So, she was surprised when she found she was pregnant?'

'Well, of course she was. Why do you ask that?'

He shrugged. 'No real reason. Just trying to get the picture.'

I tried to think back to what Megan had said to me but some of the details had slipped through my memory like false teeth down a drain.

'Why won't she tell me all this personally?' he asked. 'If she wants to bring a case, she's going to have to face cross-examination.'

'It's not just about the rape. She's frightened and still in shock.'

'Where's the baby, Kate? You've taken a single mum in, haven't you?'

'No, I have not!'

Suddenly I knew exactly how it would be for Megan if this case ever got to court. I excused myself and went to the kitchen to get myself a glass of water and talk to Hubert.

'I don't think he's taking this seriously,' I said.

Hubert carried on wiping kitchen surfaces. 'Have you told him the full story?'

'Not yet. I want him to see a picture building. And I want him to see that Whitby is as guilty as hell.'

'David isn't stupid. I'm sure he'll do his best for you.'

'It's not for me. It's for Megan.'

'Well,' said Hubert, 'Megan should be speaking up for herself.'

And, of course, he was right. If Megan couldn't hold her own with someone as easy-going as Todman, what hope was there?'

I marched to the bedroom purposefully, deciding I would take no arguments, to find her sitting cross-legged on my bed staring into space. She looked desperately unhappy but this time I couldn't allow myself to be soft with her.

'Megan,' I said sharply. 'You need to talk to David. He'll question you and you may not like it but you're going to have to lump it. Especially if you want to stay alive and maybe find your child. The stakes don't come much higher than that.'

Close to tears, she said, 'I know I'm being a coward. I'm so afraid he won't believe me.'

'You have to go in there and convince him,' I said. 'You just have to tell the truth.'

'I'm always truthful,' she said, brushing a tear away with her hand.

'Do you want me to be with you when you talk to him?'

'Oh yes, Kate. I can't do it on my own.'

David smiled at her reassuringly and we sat together like the three monkeys on the sofa. 'When did you first realize you were pregnant, Megan?' asked David bluntly. She glanced at me as if I had the answer but when I just mouthed, 'Go on,' she took a deep breath. 'I felt odd for ages,' she said. 'I thought I was ill. I was very tired and I felt sick quite often, but I was looking after Alice and I tried not to think about it.'

'But you knew you were pregnant?' persisted David.

'Sort of,' she admitted. 'At least, when I began to show, I did.'

'Did you see a doctor?'

'No. I didn't have a doctor.'

'How did you plan to have the baby?'

'Michael said he'd get me a midwife and, once the baby was born, I could still live in the house and still have a job looking after Alice.'

'Did he pay you?'

'Yes. He gave me money if I needed any. He was quite generous. He said he didn't want me to feel I was merely an employee.'

My mouth dropped. So far this was progressing as a tale of a good Samaritan. A smart barrister would have Whitby as kind but misguided, his only crime so far being one of failing to register a birth.

'You didn't manage the whole house on your own, did you?' asked David.

She shook her head. 'There was a cook and a cleaner but, a couple of weeks before I was due, he sent them away and Michael and Teresa moved in.'

'This cook and cleaner, what nationality were they?'

She gave a little shrug. 'Everyone's foreign to me.'

'Did they speak English?' He sounded slightly irritated. If Megan weren't careful, she'd come across, not as naive, but dull-witted.

'The cook didn't speak to me at all,' she said, 'but the cleaner was quite friendly.'

'Where was she from?'

'She didn't say. She did say she was sending money to her family, who were very poor. I used to give her money sometimes. She'd listen out for Alice, so that I could go out for a walk or to the shops, otherwise I wouldn't have gone out at all.'

'What was her name?' asked David.

'Katia.'

David wrote a few notes and his expression was vaguely suspicious but I took that as being natural for a cop.

'Tell me about the birth, Megan.'

She began telling him about the pains and then not remembering the actual birth. At this point Megan became tearful. 'It's all a blur, like a dream. I thought I heard my baby cry but then, sometimes, I think I hear my mother calling me.'

I glanced away from David, not wanting to catch his eye. She went on to tell him about the overheard conversation and how, later, she'd run away from the house and hitched a lift that took her to Longborough.

'Why Longborough?'

'That's as far as the lorry went.'

'So, what's happened since?'

'She's had threatening phone calls on her mobile,' I said.

Looking directly at Megan, he asked, 'What did he say?'

Megan stared at the floor and didn't answer.

'I've taken two of the calls,' I said. 'They were death threats. Saying he knew where she was. At first it was as if he was trying to get her to commit suicide. But the last one was even nastier.'

'In what way?'

'He mentioned Dr Lewis.'

'Who?'

'Dr Angela Lewis, the GP who was found shot in Criccieth.'

'I heard about the case. But what has she got to do with Megan?'

'Dr Lewis was Megan's GP. I went to see her and left her my business card. A couple of days later she was found shot dead and then the call on my mobile mentioned her, saying that soon we too would be dead.' I didn't tell him that this voice didn't sound like Whitby but I didn't want to muddy the waters any more than they were already.

'So, what have you been doing in London?' he asked me.

I told him about the Georgiana Hotel and how we'd only found one person, Rosa the chambermaid, who remembered Megan.

'So, your short stay there didn't achieve much.'

'We did go to Belsize Park to the house that Megan stayed at. It's being refurbished. Alice died soon after Megan ran away and, as far as we know, Whitby has inherited it.'

'And did you find out anything useful?'

I didn't much like his tone. He thought I was a bumbling amateur anyway, which is true, but I do try, and this time I did have evidence. Megan meanwhile seemed to have opted out and had her eyes closed. 'Is she all right?' he mouthed at me. I nodded.

'Well, I do have some evidence, David, despite your mocking tone.'

'Right, then,' he said. 'Tell me about it.'

Before I handed it over I wanted to make sure David would deal with it. If not, I would send it to a private laboratory. 'Finding the murderer of a respected GP,' I said, 'would be a real brownie point for you, wouldn't it?'

'I suppose so, but since the North Wales Police are dealing with it, I'd have to clear it with my boss.'

'What's he like?'

'New to the job and a dickhead.'

'Do you think you can swing it?'

'Just tell me what you've got, Kate, and I'll give you an honest opinion.'

I showed him the plastic bag with the circle of mattress cover. He glanced at it through the plastic. 'So?'

'So, this is the mattress cover that Megan gave birth on. There may be bloodstains on it.'

He smiled condescendingly and I felt like hitting him. 'If there are bloodstains,' he said, 'and it's proved to be Megan's blood, that will only prove she gave birth there. The only misdemeanour Whitby could be charged with is failing to register a birth. And even then, it's not clear that it would have been his responsibility.'

I nudged Megan with my elbow. 'He was present at the birth, wasn't he?'

Her eyes snapped open. 'I think so. I can't be sure. I told you it was later that I heard his voice.'

Oh God, I thought. Then I remembered my other piece of evidence. I rummaged for the envelope in my bag and opened it so that he could see it. 'What is it?'

'It's the tab from a disposable nappy.'

'Are you sure? How many nappies have you dealt with?'

'A few,' I snapped.

David continued looking at it. 'There was an old lady in the house,' he murmured.

'What are you trying to say?'

'Megan, was Alice incontinent?' he asked.

Megan shrugged, 'At night she was.'

'And what did you do about that?'

Megan's mouth dropped a little, as if realizing where the questions were going. I too had got his drift. 'She wore incontinence pads,' she said.

'Like nappies?'

She nodded despondently.

'Could this tab be from one of those?' Her hand stretched out for the envelope and she scrutinized the tab for several seconds.

'I think Alice's plastic tabs were larger.' Her face brightened a little. 'I'm sure they were.'

Hubert appeared then with coffee and a box of chocolate mints and Megan and I gobbled several in quick succession, as if chocolate held the answer to all our problems. David drank coffee and flicked through his notes. 'I take it, Kate, that this Michael Whitby is definitely Inspector Whitby, not just some bozo calling himself Whitby?'

At that moment I wished I had been a Victorian woman in a tight corset, because I could have had a fit of the vapours and been carried from the room. Instead, I grabbed another chocolate mint and sucked on it, trying to give myself a few extra seconds thinking time.

From David's general attitude, he didn't seem at all convinced that we had a case. And, once told, it seemed a bit thin. Second-guessing what he was thinking, I said, 'Don't forget Dr Lewis.'

'There's only one problem there,' he said, giving Hubert one of those man-to-man glances that seems to precede announcements which may upset a woman.

'What?' I asked, worried.

'A local man has been arrested. A gun freak.'

CHAPTER ELEVEN

I was quick to reply. 'Well, they've arrested an innocent man, then.'

David smiled at me sympathetically, which irritated me even more. No one spoke for a few moments. Then Megan surprised us all by saying, 'I know he really is an inspector. I've seen his warrant card.'

I was still staring at her when David asked, 'How did that come about?'

'My mother always checked through my father's pockets,' she explained. 'She said it was so that his suits and jackets didn't go to the dry cleaner's with money or anything important in the pockets. I knew she was just being suspicious.'

'So, you were suspicious of Whitby at this time?' he asked.

'It was when he wanted me to look after Alice. I thought I'd better check that he really was a policeman. My mother had warned me about girls in London being sold into the white-slave trade.'

'I've only got one more question, Megan, and I want you to think very carefully about the answer . . .' He paused, waiting for her full attention. 'If you were raped under the influence of Rohypnol, who did *you* think was responsible?'

Megan looked towards me as if, somehow, I could help her out. I looked away. Although I had the feeling I was letting her down in some way, she had to learn to speak up for herself.

'I remember Michael leaving me in my hotel room,' she said, sounding uncertain. 'I heard him close the door and walk away. After that I don't remember anything.'

'I'll ask you again, Megan — if Whitby didn't come back, who did?'

'I don't know. It could have been anybody . . .'

'Anybody?' queried David.

'You're confusing me,' she said. 'I meant it could have been someone from the hotel.'

'Maybe the barman or another man you met at the hotel?'

Her eyes were bright with tears but they were tears of anger and confusion. 'David — let it drop,' I said.

'They won't let it drop in court.'

'I'm going to bed,' said Megan as she rushed from the room. I didn't follow her. David was a captive audience and our sole link with information, so I couldn't afford to lose this opportunity.

'I didn't mean to upset her,' he said. 'But even if we can find enough evidence to arrest Whitby, proving it in court is another matter.'

'I appreciate that but, on what you've heard, has she got a chance? And what if her baby is still alive?'

'Don't raise her hopes on that score, Kate. She had no antenatal care. Whitby could say she refused. I don't think there is a law which states you *have* to see a doctor when you're pregnant. Maybe if she'd had proper care, the baby might have lived.'

I shut my mouth. I was in danger of losing my cool. Hubert was looking at me in a worried way. But I knew what he was thinking. He thought I was getting emotionally involved, not being clear-headed and logical. How could I remain detached? Megan was a hard-working, innocent young girl and the bastard Whitby had used her. And there the question hung in the air. What had he wanted her for?

The drug angle seemed an afterthought. The baby seemed the prime motive.

'What if the baby was born alive?' I asked. 'What's the going rate for a healthy baby of a healthy mother?'

David looked uncomfortable. 'Kate, I read the newspapers. I know that in certain countries a baby can be sold illegally for around fourteen thousand pounds. In India for a lot less. But in Longborough I haven't heard of newborns being bought or sold.'

'It's not something that's going to be advertised on a card in the newsagents. I know that,' I said, calmly. 'But that doesn't mean it doesn't happen, either here or in London.'

'Don't get upset,' said David, patting my knee. 'I'll find out as much as I can but, at the moment, I can't go through the proper channels. If the gun freak in North Wales is released, then I might be able to do something officially.'

I ignored the fact that he'd patted my knee — the patronizing twat — and smiled humbly. I would have to put up and shut up if I wanted his help and this was a case I couldn't deal with on my own. More and more I was convinced the baby was alive and we had to act quickly. Even now it could be too late. The baby could be abroad and, from Megan's point of view, her baby being thought dead might be the kindest option for her. I bitterly regretted giving her even the faintest glimmer of hope.

Hubert was looking increasingly glum and I excused myself and went to see Megan. She was curled up on her side, sobbing quietly. 'I knew no one would believe me,' she muttered into the pillow.

'I believe you, and David doesn't disbelieve you. He's the one who can get access to police files. If all of us give it our best shot, Whitby will be brought to justice.'

'And my baby?'

'We'll find out,' I said. 'We'll find out.'

Walking back to the lounge, I heard Hubert and David talking. Hubert was saying, 'If she does that, she'll have to be careful. Some ex-wives remain friendly, especially if they're being paid maintenance. It may not be in their interests to be honest.'

'I can't do it all,' David was saying, 'Most investigating I'll have to do in my own time and that's in short supply.'

Even though I'd been eavesdropping and I didn't like the tone of their pronouncements, I decided to take a positive approach. I came in all smiles. 'Did I hear you say you've found the addresses of Whitby's ex-wives?'

They both looked a little non-plussed but David rallied. 'Yes. One lives in Bedford, the other in Solihull. But . . .'

'I won't take everything they say as gospel,' I said cheerfully. 'I'm pretty good at spotting liars. I'll winkle the truth out of them.'

'You're not that good at being subtle,' said Hubert.

'Sometimes being blunt works,' I said, as I sat down less than gracefully next to David.

'There's blunt and there's elephantine . . .' began Hubert.

I didn't let him finish. 'Thanks for the vote of confidence. If you two only want to criticize — we'll manage on our own.'

As soon as I'd said it, I regretted it. Hubert glanced at David. 'Don't worry,' he said, even though David looked far from worried. 'She gets a bit tetchy when she's tired.'

Sometimes I show real restraint. This was one of those times. I ignored Hubert's remark. 'I know this makes extra work for you, David,' I said. 'But Whitby is not only very dangerous, he's a cop and, surely, catching him is worth any effort.'

There wasn't much either of them could say to that and David handed me the addresses. 'We don't want him warned off, Kate, so . . . be careful.'

Shortly after that I saw him to the door. 'I get the distinct impression,' he said, 'that I'm being used.' I kissed him enthusiastically. And, after a while, I heard him mutter, 'Use me, use me.' I knew then that he was play dough in my hands. I should have felt guilty but I didn't.

* * *

Most of that night I sat at my computer trying to work out a strategy for squeezing information out of two women who may not have a vested interest in telling me the truth. Strategies take a while to formulate but I looked at the information I had: two women, both divorced, husband in the police force — a public service. And then I had the answer. When in doubt, blame the government. It took me nearly two hours to formulate the questions and make them seem as if they might have surfaced from some government focus group.

Once the pages were fashioned together on a clipboard, the only other thing I needed was an identification badge. I knew that Hubert could fashion me one from a passport photo. I could then attach it to the front of the clipboard and give it a quick flash before I turned the first page, which stated boldly: *Divorce and Relationship Breakdown in the Public Services. Help the Government to Help You*. I then made a list of aims and objectives, without which no organization seems able to exist, as if, somehow, the words are a substitute for action and, as long as the *intention* is there, nothing else matters.

In the morning I showed Hubert my effort and he seemed suitably impressed. Within minutes he had produced two identification badges, one for round my neck and the other for the clipboard. 'No good haring down to Bedford,' he said, 'if she's going to be out.' I had thought of that and planned to ring her just before eight a.m. to make an appointment. Although I hadn't had much sleep, I seemed to be running on all cylinders and was feeling very optimistic. My optimism was misplaced — neither of the women answered their phones.

By late morning I'd walked Jasper twice and had repeatedly tried to contact them. I could have left a message on their answerphones but I decided against that, as they would probably want to opt out if given time to think about it.

Megan made an appearance at midday. She was dressed in a black skirt with a pink top that looked new and fresh. Her face, in contrast, looked crumpled and creased, as if she'd stayed in one position for too long. 'Hubert says if I want to I can arrange flowers or sit in the office with the receptionist.'

'So, you don't want to drive to Bedford or Solihull with me?'

She shook her head. 'I don't think I'd help you much. I might put my foot in it.'

I knew she'd be well looked after. The latest receptionist, Betty, was a kindly soul, with a round pink face and a mop of silvery grey hair. She was unlikely to go the same way as Leyla, who'd been so prone to fits of hysterical laughter that she'd had to be led from the building. After three warnings she had not been allowed back.

I was a little disappointed that Megan seemed to be opting out, but I was probably a better actor than her and, if she felt uncomfortable role-playing — I refuse to call it lying — then I would be better off on my own.

At just after two p.m. I finally got through to the ex-Mrs Whitby living in Solihull. I gave her the spiel and she said she'd see me in an hour, so I left immediately and, in fifty minutes, I was sitting outside a large detached house in a leafy avenue, where every garden boasted neat lawns and daffodils, crocuses and snowdrops, all in serried, neat clumps. There wasn't as much as an empty crisp packet to sully the paths.

On the hour, I made my way up the flower-lined front drive to pull the medieval-style bell at the door. When she opened the door, I gushed, 'Thank you so much for seeing me, Deborah. I'll make it as quick as I possibly can.'

'No problem. It's Kate, isn't it?'

I guessed she was born south of Watford. She was in her thirties and wore a grey pinstripe trouser suit as if she'd just left her office. Her red hair reached to near her shoulders and her make-up and nails were immaculate. One thing I didn't need to guess was if she did any housework. The nails would never have survived anything more arduous than filling the dishwasher.

As she was showing me through to the sitting room, I admired the wood panelling and the parquet floor and the glimpses of fine old furniture. Some houses not only smell of furniture polish, they also look polished. I find, following my mother's dictum, that a quick spurt of Mr Sheen into the air is plenty good enough to fool the senses. Deborah had either fallen on her feet or she'd always been standing. Everything about the house reflected money. It wasn't just the fine wood. The wealth was underlined by the fine wall hangings and the oil paintings that graced the long hall.

'It's a wonderful house,' I said.

'Yes, love it. We've only been here two years. Would you like to look round?'

'I'd love to.' I wasn't lying. I'm really nosy and interested in how people live.

Deborah showed me every alcove and room, pointing out the splendid four-poster bed in the master bedroom, although I couldn't have missed it. I was suitably impressed and praised her taste.

Finally, after the grand tour, she decided the study might be the best place to fill out the questionnaire. She moved a heavy antique chair, so that we sat either side of a desk that was so large it almost filled the room.

'I'd like to explain a few things about the questionnaire,' I said, as I flicked to the first page. 'Just in case you don't wish to proceed.'

'Fine,' she said.

'You've been allocated a number and the form is anonymous. Your name and your ex-husband's name will not be mentioned. This form just uses *ex* and *husband* if you have remarried.'

'Fire away.'

'Some of the questions will seem very personal but, as you know, the government does seem interested in families and they've started with the public services because they have identified more marriage breakdowns in the public sector than the private. The hope is that, by collating more information, they can identify the causes, which may be work-related, and then they can take more positive action in the future if they have the information to work on.'

I took a deep breath then. I could get carried away. I hadn't mentioned focus groups, or grass roots, and I hoped my spiel was both coherent and reasonably convincing.

'I've got no problem with that,' she said. 'Sounds like all their ideas. Plenty of words and no action.'

I started with the more mundane questions — date of birth, place of birth — then moved on to the wedding day.

'Which one?' she asked. 'First, second or third?'

'Could we start with the first?'

Deborah, it seems, had married at eighteen in 1984 and was divorced in 1986. She didn't go into any details but thought she'd been far too young.

'In 1988 I met Michael. I met him in a supermarket. He's the one you're interested in. He was a police sergeant in the uniformed branch at the time. I was really smitten. He was tall and handsome and he made me laugh. He was great in bed, hard-working and generous. My family thought he was wonderful. We got married in 1990. The first two years, we were really happy. We didn't have much money but we managed because I had a job. He did shifts and I knew when he'd be home.'

She stared thoughtfully for a moment at her hands. 'Do you fancy a coffee?' she asked.

I did. When she'd gone to the kitchen, I looked round the room. There were a couple of photographs on a small oval table in the corner of the room. One was a photo of her most recent wedding. The groom, silver-haired and looking considerably older than her, was smiling broadly. She looked pensive in a cream sheath dress. The other photo was of an older couple, presumably her parents, on their wedding day.

When she returned with the coffee, I flicked over a page and sat with pen poised, trying to look professional. Her expression was a little pensive now. 'Some things,' she said, 'you try to forget. I've tried to forget Michael but it's not easy.'

'Take your time,' I said. 'Just tell me about what went wrong and I'll scribble away. There's plenty of white space on the form.'

We sipped the coffee and I was disappointed it wasn't ground and that there were no bickies.

'In 1993 he joined the CID in London at Coram Green,' she said, in answer to the question devoted to his career moves. 'That's when he changed. He worked sixteen hours a day, or at least he told me he was working. Most of the time he was in various pubs and clubs getting drunk. As he drank more, he became violent. And, drunk, he was a different person. I eventually lost my job. I was a beauty consultant and you can't do that job with black eyes. I begged him to join AA but he denied being an alcoholic and refused.'

'But *you* thought he was an alcoholic?'

'I think he liked drinking with his mates and certain criminals. I don't think he *needed* to drink like a real alcoholic. He just enjoyed it and he liked living on the edge. Gradually he began to talk about making real money.'

'What did you think he meant by that?'

She shrugged. 'To be honest I was scared of him by then. I was frightened to say too much. If I questioned him about where he'd been or what he'd been doing, he'd go mad. Afterwards he'd be really loving for a while, telling me about the stress of the job and he couldn't do his job without being in the pubs and clubs. And then . . .' She broke off suddenly, looking haunted. She began again. 'And then I got pregnant.'

There was a long pause and her hand went to her mouth as if she wanted to keep the words back but couldn't. She gave a huge sigh. 'I don't know why I'm telling you all this. I suppose it's because you're a stranger and I want to. Even my present husband doesn't know the full story. He knows I lost a baby but that's all.'

'I won't write it down if you don't want me to.'

'No,' she said bleakly. 'It doesn't matter. It was all my fault anyway.'

'How do you mean?'

'I was so stupid. I thought he wanted children. I didn't ask and when I told him I was pregnant he seemed pleased. He acted pleased for a few days. But he started getting nasty even when he was sober. I should have seen the danger signals. But I chose to ignore them. He wasn't really violent until I began to show and then one night he came home very late and very drunk. I was in bed asleep. He pushed me out of bed and told me to make him something to eat. I was half asleep and struggling to get up off the floor. Then he started kicking me in the stomach and screaming "Die, you parasite — die!" He meant the baby, of course. I stumbled out of the room and he came after me and kicked me down the stairs.'

'But none of that was *your* fault,' I said emphatically.

She stared at me sadly as if I was naive. 'Of course it was my fault,' she said sharply. 'I'd stayed with him. I thought he might change. When he was in a good mood I thought I still loved him. I was old enough to have known better. I was a coward. Battered women become cowards. They fear being on their own more than they fear being beaten.'

'Violent men operate like that,' I said. 'They work at destroying your confidence and you probably spent your time working out how to please him, how to avoid upsetting him. That saps your resolve and your energy.'

She gazed at me for a moment as if trying to work me out. 'I've studied some psychology,' I said, by way of explanation. That was true in part. Saturday night in the Accident and Emergency Department had been my training ground. Husbands and partners bringing in injured women who'd fallen downstairs or walked into door handles or fallen over the cat. I'd heard all sorts of excuses and most were just accepted, the man involved not leaving the woman's side. *Two left feet*, they'd say with a smile. Or, *Born clumsy* — and then add, *You should be more careful*, and the woman would smile feebly and say nothing.

'Anyway,' she continued. 'I had a broken right wrist and I lost the baby. But I had nowhere else to go. I had plaster of Paris on my arm and I had to go through an induction. I needed help even getting dressed. My mum and dad are dead. I didn't have much choice but to stay with him until I'd recovered.'

'But then you left him?'

'Not straight away. It was about six weeks later when the plaster came off. But before that I went to see the chief inspector at Coram Green Station. I suppose I thought one last ditch attempt might be worth a try. And after losing the baby and needing help because of my wrist, Michael was being an angel. He was like a different person but I knew once I was better he'd start again. I needed an ally, I suppose. Michael had always spoken well of him, so I went to see him.'

'What happened?'

'He listened. I don't know if he believed me or not, but he told me what a wonderful officer Michael was and that he could well be promoted very soon. Did I want to jeopardize such a promising career? I soon felt that I was the one in the wrong.'

'Then what did you do?'

'I left the station in tears. It was raining, so I went into a café and sat sniffling in a corner. An old lady came and sat with me and started talking and then I told her everything just like I'm telling you. She said, "Don't go home. His boss will have told him. He'll half kill you. Go straight to this place." She wrote down an address on a scrap of paper. It was a women's refuge. I told her the police knew all the refuges but she said they would look after me, I'd be safe. So, I walked there in the pouring rain and they took me in. Two days later I saw a solicitor and she said I should immediately file for divorce. I qualified for legal aid and the solicitor did a wonderful job. Michael capitulated on every point she made. So, I got the house and he agreed to a lump sum. It was either that or I would press charges.'

'Did you ever see him again?'

She shook her head. 'I heard that he'd remarried a year after the divorce. If I'd known before, I would have warned her.'

'I don't suppose she would have believed you.'

'No. If someone had warned me, I wouldn't have believed them.'

'Do you think that working in the CID changed him?'

She paused for a moment. 'I think working on the drug squad corrupted him. I think he was making money selling drugs on. I think he drank to forget and he took his guilt out on me.'

'Shouldn't he be stopped?'

'Of course he should, but there's something I've realized about him.'

'What's that?'

'He knew or guessed other people's weaknesses. He was talking once about a senior officer, saying he was a paedophile. I was shocked. Michael laughed at me, saying I was stupid and that the police were only a cross section of society and very few were saints.'

I stared at my scrawled notes.

'Do you know?' she said. 'I realize for the first time what a dangerous, evil bastard he is.'

I put down my pen and closed my notes as if my survey was at an end.

'I bet you wouldn't be willing to say that in court,' I said lightly.

She paused briefly. 'I think I would. I have a good husband now and the confidence. I don't know what he's up to now but I think he's capable of almost anything.'

'Even murder?'

'Yes. He murdered my baby.'

CHAPTER TWELVE

David had left me a brief message on my mobile answering service saying the cottage was sorted but I'd need a new sofa etcetera. I couldn't bear to think about the etceteras but an Argos catalogue and home delivery would sort that. I was delighted and surprised that two minor criminals seemed as fast as television professionals.

My visit to Deborah gave me something else to think about on the way home. A picture was building of an extremely dangerous individual who might have friends in high places. David would do his best but he didn't have either the time or the resources to make it his major priority. It was down to me but, if I was honest, I had to admit I didn't know what to do next. Apart, that is, from seeing his second ex-wife in Bedford. Whitby's address would help but knowing where he lived would mean breaking and entering, which wasn't my strong point.

Jasper's greeting was on its usual par but one look at Hubert's face told me something was wrong. 'He's rung here,' he said. 'The office number. Betty answered the call. I had to send her home because she was so upset. I doubt we'll see her again. She's bound to tell her husband.'

I didn't need to ask what he'd said. It was enough that he did indeed know where we were.

That news cast a shadow over the evening. Megan was more quiet and subdued than usual and went to bed early, while Hubert and I sat together drinking copious amounts of wine to fuel our resolve. Alcohol always seems like an answer but never is. We just got sleepy and depressed and neither of us could think straight. 'I've rung David,' he said. 'If he rings again, they'll try a trace, if we can keep him talking, but it's unlikely that will work — the caller doesn't wait for a reply.'

'What are we going to do?' I asked, not expecting an answer and only getting a blank look from Hubert. 'Find him before he finds us,' I said. 'That was my plan but it's easier said than done. And if we did find him, apart from Megan's identification of him and testimony, we don't have any evidence.'

'A doctor could tell if Megan had given birth, couldn't he?' enquired Hubert.

'Yes. That's the next step,' I agreed, not wanting to acknowledge I'd let that drift. 'Megan will have to agree, of course, but she seems more willing now to participate.'

Hubert looked round the room. 'She's opted out this evening, hasn't she?'

I too was worried by her absence but I didn't let on to Hubert. 'I'll make her an appointment at the health centre. She can be seen as a casual.'

'I have got one idea,' said Hubert. 'Security cameras above your door and the main entrance.'

'Has it come to that?' I said.

'What else can we do? Longborough Police can't afford to offer us round-the-clock protection.'

I told him about my visit to the ex-Mrs Whitby and he listened in horrified fascination. 'There's no honour among thieves,' said Hubert.

'What's that supposed to mean? Or are you just being philosophical?'

'I mean that good cops outnumber bad. One of his colleagues must know or guess that he's bent. With a little encouragement, they might blow the whistle.'

'But that means going up to London and talking at random,' I said. 'Knowing my luck, I'd pick the lowliest, least bright spark in the force.'

'I wasn't thinking of involving anyone else.'

'Enlighten me, O wise one.'

'We do it anonymously . . . A few letters to senior officers planting doubts. They'd have to take some action.'

I thought about that. Anonymous letters seemed underhand. But who was I kidding? We were dealing with a man who didn't appear to have scruples, so I concluded that all is fair when self-preservation is at stake. And not only was Megan in danger, we all were. Poor Dr Lewis had died because I went to see her. A few anonymous letters seemed mild in comparison.

'OK,' I agreed. 'I'm up for it. I'll start composing a letter tomorrow.'

Just as we'd decided to call it a night, Megan wandered in. She'd been crying. 'I feel terrible,' she said. 'I just can't stop crying. I seem to be getting worse rather than better.'

On cue, I said, 'See the doctor tomorrow. Maybe some antidepressants would help.'

She nodded in agreement, muttered, 'Goodnight,' and walked slowly out of the room.

'Poor kid,' said Hubert.

'Yeah. But at least she's got us trying to help her.'

'We haven't made much headway so far.'

Hubert was usually more positive than me but I had to agree that things were bleak at the moment. And one thought was particularly bleak. If Megan's baby was still alive, it could by now be anywhere in the country or — the worst scenario — had been taken abroad.

To take my mind off the situation I began glancing through the Argos catalogue. Hubert soon joined me and we argued a bit about style and colour but eventually I decided and Hubert, just to cheer me up, said he'd place the order and make sure it was delivered and arranged in the best possible taste. I couldn't argue with an offer like that but strangely the interior of my cottage didn't seem important. As long as there was a sofa to sit on, a table to eat from, a bed to sleep on — what else mattered?

* * *

I was up early the following morning to catch a kindly receptionist at the health centre. I rang for ten minutes before it was answered. 'We are very busy today,' she said, sounding harassed. 'We're a doctor short.'

'The female doctor?'

'She's on holiday. Is it urgent?'

'Yes — very.'

I wasn't in the mood to plead and maybe my tone suggested that. I explained that the patient was a casual.

'Come back towards the end of surgery and wait. Dr Darby will see you.' I'd never met Dr Darby but I was suitably grateful.

By nine a.m. I had managed to contact the second Mrs Whitby. At first she seemed reluctant but I kept pressing her relentlessly, even using emotional blackmail, suggesting that my job was on the line. I could have added my life might be on the line. My tactic worked. 'Oh, all right,' she said eventually. 'Come at four. I'll be back from work by then.'

I started composing an anonymous letter but wanted Hubert to vet it and help me decide if we should cut out the middle man and go straight to the top with the Chief Constable.

Megan's mood hadn't much improved and she mooched backwards and forwards between rooms like a lost soul. She didn't want to walk Jasper or eat breakfast and I was relieved when it was eleven thirty and we were on our way to the health centre. Three desolate-looking souls were booked in before Megan. I hadn't told her the doctor was male and I half expected her to make a fuss when she found out.

When Megan was finally called, she grabbed my arm. 'I want you with me,' she said. At the sight of the portly Dr Darby she turned and made a bid for the door but I yanked her back, whilst the doctor looked more interested than perturbed. 'Is . . .' He paused to look at the name on the temporary notes. 'Is Megan your daughter?' he asked, looking straight at me. To say that I was outraged would be an understatement. 'She is a friend and client,' I managed to splutter. He murmured something into his double chin but he'd plummeted so far in my estimation that if I found out he'd won the Nobel Prize for medicine I wouldn't have been impressed.

Megan still clung to me irritatingly and I had to disengage her hand and sit her down. 'Megan is very nervous,' I explained. 'She's been a victim of rape under the influence of Rohypnol, which resulted in a pregnancy. She gave birth less than two weeks ago . . .'

His piggy blue eyes showed his interest and, I suppose, compared to backache and haemorrhoids, Megan's history was a damn sight more interesting. 'And the baby?' he enquired.

He might have an eyesight problem but perhaps he was sharper than he looked. Give him the benefit of the doubt, I thought. 'The baby's whereabouts are a mystery. Megan was told the baby was stillborn.'

He looked confused now but he smiled at her. 'I'll need to take a medical history,' he said, 'before I examine you.'

Megan, it seemed, had had the full range of childhood diseases. He then asked her about her menstrual cycle, which was regular, virtually to the day, every twenty-eight days from the age of twelve. It was obvious she was uncomfortable answering his questions but he was patient and I could tell he was going to give us plenty of time.

'Just slip your top and jeans off,' he said to her, 'and lie on the couch.'

Megan hesitated but I tugged at her sleeve and she stood up slowly and reluctantly to get undressed behind the portable screen.

Dr Darby smiled at her reassuringly as she lay with a pale-blue blanket pulled up to her chin. 'I'll take your blood pressure first,' he said. 'Have you had it taken before?'

She nodded and then announced abruptly, 'My last doctor was murdered.' He looked immediately at me for confirmation. 'It's true,' I said. 'Dr Lewis in Criccieth.' He began applying the cuff to her arm. 'I read about that. Have they caught anyone yet?'

'No,' said Megan swiftly. 'And if they have, they've got the wrong person.'

'Just relax now,' he said, 'while I do this.'

I was beginning to feel sorry for the doc. Two strange women arrive with tales of a missing baby and murder. I had a feeling it was all getting a bit much for him.

More general questions followed on the lines of bowels, bladder, appetite, sleep and previous medication. He raised an eyebrow a fraction when he heard she'd been on antidepressants but he didn't press the point.

'My hands are warm now,' he said, after rubbing them together for a few seconds. 'I just want to feel your tummy.' Megan clutched my hand but managed a smile when she realized it was not going to hurt.

He felt the fundus of her uterus. 'Your womb is still bulky,' he said. 'But it takes a few weeks to get back to normal. Are you doing your post-natal exercises?'

She looked at him blankly. 'Megan had no ante or post-natal care,' I explained.

'Why not?'

'She hasn't been in a normal situation.'

I didn't think he thought either of us was normal but he then examined her breasts, which he described as *still active*. 'I won't do an internal, Megan,' he said. 'If you're still living here, we can do that at six weeks. Get yourself dressed and I'll do a blood test.'

He took blood and Megan didn't flinch and I didn't mention HIV, because I thought that Megan had more than enough to cope with at the moment. Then he wrote copious notes and eventually said, 'You seem fine, Megan, but you're obviously depressed and anxious. I don't want to start you on antidepressants at this stage. How are you sleeping?'

'I have nightmares and I wake up very early in the morning.'

He picked up his prescription pad. 'I'll prescribe a mild sleeping pill for a couple of weeks and some vitamins.'

She murmured her thanks. Then he turned to me. 'What's happening about the baby?'

I couldn't resist saying, 'We're in fear of our lives but we're doing our best to find out what happened.'

'Are the police involved?'

'Oh yes,' I said, 'very much so. You wouldn't believe how involved they are.'

When we got back to Humberstone's, I had to leave immediately and, although I invited Megan to come with me to Bedford, she refused. 'Keep my front door bolted,' I warned her. 'And don't answer the phone. I'll ring David for an update.' I was halfway down the stairs when I turned. 'The midwife, Teresa, is a key witness. I want you to remember anything you can about her. Her accent, the colour of her eyes, what she wore — anything.'

'I could do a sketch of her.'

'Great — do that. I'll be back late evening.'

It was as I was driving away that I realized I hadn't seen Jasper. Usually he was around for arrivals and departures even if he acted the sleepy mutt the rest of the day. The thought niggled me for a few miles but Hubert or one of the staff could have been out walking him, so I put the worry to the back of my mind and drove on, noting the ominously grey clouds building.

It took two and a half hours to get to Bedford and, once I got there, I asked two people for directions. One was convinced Baptist Road was on one side of the river and the other was equally convinced it was on the opposite side. In the end I ignored them both, drove out of town a short distance and stopped at a petrol station. The assistant there had a decent local map and, from what she said, my destination was nearby.

Baptist Road was made up of numerous tiny terraced houses that had seen better days. Yvonne, the second ex, lived on the wrong side of the river and had obviously not fared as well from the divorce as Deborah. Yvonne's house was freshly painted and so was she. She was short, thin as a boy, elfin-faced, wearing jeans and a check shirt, and either her eyelashes were abnormally long or she wore falsies. Her lipstick was a brilliant red and her hair, thick, curly and blonde, seemed to belong to someone else.

She'd already made a pot of tea and we sat in her front room to drink it at a coffee table. She'd made the best of a small room, with throw covers on sagging armchairs and framed posters on the walls, but it contained such a variety of old and shabby pieces that she'd obviously been to a few car boot sales and money was a problem.

'Are you married?' she asked.

'No. So far I haven't met the right man. I haven't totally given up though.'

'Take my advice,' she said. 'Stop looking.'

I asked her the usual questions and she didn't elaborate much until we got to Michael Whitby. 'I thought marrying a copper was a step up from the fireman I was with before. How wrong could I be? I'd only known him three months when he asked me to marry him. He was good in bed, earned good money and he liked a drink and I do too — and he seemed like a nice guy.'

'When did he change?'

'He was in the vice squad when I first met him. He worked undercover for some time. So, I didn't see him very often. When I did see him he was often drunk.'

'Was he violent?'

She flashed me a quick glance, as though suggesting I was stupid. 'Oh yes,' she said. 'One minute he'd be fine but if I asked him a question about his job he'd go mad.'

'Did he injure you badly?'

'Depends what you mean by that. He was called Mad Mick at the station, so they knew what he was like, but cops always stick together. I knew I was going to leave. I began saving as much money as I could. We were renting a house at the time. I think he got wind that I was planning to go, because I'd got a job in the office of a garage and then for some reason they laid me off. I wanted to go for unfair dismissal but when Mick was so against it, I guessed he'd had something to do with me losing my job.'

'Did you have any family you could turn to?'

'One sister with four kids and no money living in Sheffield and that's all.'

'What about girlfriends?'

'I was living south of the river when I met Mick. They warned me I didn't know him well enough but over that first year we gradually lost touch.'

'So, you were isolated.'

'Yeah, and depressed. I lost stones in weight, haven't managed to put it on yet.'

'So, how long did the marriage last?'

'Two years. I've been free of him now for eighteen months. I was so relieved when I got my decree.'

'You divorced him?'

'Oh yes. I finally got the strength to see him off.'

'What did you do?'

'I was working in a chemist's when he met me. So I crushed up some laxatives and put them in his food. I didn't tell him, of course, not straight away. Then I began to hint that maybe I was poisoning him.'

'I thought he'd beat the hell out of me. But he didn't. For once he looked scared. I even told him I could get hold of insulin and, if he ever touched me again, he'd never be able to close his eyes, because I had a syringe full of insulin just waiting for him.'

'And did you?'

She laughed. 'No. But he believed me. I think he knew I'd reached the end and there was nothing he could do to frighten me anymore.'

'So, you left?'

'No, he left. I stayed on in the house for a while but I couldn't afford the rent. He coughed up thirty-five thousand for this little place.'

'How did he get that sort of money?'

'He was bent, of course. And he didn't want a fuss. I threatened to go to the station with a placard round my neck saying: *This is what Whitby did to me.*'

She gave me a wry smile and put her hands to her hair and raised them in the air. She placed the blonde wig in front of me. Her head was totally bald.

'The stress of living with him caused that. I lost my eyelashes, my eyebrows. All my body hair. For ages I felt a freak; now I've got used to it.'

'You've been very brave,' I said.

'Yeah. I'd have been braver still to have gone before this happened.' She slipped the wig back on her head.

'Do you think the pressures of his job in the police had a bearing on his behaviour?' I asked, reverting to my questions.'

She laughed, dryly. 'You've got to be joking. A bastard like Mick can be in any job and he's still a bastard.'

'Did you try talking to his senior officers?'

'Who writes these stupid questions?'

'A civil servant somewhere,' I said, apologetically.

'Well, they should be out in the real world. I did once say I'd tell his boss. He very nearly killed me that night. And he told me that he'd already told those he worked with that I was a slovenly bitch who couldn't keep her knickers on. And he always made sure he didn't mark my face, so that no one seeing me would know.'

'What about children? Did he ever say he wanted children?'

'No. Thank God. I'm only twenty-five — maybe one day with a good man, who knows?'

I was about to leave but I still wanted to ask her the same question I'd asked Deborah. 'Do you think your ex-husband is capable of murder?'

She stared at me hard for a moment. 'Where did that question come from?' she asked, suspiciously.

'Just curiosity,' I said, standing up and collecting my notes.

'You just sit down again,' she said. 'Who the hell are you anyway?'

CHAPTER THIRTEEN

I sat down promptly. Yvonne was small but feisty and, if she was telling the truth — and it certainly seemed like it — she might make a useful character witness in court. 'OK,' I said. 'I'll come clean.'

I told her the real reason for my visit, explaining about Megan and the baby. She listened intently. 'Oh my God,' she said. 'The poor kid.'

'He and an associate are making threats against us. Death threats.'

'So, that's why you asked if he was capable of murder?'

I hesitated. I wasn't sure if she needed to know about Dr Lewis. Her murder could have been a horrible coincidence. Maybe it was a robbery that went wrong or a disgruntled patient or lover, but I didn't believe that. However, if it was connected with Megan, a shooting seemed very extreme for a man more used to using his feet and his fists.

'Yeah. I think he may have killed because of a connection with Megan.'

Yvonne sat silently for a moment. 'If he did murder someone, how did he do it?'

'With a gun.'

'I don't think he'd risk using a gun,' she said, thoughtfully. 'Especially if it was police-issue. I think he'd get one of his criminal cronies to do it.'

That made sense to me, but was he taking huge risks to protect himself from a rape charge or was the baby the real reason? There was another angle, of course, that the baby was a pure accident, evidence of rape. Get rid of the baby and then use the innocent-looking Megan as a drug runner. How are drug runners recruited anyway? I didn't know. But the vast amounts of cocaine and heroin getting into the country didn't all come from huge consignments. Some of it must come in small amounts. Someone like Megan, telling of a rape she didn't remember, a baby that she never saw, and with a psychiatric history, could have become both a user and a carrier. Easy meat and with no family to worry about her or fight for her in some foreign jail. Or, perhaps worse, she could have landed up on the streets in the vicious thrall of some pimp.

'When you were married to him, Yvonne, did you ever suspect he was involved in the drug scene?'

She smiled uneasily. 'He once said that vice and drugs were naturally intertwined and he didn't know why they were different branches of the force.'

'Was that because it would have been easier for him if they were?'

She nibbled thoughtfully at her thumbnail and then said, 'Maybe. I think that, whatever scams he's up to, he's in it with someone higher up. That way they cover for each other.'

There wasn't much to be achieved by staying any longer, so I said, 'I'd better be off now.'

'What are you going to do about him?'

'I wish I knew. The answer is in London but, if we get too close, he might get even more rattled.'

'Be very careful,' she said ominously. 'You could be on to something bigger than you think.'

Did she know more than she was saying or was she just guessing? 'What are you trying to tell me?'

She shrugged. 'Sometimes he'd talk about crime as if he were whiter than white. I think he might be using illegal immigrants for all sorts of purposes. They're easy enough to blackmail. Amongst his other personality traits, he is a racist — he'd think they were expendable.'

'Thanks, Yvonne. That might be useful.'

I left Yvonne then, telling *her* to be careful.

I drove homewards under an ever-darkening sky that threatened a deluge and glanced nervously into my rear mirror so often that I was in danger of losing my concentration for what was ahead. Michael Whitby, although a shadowy figure, had been our major worry. Now it was becoming obvious that there could be others with neither names nor faces. When, I wondered, did paranoia become a normal reaction? Was I being paranoid that the black car behind me was following me? When it eventually turned off, I decided I was. But I felt increasingly nervous, a premonition of things to come, perhaps. I drove faster, ignoring forty-miles-an-hour warnings. At one camera point I saw a flash, but what was a mere speeding fine compared to life itself?

The journey seemed long, and twenty miles from Longborough the heavens opened. I slowed as the driving rain slashed at my windscreen. In my rear mirror a silver car slowed too. Don't get fraught, I told myself, he or she is being as cautious as you are. They wouldn't even try to overtake in these conditions. The fact that they're behind me, I tried to convince myself, does not mean they are following me. And anyway, the silver car, make unknown because I don't recognize makes of car unless they are very distinctive, has no choice on a wet, bendy road but to follow. We were both on the road leading to Longborough — so what? No ill intent intended. But all the positive thinking in the world failed to override my fear that my life could be on the line.

When at last the silver car disappeared in the middle of Longborough, I sighed audibly. I'd been wrong. It was just another person going homeward in the dark. And dark and dismal summed up Humberstone's that night. Normally there was a lamp standard outside and usually a light on in the reception area. Bodies turned up day and night, so it had to be well lit. It was a bad omen. I was sure of that. I slipped my key in the door and was grateful that the hall light was on. It doesn't take any effort to switch on a light but I'd never liked entering dark places and often left a light on if I was going out. I shook my wet hair and waited expectantly for Jasper's excited yapping. But there was no sound at all. 'Megan!' I yelled. 'Hubert?' There was still no sound. A hollow sensation hit my stomach, a desolate feeling like feeling abandoned as a child. I rushed up the stairs and swung open doors, flicking on lights, afraid of what I might find in the dark. It was then that I noticed Jasper's lead was not hanging from the kitchen door, but surely even Jasper would baulk at a walk in torrential rain? I stood in the hall uncertain of what to do next.

Take a deep breath and try to think logically, I told myself. Then I dialled Hubert's mobile number and waited and waited. There was no reply. It was either switched off or he hadn't even taken it with him. I thrust down the receiver, grabbed my mac and an umbrella and rushed down the stairs.

Where exactly I was going to look for them, I didn't know. I was already outside in the pouring rain when the thought crossed my mind that they may have been taken — kidnapped — abducted. Then common sense rallied. There was no sign of a struggle and surely Jasper wouldn't have been included. I was convinced Hubert would have put up a fight anyway, although, if he was staring down the barrel of a gun and had Megan to think about, he might go quietly.

I started at a trot but I wasn't fit enough to keep it up for long and the rain and the cold night air seemed to sap my energy, so I walked briskly towards the river, because that was the only place I could think they might be.

The town was bathed in watery desolation. There wasn't a soul about. An occasional car passed me by, hissing through the puddles. I walked on, peering under my brolly for any signs of life. I was nearing the river when I saw them. They seemed to be holding each other up and I wasn't sure who was most in need of support. I was so relieved to see them that even the absence of Jasper didn't spoil that sense of relief.

As I got nearer I could see they were drenched. Megan was sobbing silently and Hubert looked distraught but he did manage to say, 'Why didn't you bring the car?'

Because I'm stupid, I thought, but I didn't answer or ask any questions. They both looked grey with cold and normal speech seemed beyond them. As I took hold of Megan's coat sleeve, I realized she wasn't just wet from the rain — she was soaked through. I knew then that for some reason she'd been in the river and visions of Jasper being swept away filled my eyes. I tried to hurry them but water squelched in their shoes and their footsteps were slow and leaden. Megan had begun to mumble in Welsh and I wondered if both of them were in the first stages of hypothermia. 'Come on,' I urged. 'We're nearly there, you'll soon be warm.'

I had my key at the ready long before we reached my door. I ran ahead of them up the stairs to grab warm towels from the towel rail and start running the bath water. I rushed back to hand out the towels and start removing their sopping coats. Hubert squelched away to his bathroom and I dealt with Megan, whose face was a ghastly mottled-grey colour. She seemed in a trance-like state, letting me undress her and help her into the bath. The hot water soon worked its magic and her face gradually became pinker and she stopped mumbling in Welsh.

'It was all my fault,' she announced in a rush, as I briskly towelled her down and then slipped my winter-weight towelling dressing gown on her. She seemed oblivious to my ministrations. 'Jasper wanted to go out. He kept barking at the door. I told him it was raining but he wouldn't stop.'

'Come on,' I said. 'I'll put the fire on and make you some toast and hot cocoa.'

She protested, but only mildly, as I led her into the lounge and turned the coal-effect gas fire on and moved an armchair nearer to the fire. 'I'm so sorry, Kate,' she said.

'Just get warm,' I said. 'You can tell me all about it in a few minutes.'

In the kitchen, I made a huge pile of toast and three mugs of hot sweet cocoa and, by the time I returned with the tray, Hubert too was sitting close up to the fire and staring into the mock flames. I handed out the cocoa and they both started eating the toast like automata and so I waited and nibbled at my toast and sipped at my cocoa without really tasting it.

'I thought we were goners,' said Hubert.

'Is Jasper in the river?' I asked, my voice barely a whisper, as if speaking quietly would make a difference.

'We don't know—'

'It was my fault,' interrupted Megan, her face now flushed with the warmth of the fire. 'I put his lead on and I was just going to walk him round the car park but something frightened him and he pulled really hard and the lead slipped from my grasp and he ran off. I ran after him and I thought he'd gone to the river . . . So, I went down there and I thought I saw him in the water . . . So I waded in a bit to where I thought he was caught up among the weeds but it wasn't him. It was just an old shoe. In the dark, I couldn't see properly. Then the force of the water knocked me over and, if it hadn't been for Hubert, I'd have drowned.'

I turned to look at Hubert, who looked embarrassed. 'I saw her go out and I followed her. I was just in the right place at the right time.'

'You're still a hero.'

'Don't be so silly, Kate. I didn't have to swim, I only waded in.'

'It wasn't that easy against the current,' said Megan, looking adoringly at Hubert.

'Let's forget it,' said Hubert. 'Jasper's still missing and he's never run off before, so I think someone was hanging around.'

No one spoke and in the silence we could hear properly the sound of the wind and rain outside. It brought it home to us that Jasper was alone in that big, cold, wet world and we were now warm and cosy. 'Jasper's a canny soul. He'll find shelter,' I said. 'And he'll find his way home.'

Both Hubert and Megan looked at me as if I was crazy. 'I hope you're right,' said Hubert. 'I hope you're right.'

We sat for a while in miserable comfort and, after a while, going to bed seemed the only option. 'We'll go out really early in the morning looking for him,' I said. 'And he's wearing a collar, so there's every chance someone will ring us to let us know he's been found.'

Neither of them looked convinced and, as we trooped silently to bed, I had a strong feeling that we'd never see Jasper again. It would break Hubert's heart. I knew that. Jasper had become part of our lives and, even as I walked to my bedroom, I expected him to be at my heels. It was like missing a limb.

During the night it continued to rain and, as I dozed, I heard Megan calling out in Welsh twice and in English once, 'I'm here, I'm coming.' I didn't know if she was answering her mother, her baby or Jasper. A great pall of misery seemed to have fallen over us and, as far as I could see, it could only get worse. Something had really spooked Jasper. He'd never run off like that before. I lay for hours listening to every noise and rattle. At two thirty I was up and out of bed when I heard creaking on the stairs. I crept to the kitchen, picked up a frying pan and walked to the top of the stairs. There was nothing, even the creaking had stopped. For the first time I worried about the spirits of the dead being so close at hand. Was there an unquiet spirit in the cold room or the chapel of rest?

You're already paranoid about the living, I told myself, now you're getting paranoid about the dead. I went back to bed, pulled the duvet over my head and it seemed that, in a brief lull when the house became quiet and the wind outside dropped, I fell asleep.

Vaguely aware of it being morning, I heard my door open quietly, but somehow my eyes felt glued-down and I couldn't manage to rouse myself. When I heard my front door close, my eyes suddenly snapped open. I sat up feeling dizzy and thick-headed and saw that a note had been pinned to my bedroom door. I staggered out of bed and snatched the note: *Gone out to look for Jasper. Megan.*

I threw on a pair of jeans and a sweater, grabbed a coat and ran after her. It had stopped raining but there were puddles everywhere and no sign of Megan. I began making my way to the town centre and wondered if she was making for the river. I decided she was and I broke into a run to try to catch up with her before she had another mishap. Then I struck lucky. I saw her in the main street. I was too far away to shout, so I hurried towards her. It was then that I saw a silver car moving slowly through the main street and stopping alongside her. The window wound down and a man's head emerged. She leant towards him and spoke and, as I stopped running and paused to collect a screaming breath, the man got out of the car. 'Run, Megan!' I screamed. 'Run!'

CHAPTER FOURTEEN

Megan looked towards me but the man was by now out of the car and opening the passenger door. I tried to scream again but I was out of breath and had to stop running momentarily. As I got to within a few yards of the car, he had his hand on Megan's back and was pushing her towards the back seat.

'You bastard!' I gasped, banging him hard on the back. 'Let her go!'

He turned round in surprise. Megan's mouth was open in surprise. 'Run!' I tried to shout but it was more of a croak than an instruction.

'Who rattled your cage, love?' he asked, as I pushed Megan away from the car and he fended me off with one arm. I kicked at his shins but missed and Megan cried out, 'Stop it, Kate — he's found Jasper.'

I stopped and looked at him. He was about fifty, with a round good-natured face and sparse hair. Appearances aren't everything but there was no mistaking the fact that he looked harmless.

'Calm down, love,' he said. He seemed vaguely amused, as if women lashing out at him wasn't that abnormal. 'The little dog was at my door last night. We took him in out of the rain. He wouldn't let us look at his collar until this morning.

I was just trying to find the address and I stopped to ask this early bird.' He looked towards Megan and from the back seat of the car she lifted out Jasper, who was wrapped in a blanket and seemed barely able to open his eyes. 'Is he OK?' I asked.

'He's been awake most of the night. Kept whimpering at the door. Why he came to us, I don't know.'

'I'm sorry I attacked you. I thought Megan was being abducted.'

He glanced at me with a hint of pity, as if I was slightly mad, and — if being paranoid counts — I was. 'Whereabouts do you live?' I asked him.

'Aspen Way,' he said. 'We moved in a few weeks ago.'

'That's where Jasper used to live.'

'That explains it, then,' he said.

I apologized profusely, thanked him several times and, with Megan clutching Jasper, we walked back towards Humberstone's. He still looked dozy and, if it hadn't been so early in the morning, I'd have gone straight to the vet's. As it happened, just as we approached Humberstone's, he began to sniff the air and started to wiggle in Megan's arms. At my door, she was forced to put him down and he surprised us both by bounding up the stairs. Hubert, with his coat on, stood in the hall, his face wreathed in a smile. He bent down to scoop up the excited dog and it was one of those moments when everything else is eclipsed. Even Megan, smiling broadly, looked for an instant as if she too didn't have a care in the world.

Nothing lasts, though, and a phone call from David put us squarely in more serious mode. He'd made further enquiries and Whitby had been investigated internally when he was working in the drug squad but, even though he had been suspended for a short period and his bank accounts looked into, nothing untoward was found.

'Well, thanks for trying.' I said, unable to hide the despondency in my voice.

'There is another avenue to try but I can't do it for you.'

'Fine, tell me.'

'An unofficial source told me he'd been seen at the Tree Tops internment camp at Lettering-on-Sea. It seems he saw a woman there on a few occasions.'

'You're an angel.'

'Be careful, Kate. The officer on the gate today is. Bill Oldman. Make sure it's Bill. Give him my name. I've told him you have police permission to look round, because you're a lawyer. So, for God's sake look like one and act like one. If Megan's with you, she's your assistant. Security is not that hot there. It's not a prison but some internees are regarded as risky, so take care.'

I checked on the map. Lettering-on-Sea needed a magnifying glass to be found. We'd need to stay the night and I had things to do before we left. Most importantly, I had to send off the anonymous letters.

Hubert thought my draft copy was OK and offered to print a few off and post them. I gave him a big kiss on the cheek and urged Megan to pack an overnight bag.

Within an hour we were on our way. 'Why are we going to this camp?' asked Megan, just as I turned the key in the ignition.

'Whitby's been seen there. I think that's where he may have met Teresa — the midwife.'

'But she won't be there, will she?'

'Not unless she asked to go back in.'

'I did those drawings you asked me to do,' said Megan.

In the trauma of losing Jasper, I'd forgotten all about them, not that I'd placed much emphasis on them. Most people I know have the drawing ability of a five-year-old. I switched off the ignition. 'Have you got them with you?'

She produced them from her holdall, carefully rolled and secured with an elastic band. I looked at each of them carefully. They were terrific. 'You're an artist, Megan. They're amazing.'

Teresa had solemn dark eyes, heavy brows and thick black hair in a plait. She'd drawn two views of her and the detail was impressive. Teresa had a hairy upper lip. Whitby was attractive in a craggy way and his nose was slightly bent. She'd made his eyes look positively evil but maybe that was mere artistic interpretation. 'I was good at art at school,' she said. 'I wanted to go to art school.'

'Believe me,' I said, still looking at the drawings in admiration, 'you still could.'

The drive to the sea seemed to relax Megan, as though the sea was where she belonged, and she talked about how much she loved to draw and paint. 'Well, you kept that light under a bushel, didn't you?' I said.

'I'm not much good at anything else.'

'Don't put yourself down. You're a good carer and a good cook.'

'Yes, but I can't drive and I missed a lot of schooling. I had to stay at home quite a lot to look after Mam. I sometimes thought she didn't want me to go to school. She didn't even want me to learn to drive.'

'Now you have all the time in the world to do those things.'

'I do hope so. Sometimes I feel optimistic and then I think about *him*. He's not going to let us get away, is he?'

'Don't think like that,' I said sharply. 'We're going to beat him.'

'I hope you're right,' she said in her languorous Welsh way.

We stopped for a pub lunch on the way and Megan seemed quite thrilled with its coal fire, dim lights and low beams. I was more thrilled with the bowl of real chips that came with our well-stuffed baguettes.

The food made Megan sleepy and, for the second leg of the journey, she slept, her head resting on my shoulder. I too felt very sleepy and opened the window a fraction in case I fell asleep.

As we neared Lettering-on-Sea, the sun shone with a glorious spring brightness and I became more alert as the traffic grew heavier. No problem, I thought, until, that is, I became convinced I was being followed by a dark-blue car, a small one, similar to a Fiat, I thought. But what self-respecting criminal would pursue someone in a Fiat? I tried to relax. They were probably going the same way as us and, as usual, I was being paranoid. I'd driven through the main street, which was so dreary that I was out of town before I knew it, and the same car was behind us. Then, thankfully, I saw a sign to the right saying: *Tree Tops Holiday Camp welcomes you!* Ironically, this was now an internment camp for asylum seekers who'd fled from France's camp the other side of the Channel Tunnel at Sangatte. I continued to drive along a narrow lane with bushes and fields on both sides and still the blue car was behind us. I nudged Megan and shrugged her head from my shoulder. 'Megan. Wake up. I can smell the sea.' She opened one eye slowly and licked her dry lips. 'I can't see it.'

'It's there somewhere,' I said.

'I need a wee,' she said. 'I'm desperate.'

'No problem. I'll stop, but you'll have to go behind a bush.'

'Beggars can't be choosers,' she said with a smile.

I didn't tell her about the beggar behind us who'd been following us for at least ten miles. I signalled left at the first lay-by I came to and told Megan to wait until it was clear before stepping out into the road, because the best bushes with a little gap between them were on the other side. There were occasions, I thought, when — horror of horrors — I *did* feel like her mother.

The suspect blue car — a Fiat, I noted — passed straight on by and I caught a glimpse of the driver — young and male. I clocked the registration number, just in case, because, apart from being a young white male with dark hair, I wouldn't have been able to recognize him again.

There was one other car — a dark-grey saloon — behind him and then the road both ways was completely clear. Megan crossed the road and disappeared into the gap in the bush. If I didn't have a view, then at least no one else could, not that there was anyone else around.

I sat looking at the map. Lettering-on-Sea was, I guessed, within fifty miles of London, but, judging by its relative isolation from any large towns, it could well have been in the Outer Hebrides. Which is presumably why refugees were sent there.

I glanced up from the map to see the blue Fiat parked further up the road. I put my paranoia aside. Maybe Tree Tops was a dead end and he'd made a mistake. Maybe he too was reading a map. When the car moved slowly forward, too slowly, the moment was one of paralysing fear. I wound down the window just as Megan appeared at the gap in the hedge. I screamed, 'Quick!' and simultaneously the car revved. Megan hesitated at the side of the road as she saw and heard the car. She'd only put one foot out by the time the car had rammed her with a sickening *thunk*.

How long it took me to move, I don't know. She lay crumpled half on, half off the road. The force had thrown her ten, maybe twenty feet. I didn't know how far. The car had driven on but I was trembling so much that I could hardly open my door. I didn't stop to close it. As I rushed to her, I glimpsed the car further down the road about to turn — about to come back for me. Should I drag her back through the gap? If she wasn't already dead, that would kill her for sure. I knelt down beside her, my mind a blank. What should I do? She was on her side, with blood pouring from her nose and her head. Airway, I thought, make sure her airway is clear. It was clear but I wasn't even sure if she was breathing. I hadn't even got a handkerchief. I pressed my bare hand to her head wound. Time had no relevance. Even as the Fiat now moved towards us, it seemed everything was in slow motion. I had to make a decision. If I did move her, she could die. If I didn't, she'd die or we'd both die for sure. There was no contest. I bent down, took her shoulders and pulled her with all my might through a gap in the hedgerow. And I carried on pulling her into the field. She made a gurgling, groaning sound and I called out her name as if, somehow, that would give her the will to live. I glimpsed the blue Fiat stopping.

If he got out of the car and came after me, he might assume Megan was dead and settle for me. I didn't want to leave her, but if I had to run, I'd run.

Then, thank God, I heard another sound and there, like the cavalry, crossing the field towards us, appeared a Land Rover. The Fiat drove off at speed and I began screaming, 'Help! Help!' like someone demented.

The ruddy-faced farmer who came to our aid was big and lumbering and already on his mobile phone. 'Don't you worry, me dear,' he said. 'Ambulance is on its way. And I'll fetch my first-aid kit.' He lumbered back to his Land Rover and, strangely, his slowness was reassuring. I was on my knees by Megan, telling her to hold on, but she wasn't responding. By now the blood was beginning to clot but the glimpse of skin was pure white. I took her radial pulse. It was fast and thready. The external wounds looked dramatic but the real danger was internal bleeding, even a ruptured spleen maybe. Then I noticed her right leg was at a funny angle and was probably broken. Her pelvis too was likely to have been damaged. I tried to think like a nurse but I could hardly breathe properly and fear clogged my thoughts. However, the sight of the big farmer coming back with his first-aid kit and a blanket rallied me a little. I knew I was near to passing out but I tried to breathe normally and not get into a state of pure panic. I covered Megan with the blanket and began fumbling with the packets of sterile dressings. 'They won't be long now,' he said. 'How did you get out here in the field?'

'The man in that Fiat was trying to kill us.'

'Was he indeed? I'd better call the police, then.'

He used his mobile once more. 'They'll be here soon,' he said. How long was *soon*, I wondered, in this neck of the woods? Time was standing still. Megan was still breathing but only just. She needed oxygen, an intravenous infusion, splints and a neck brace. Please God I hadn't damaged her neck in the process of moving her.

The sound of a siren filled the air and I hoped it was the ambulance but it was the police. One man, one woman, running from their car across the field towards us. 'You made good time,' said the farmer. Had they? I didn't know. They both checked on Megan and then I felt my fingers being prised apart from Megan's hand. For some reason, I'd thought she was gripping me. The woman officer started to lead me away. 'Come and sit in the car,' she said. I tried to resist but I had no strength left. Inside, I felt like a watery sponge.

'My colleague is a great first-aider,' she said, gripping me by the arm in an attempt to hold me upright. 'He'll look after her until the ambulance comes.'

I allowed myself to be led to the car, where — embarrassingly — just before getting in, I vomited all over the road. I kept apologizing but she said, 'I'm just grateful you didn't do it in the car.'

Once I'd been sick I felt more clear-headed. 'I'm Constable Jacky Gordon,' she said. She was young and pretty, with a warm smile and film-star teeth. 'And you are?'

She wrote down our names and addresses in her notebook but she was so slow and meticulous that I began to get agitated. 'If Megan's dying out there in that field, I should be with her, not some stranger.'

'Is she a relative?'

I hesitated. 'Yes. She's my stepsister.' I don't know why I said that, but it might have been hard to prove she wasn't and what the hell anyway? 'Let me go back to her.' She put a gentle but restraining hand on my arm. 'You have to tell us what happened.'

I didn't go into any real details except that the blue Fiat was behind me for ten miles prior to him deliberately running down Megan.

'Do you think it was road rage?' she asked. 'Did you drive extra slowly and he lost his temper?'

'No! Definitely not. We were targets. He was out to get us. He'd already passed us. He turned round up the road and came back . . .' As I spoke, my mind went into instant replay of the car revving. If only I'd shouted for Megan to run in the opposite direction.

'So, you know the driver?'

'No.'

'Would you recognize him again?'

'Possibly not. Dark-haired, white, male — that's all.'

'Where were you headed for?' she asked.

'Tree Tops. My . . . uncle works there.' At least I was keeping up with the family tree, but I wasn't sure anything I'd said had convinced her anyway. Soon I'd have to ring Hubert. Was I going to describe him as an uncle?

Somewhere in the distance I heard the steady *der-der, der-der* of a siren, then eventually I saw the flashing blue light. I tried to open the car door but again the law restrained me. 'You'll only get in their way,' she said. 'Give them a few minutes.' Then she added, 'Could you tell me, if Megan was hit at the road side, how come you were so far into the field?'

'I dragged her there,' I explained. 'I had to take that chance. I knew I was risking her life but he was coming back again to finish us both off.'

By the old-fashioned look she gave me, I knew she either didn't believe me or she thought I was in shock and talking nonsense. 'I've remembered the car number,' I said. As I rattled it off, I felt I'd redeemed myself a little in her eyes. 'I'll get it checked out.' She gave the details on her car phone and then said, 'Come on, let's see how your Megan's doing.'

The paramedics were stretchering Megan towards the ambulance and I burst into a run, because there was no way she was going on her own. 'How is she?' I managed to gasp out. Even that short run had stolen my breath. 'Are you the driver?' the one at the head of the stretcher asked. 'Are you OK?'

I nodded and walked along beside them over the rough ground, staring at Megan as though I could guess her condition merely by looking at her. An oxygen mask covered her face. A red blanket covered the rest of her. 'Is she going to make it?' I asked no one in particular.

'She's holding her own, love. She's young. She's got a chance.'

A chance? A chance? What does that mean? These days they consider everyone has a chance unless rigor mortis has set in.

I was about to board the ambulance when WPC Jacky barred my way. 'You come in the police car with us — we're following on to the hospital. We need to ask you a few more questions. If this man *is* out to get you — he may try again.'

Why was it I felt she didn't believe me? If I told her the whole story, would she be any more likely to believe me? I didn't think so. 'What about my car?' I asked.

'We'll see to that later. Is there anything you want to collect from it?' And, of course, there was — our overnight bags and our handbags. If Jacky hadn't reminded me, I'd have forgotten them. Gratefully I retrieved them and, strangely, being reunited with my handbag made me feel more normal, a little nearer to gaining control of my shattered senses.

As we drove behind the ambulance, a call came through on the car phone. She listened and nodded. 'Well,' she said. 'The Fiat owner seems to be a Mrs Entwhistle.'

CHAPTER FIFTEEN

Somehow Entwhistle didn't sound like a criminal name, but not every criminal was called Kray and the Yorkshire Ripper was a Sutcliffe, which sounds innocuous enough. 'It must have been stolen,' I said.

'We'll find out,' said Jacky. 'Are you sure you're feeling OK?'

'I've known better days,' I said, forcing a smile. 'Am I allowed to use my mobile phone to ring a relative?'

'Fine, go ahead.'

Hubert answered the phone straight away. Even before I could get the words out, he was saying, 'I had a premonition. Where are you?'

'In a police car.'

'You've been arrested?'

'No . . . Megan's been . . . badly injured.'

'And you?'

'I'm fine.'

'Which hospital?'

Jacky intervened. 'The Royal Hospital — it's to the north of the town.'

'Right,' said Hubert. 'I heard that. You hold your nerve, Kate. I'm on my way.'

It was then that I broke down. Jacky patted my shoulder but, try as I might, I couldn't stop crying until we neared our destination and then I managed, with a lot of gulping and sniffing, to compose myself.

The hospital, a Victorian building, was showing its age and I feared for Megan's safety. As if reading my thoughts, Jacky said, 'It's old but it's got a very good reputation. They don't do organ transplants but the A&E is pretty good — mainly because it's not busy.'

As the ambulance stopped, Jacky urged me to wait a few minutes or we'd get in the way. So, we sat in the police car and I impatiently looked at my watch as the minutes ticked past. 'What do you do for a living, Kate?' Jacky asked me. I noticed that our driver hadn't said a word, probably my outburst had something to do with that, or he was merely the strong silent type. This time I couldn't be bothered to lie. 'I'm a private investigator.'

'That's interesting,' she said. 'So, could the driver have been an irate husband?'

'He might be an irate husband,' I said flatly, 'but it's got nothing to do with me.'

Jacky was right about A&E not being busy. There were only three people waiting in the main bay. With the three of us sitting in a row together, it still didn't look crowded.

'I'll give them a bit more time,' said Jacky. 'Then I'll see if one of the docs will have a word.'

'Do you fancy a tea or a coffee?' asked the male PC in a theatrical whisper.

'Yeah, anything. Thanks.' As he left to find a drinks machine, I said, 'He can speak, then?'

'Vince is on voice rest. He keeps getting laryngitis.'

'There we are, then,' I said. 'Another mystery solved.'

'Are you good at being a private 'tec?' she asked.

I laughed. 'Not really. I try hard to do the best for my clients but, along the way, disasters seem to overtake me.'

'Like this one?'

'This is the worst ever.'

'I would have thought,' she said, 'it would be less dangerous than the police.'

'It's just me.'

'Oh well,' she said. 'No pain, no gain.'

'I'll tell Megan that, shall I?'

Laryngitis Vince reappeared with three plastic cups of coffee. I'd just taken the first reviving sip when a young woman in a white coat with a stethoscope draped around her neck advanced towards us. I tried to read her expression but couldn't. 'Kate?' she enquired. 'I'd like to have a chat about Megan — in private.'

'She's not dead?' I blurted out.

'No. No. Don't worry. She's stabilized. Her vital signs are improving.'

In an empty office, Dr Melanie Gooding told me that, although Megan's condition had stabilized, she would need to be operated on as soon as a theatre was free. Her right leg was fractured, possibly her pelvis, and there might be internal injuries. She didn't put it as simply as that and I realized I only really wanted to know two things — would she pull through and was she conscious?

'I'm sure she'll be fine,' she said. 'Now her blood volume is up, she's beginning to come round. She's answering questions. After surgery, she may need to be in intensive care for twenty-four to forty-eight hours.'

In my opinion being in ICU for two days was good news. The nurse patient ratio was higher and Megan could be better observed.

'May I see her now?'

'Yes, of course.'

Having been reassured by the doctor, albeit a doctor who looked barely old enough to be qualified, I was disappointed when I actually saw Megan. She lay slightly propped on a high trolley, her face still bloodied, her hair matted with blood and, although she opened her eyes when I called her name, her eyes were glazed and she obviously found it hard to focus. Her lips too were caked with dried blood and she murmured, 'I'm in such pain. Am I going to die?'

I took her hand. It felt cold and I automatically started trying to rub warmth into it. 'I've just spoken to the doctor. You're not going to die. She says you'll be fine. You'll be operated on soon. That'll help the pain. I'll catch one of the nurses and ask them to give you something—'

She didn't let me finish. She squeezed my hand tightly. 'Don't leave me. Please don't leave me. He might come back to finish me off.'

I stayed holding her hand and, after half an hour or so, a nurse appeared with an injection. I told her I'd been a nurse and she smiled and nodded and gave Megan a jab.

'When that's taken effect,' she said, 'we'll get her cleaned up.'

As the painkiller took effect, Megan gradually relaxed her grip on my hand and she fell asleep. I crept away, feeling guilty, but I had to make my exit while I could.

In the reception area, the two PCs sat waiting for me. I walked up to them purposefully. I'd almost made a decision. Megan needed protection and I needed help. But would a full statement just confuse the whole issue? In the end I decided that David Todman could at least talk to Jacky or a senior officer at Lettering Police Station. I explained to Jacky and Vince that I had to call a police inspector in Longborough.

'No mobiles allowed in here,' she said. 'We can go outside.'

Outside, the sun shone but a strong wind gusted and I huddled against a wall to ring David. Just as I was giving up hope, he answered his mobile, but he didn't sound pleased. 'It's not a good time,' he said.

'I don't care,' I said in a rush. 'Someone has tried to kill us. Megan is at death's door and he might try again. I haven't even got to the camp and I'm here at the Royal Hospital with two PCs who probably think I'm mad . . . and I need your help.'

'Right. What do you want me to do?'

You're supposed to be the law, I thought, you should have some idea — but I took a deep breath and said, 'I want you to ask the local police to provide twenty-four-hour protection for Megan.'

'What about you?'

'I'll take my chances.'

'OK. Get one of them on the phone.'

Jacky walked a few steps away with my mobile, as if she didn't want an audience. I couldn't hear much of what she was saying but I did hear her call him sir and she seemed to be taking it seriously.

Vince, meanwhile, was looking bemused. 'What's going on?' For the first time, I looked at him properly. He was actually quite good-looking, with friendly green eyes, and his husky vocal cords made him sound quite sexy. 'I think one of you could be on protection duty,' I answered.

'That'll be me,' he whispered with a grin. 'Voiceless Vince falls lucky again.'

'Vince,' called out Jacky. 'Guess who got the short straw?'

'Is that definite?'

'Yeah. Inspector Todman's getting in touch with our guv — you sit guard and I follow up the hit-and-run merchant.'

Jacky turned to me, took my arm and drew me away from Vince. 'I don't want him to hear, because he'll get a big head. Vince is a great bloke. He'll look after Megan really well. And I'm driving you to the camp. I'll come in with you if you think I can help.'

'I'd rather go in on my own. The refugees may not trust the police.'

'Yeah. Good point. That inspector friend of yours says this is all a bit hush hush. Big case, is it?'

'Could be.'

Tree Tops was an ex-holiday camp with a row of plane trees visible above the half-derelict chalets. The walls were festooned with barbed wire and, apart from the absence of armed guards in watchtowers, it had the look of a Second World War prisoner of war camp.

'This place thrived once,' said Jacky, 'until about twenty years ago, but the accommodation wasn't good enough. It rains a lot down here and families wanted Florida, Disneyworld and Spain. A week in a damp old chalet with a black and white TV and canteen food just couldn't compete. Now it's home to these poor buggers. And it's not just two weeks of misery for them. Some of them have been here for two years.'

At the main gates the security man, knowing Jacky, waved us through immediately and for once my luck was holding. In the reception area, a balding, stocky man in his late fifties, wearing a dark navy-blue uniform, greeted me with, 'You must be Kate. I'm Bill.' As he seemed to expect me, I didn't give him any false patter. 'What can I do for you?' he asked. I showed him the drawing of the woman first. He stared at it carefully for some time. 'I wish I could help you,' he said. 'We have more men than women here. They seem to get clearance quicker, but a lot of women have dark hair and dark eyes. And, to be honest, I don't reckon I've seen every one of 'em anyway. Mostly they run things on their own. They do their own cooking and cleaning and running the laundry. We try to give them a bit of freedom inside the camp. It's not run like a prison, even though they're not free to leave.'

'She might be calling herself Teresa.'

He shook his head. 'Sorry Kate — it still means nothing to me.'

'I think she's a midwife.'

'In that case,' he said, 'it might be worth your while going to house seven. That's the medical unit. Somebody there might know her.'

He rang an internal number and, within a few minutes, Man Mountain turned up. His name was Finbar O'Donnell, he stood about six foot five and he had the biggest feet and hands I'd ever seen. When he put his hand out to shake mine, I feared I'd never see my mitt again.

We walked along muddy pathways between chalets, occasionally meeting small groups of young men standing about aimlessly and reminding me of old photographs of the depression years of the nineteen thirties. The flat caps had gone and these men wore jeans but the facial expressions were the same. Finbar greeted a few by name. Occasionally he received a smile or a wave in return. He told me he'd worked at Tree Tops for two years. 'I don't get a lot of trouble with the men,' he said. 'It's the women that give me the trouble.'

House seven had once been an entertainment area, but now the red carpet was stained and threadbare, the bar was selling Marmite and orange juice and the small raised dance floor was filled with chairs and men and women sat waiting to see a medic. 'A doctor comes from outside once a week,' explained Finbar. 'But some of the refugees have medical knowledge and they interpret for the others.'

A woman in her twenties approached us. 'Finbar,' she said, clutching his huge arm. 'Finbar, my friend.' He blushed slightly and I could see why he had more trouble with the women. He was one big softie.

I showed my drawing of Teresa to as many people as I could, all with no response, until, that is, a heavily pregnant woman showed her recognition. Finbar told me she was called Ulima. Her olive skin looked pale and her fingers looked slightly swollen. As Finbar directed her to a table, I noticed she walked as if in pain and, once we'd sat down, she smiled with relief. Ulima spoke only Arabic, but Finbar soon found a young Muslim woman to interpret. 'I'm Zada,' she said. Although she wore a plain scarf covering her hair, somehow it accentuated the beauty of her eyes and the clearness of her skin. 'My English is good,' she said. 'Please ask Ulima what you want to know.' I again showed Ulima the drawing of Teresa. Then I turned to Zada. 'Please ask her where she met Teresa.' The answer was fairly short. 'She says she met her here more than a year ago. She was visiting her young sister, who had escaped from Sangatte.'

I was shocked that anyone should have been stuck in a place like this for more than a year. Legal processes, I knew, moved slowly, but these were people's lives seeping away in dreary confinement. It didn't seem just, but then, I didn't know the answer.

'Why does she remember her if she was only visiting?' I asked and Zada re-asked the question. Ulima looked at me as she answered in Arabic.

Zada told me: 'I knew her sister, Ilka. She was only seventeen. Teresa was trying to get her out of here. Two months later she was given her clearance and she left.'

'Does Ulima know where they went?' I asked.

The answer came back — London. On an off chance I enquired, 'The Georgiana Hotel?'

Ulima, recognizing the name in English nodded. 'Yes. Yes. Georgiana.'

Merely on a hunch, I showed her the drawing of Whitby. Ulima smiled. 'Good man. He help Ilka and Tersa.'

I guessed she meant Teresa. 'Would you ask her,' I said, 'if she knows his name or his job?'

Zada said her piece and then gave a little shrug at the answer. 'She says she only know he is a rich man and she thought he was a lawyer.'

Very quietly, so that Ulima, who obviously spoke some English, couldn't hear, I said, 'He is not a good man. If he comes here again, perhaps you should warn the other women.' Zada nodded solemnly. 'And one more thing,' I said. 'Would you ask her if she ever heard from Ilka again?'

The answer no seems to be the same in any language. Ulima's shoulders shrugged slightly, she shook her head, looking disappointed, and then she explained something to Zada. The two women hugged each other and as we walked away Zada said, 'She was a good friend to Ilka. They could only speak a little English together but Ilka had promised to write. She never did. Ulima was hoping you brought news of her and now she is worried.'

I couldn't reassure her on that. There was no point, but I did say that if I found anything out I'd let her know.

* * *

On the way back to the hospital, Jacky, who had waited patiently for me, told me she had news of the blue Fiat. Mrs Entwhistle had parked the car at the back of the Crown pub. She'd gone off to do some shopping and then met her friend for lunch at the Crown. She'd left the car there because she didn't like the multi-storey car park and she wasn't going to be doing any heavy shopping and she always parked there when she was lunching with her friend Milly.

'And here's the crunch,' said Jacky. 'When she went back for her car, at least two hours later, it was in the same spot. And wait for it — the front is well dented but she wasn't sure if it was a new dent.'

'You're telling me she has an IQ a point short of the average.'

''Fraid so. But we've got forensics in to have a good look at the car. There might be fibres.'

'The Crown didn't have cameras?'

'No. The multi-storey does but not the pub.'

Two hours was more than enough time for the ten miles or so he'd driven following us in a borrowed car, with time to re-park it and make his escape.

'It's not all bad news on the Entwhistle front,' said Jacky, as we neared the hospital.

'Why's that?'

'Well, cars may not be her strong point but she saw a man loitering in the car park just before she left to do her shopping and hers was a better description than yours. She considered him to be foreign-looking, said he might be a young "A-rab". She describes him as tall but she's eighty-six and four foot ten, so most people look tall to her. And she did notice she had to readjust her car seat before she could drive away.'

Mrs Entwhistle was going up in my estimation and went even higher when Jacky told me she had described the man as wearing black cords and trainers and a grey bomber jacket. His nose was longish and his eyes dark. All in all it was a pretty impressive description.

'Good old Mrs Entwhistle,' I said.

As we walked into the hospital and that unique indefinable smell hit my nostrils, my fear for Megan resurfaced. Fear for her medical condition and fear that *he* might have one more try.

In A&E, my heart nearly stopped when I pulled back the curtain of her cubicle to find someone else there. But a tiny bird-like nurse tapped my arm. 'It's OK,' she said. 'Megan's in theatre.'

'How long will the op take, do you think?' I asked.

'She's only just gone but I should think she'll be at least three hours.'

Jacky, who was right behind me, asked about Vince. 'He's in the hospital restaurant,' said the nurse. 'Says he'll see you there.'

We followed the signs along dim corridors, whose walls were lined halfway up with drab green tiles, until we reached the restaurant, which, surprisingly, was bright and modern and smelt good. Vince sat at a corner table with three nurses and looked in his element. We patrolled the food selection but, although the food looked good, I felt a bit queasy and didn't know if I was hungry or not. Thoughts of Megan's dry cracked lips and bloodied face kept floating into my mind like the finest, most irritating cobweb. 'When did you last eat?' asked Jackie. 'You really ought to have something.'

'Breakfast,' I said. I looked at my watch. It was five p.m. It was probably the longest I'd ever been without food. No wonder I was feeling peculiar. In the end I settled on sandwiches and a Danish pastry.

As soon as I started eating I felt better. I needed to talk and Jackie was there and she was easy to talk to and friendly, so I began telling her about Megan. I'd got as far as the night of the Rohypnol when she said, 'We don't get much crime down here but there is a drug problem at the camp. Someone's supplying and I've heard rumours that there's an undercover cop in there, but there isn't much that can be done.'

'Are there any rumours about the women that leave?'

'One or two,' she said. 'The pregnancy rate is high. Some are already pregnant when they come to the camp, others get pregnant whilst they're there. They are supposed to be segregated but it doesn't work. Security turns a blind eye. Once pregnant, by rape or by choice, some seem to get clearance sooner, or at least they think they will.'

Jacky glanced across towards Vince and I wondered if she not only rated him but fancied him. He obviously still wanted to play the field and I supposed Jacky was the faithful work partner and he didn't see much beyond her uniform. I'd been in a similar position many times. The ones I really fancied saw me as a good mate and the slime balls wanted me like crazy.

She'd been watching him for a couple of minutes when I said, 'I heard of a young girl named Ilka in the camp. I don't think she was pregnant but she left the camp promising to write to her friend and there's been no word in six months. And the Georgiana Hotel cropped up. Her friend had heard of it.'

Jacky drank some more of her coffee. 'I probably shouldn't tell you this but other girls haven't been heard of since leaving the camp. The rumour is, someone is putting them on the game or using them to run drugs.'

'What about the pregnant ones?'

Jacky looked uncomfortable and shifted uneasily in her chair.

'What is it?'

'It's just another rumour circulating on our patch. I'm sure it's not true.'

'Tell me,' I said. 'It could be important.'

'It *is* just a rumour. Rumours are rife in a sleepy backwater like this.'

'Come on, Jacky. A life might depend on it.'

She still hesitated.

'Please.'

CHAPTER SIXTEEN

My pleading tone did the trick. Jacky looked round in case anyone was nearby, sighed, and said, 'Don't tell anyone where you heard this from, will you?'

'I know when to keep my mouth shut. I'm grateful.'

'You might not be when I tell you what the word on the patch is.'

She leaned forward and rested her hand on her chin. 'Ilka isn't the only woman to have left Tree Tops and not be heard of again. Three other women, in various stages of pregnancy, haven't been heard of again either. Two of them had no memory of having intercourse but didn't make formal complaints because they didn't know who was involved. It seems likely that they were an embarrassment to the authorities, so their applications were hurried through.'

'No one suggested abortion?'

'It was either too late or the girl was RC. So, they were released into the big wide world and there the facts end and the rumours begin.'

'Which are?'

'Most people assumed the babies must have been put up for adoption.'

'Because the mothers couldn't afford to keep them?'

'Partly, yes, but these girls were ashamed of their condition, especially the girls who were raped. Rohypnol was found in the camp — where it came from, nobody knew — but one of the security guards was sacked on the spot, so suspicion had obviously fallen on him, although there were no charges brought. Most of the refugee women, especially the Muslim girls, have been very strictly brought up, so, even with opportunity, the men have little chance of any sexual relationships with them — unless they are raped or drugged.'

'So, what happened to the babies?'

'A drug dealer and pimp was willing to do a deal. He told of babies being sold for thousands of pounds, not for rich couples to adopt, but for other purposes.'

'What purposes?' I asked. I was beginning to feel a chill creep up my spine. Jacky hesitated. 'The grass told of these and other babies being sold to paedophiles and for medical purposes — organ transplants or their bone marrow. When he wasn't believed, because there was no corroboration, he gave one name and only one — Teresa — a midwife.'

'Oh my God!'

'He said two of the girls were told their babies had died. Two others were told that rich Americans had adopted their babies and they were given some money to start a new life. Other girls were either put on the game or they became drug pushers after becoming addicted themselves.'

'So, you're saying there were no witnesses and therefore no case.'

'That's what it amounts to. A known criminal mentions a first name and no trace can be found of her. What can the police do? They just play a waiting game.'

'But what about the babies?'

Jacky shrugged. 'Who knows? Thousands of adults disappear every year — much easier to hide a baby. It seems that they only keep them for a few months, then they are moved on.'

'Where to? Abroad?'

'Some, I suppose. I don't know. As I said, it's only rumour.'

'Well, I think your rumour might well be fact. And Megan could be the only witness willing to give evidence.'

I hadn't told Jacky about Megan's baby. I'd told her about the Rohypnol and the rape. But I hadn't told her who was responsible and, even now, I wasn't sure that I should. The decision was taken away from me by the arrival at our table of Vince, all smiles and looking pleased with himself. 'I've got a date with a little smasher. Nineteen and loves cops.'

'Baby—' Jacky broke off in embarrassment and confusion. She was obviously going to call him a baby snatcher.

'What?' asked a puzzled Vince. 'Have I got egg mayonnaise on my chin?'

'It's not you, Vince,' I said. 'Just a conversation we were having.'

'Oh,' he said. 'Girly talk? Make-up, clothes and what bastards men are?'

'Yeah, something like that,' I said.

Jacky left then, saying she was going back to base but she'd see us in the morning. She'd got to the door of the restaurant when she turned round and walked back. 'Where are you going to stay tonight?' she asked.

'I haven't made any plans yet.' If I was honest, I hadn't even thought about it at all. If Megan was OK, I supposed I could leave her for a few hours. 'Can you recommend anywhere?'

'Most of them are grot boxes,' she said, 'but the Fortune Guest House on the Sagley Road is about the best.'

'Great, thanks.'

On the way to intensive care, I mentioned to Vince how attractive Jacky was.

'Yeah, I suppose she is,' he said. His voice remained scarcely above a whisper but that hadn't detracted from his success with the young *smasher*. Then he added, 'I've never really thought about it.'

'Perhaps you should.' He gave me a sidelong glance, as if wondering if the hit-and-run had affected my brain in some way.

Hubert was standing outside the unit when we arrived. To my relief, he wasn't wearing black. He wore a maroon cardigan with a white shirt and beige trousers, his remaining hair slicked down neatly. 'I suppose you've been feeding your face?' he said. Hubert was never overly emotional and, although I was so pleased to see him that I could have cried, I didn't. I just squeezed his arm and said, 'Thanks for coming.' He gave a sort of grunt in reply.

Half an hour later we were allowed to see Megan, who'd been pinned and plated, transfused with blood and was attached to a monitor. For all that, she looked slightly better. The grey pallor had gone. Her face was clean, except for various grazes and the odd bruise beginning to surface but, best of all, she was opening her eyes and trying to focus. 'Hi there, Megan. You're doing well.'

'Am I?' she said, her voice as much of a whisper as Vince's. Normally only two were allowed at the bedside but, because Vince was on protection duty, he wasn't counted. The nurse in charge was brisk, cheerful and Scottish. 'Your wee girl is doing fine,' she said to Hubert. 'If she's doing as well tomorrow, she'll be back on an ordinary ward in no time.'

Hubert merely nodded. When she was out of earshot, he said, 'Have you been saying she's my daughter?'

'No,' I said, feigning minor outrage that he should suggest such a thing. 'It's a presumption on her part. I only said she was my stepsister — and can they prove otherwise?'

Megan slept an untroubled sleep and I slipped away to ring the Fortune Guest House to book two single rooms. They didn't seem at all grateful for the business and there was a suggestion I should have given them more notice. Tough, I thought.

At ten o'clock a relief PC arrived. He wore rimless glasses and someone had once broken his nose. It seemed to have affected his ability to smile. I didn't want Megan to wake up and see such a miserable face but, by now, I was feeling so shattered that, if I was going to be fit to do anything for

Megan the next day, I needed sleep. The nurse in charge reassured me that Megan's pain would be well controlled and she should have a comfortable night. My idea of a comfortable night was one where I slept unbroken sleep for at least seven hours and I hoped hers was the same.

The drive to the Fortune Guest House wasn't far and Hubert informed me on the way that I looked in nearly as bad condition as Megan. Since I hadn't looked in a mirror, I couldn't argue and I couldn't care less. The bar, boasting one sofa, two bucket seats, a mere two optics and two types of bottled lager and beer, was at least still open, if empty of customers, so we had a double brandy each and tried to unwind. I'd slumped on to the sofa alongside Hubert and, although I was shattered, I felt wound up and the brandy, instead of relaxing me, edged me towards depression.

'I just don't know what to do next,' I said to Hubert.

'You could subcontract,' he suggested.

'What do you mean?'

'I mean, get in another PI.'

I wasn't impressed with that idea but I felt so jaded, the more I thought about it the more it began to seem like a possibility. 'I dunno,' I said. 'How *can* we manage alone to bring a bent copper to justice stuck here in this backwater?'

'I reckon you're aiming too high,' said Hubert. 'You want to expose his corrupt activities but, if he's been at it for a while, he's a clever sod. You need a simpler approach. If Megan makes her complaint of rape, then at least he'll be suspended pending further enquiries.'

'Brilliant!' I said. 'Give her two or three weeks and she might just be able to talk to the police from either a wheelchair or crutches.'

'Don't be sarcastic,' he said. 'She could make a statement from her bed. Police forces have specialized women officers to deal with rape, don't they?'

I agreed that they did. But it would still be a few days before she'd be fit to do even that. And how long could they spare an officer to protect her unless she told the full story?

'Your last idea — the anonymous letters — doesn't seem to have stopped him, does it?'

'Early days yet. You can bet someone is looking at him sideways.'

'If he's as clever and cunning as you say, he'll convince his superiors Megan is a mad ex-girlfriend. He knows she's had psychiatric treatment.'

'How? Did Megan tell him?'

'Just a guess. Whoever killed Dr Lewis must have stolen the notes or at least had a look at them.'

'Your guesses are often wide of the mark.'

'Not this time.'

Hubert then decided he needed another drink, so, to keep him company, I had another one too. Luckily the bar was about to shut down, so at least we'd both be sober enough to climb the stairs. As Hubert sat down, I said, out of the blue, 'If you had stolen a baby and you had to keep it for a while, what would you do with it?'

'More to the point, Kate, what would *you* do?'

'Well, I couldn't stay in Longborough, could I?' I said. 'Unless I'd been well padded up.'

'Would anyone notice?' asked Hubert with a grin.

'You're a cheeky sod,' I said. 'Well covered I might be, but I do *not* look pregnant.'

He apologized then, but I wasn't roused by his sarky comment. I was thinking hard. Eventually I said, 'I'd go somewhere that didn't need a passport. I'd go to Scotland, Ireland or maybe the Isle of Man or the Isle of Wight. Anywhere where I wasn't known. Just a woman with a baby and a bit of a sob story.'

Hubert looked downcast now. 'It's a tall order, Kate. If Megan's baby is still alive, it could be lost for ever.'

I finished my drink. A heavy weariness had settled over me. This case was doomed. So far a doctor had died, Megan had very nearly died, and now any thoughts of finding her baby were fast receding. I had to carry on. I knew that, because Whitby had to be stopped, and Megan, who'd never had much luck, wasn't getting any luckier.

As we made our way up to our rooms, Hubert said, 'By the way . . . there's bad news and good news.'

'Tell me the good news first.'

'David Todman is planning to take some annual leave and stay at the Georgiana in the hope of finding out more than you did.'

I ignored the implicit criticism. 'And the bad news?'

'Your mother is back and living at your place in Farley Wood.'

I sighed deeply. At that very moment, even my mother's unexpected return was of no consequence. I needed sleep more than I needed to worry about her.

I hardly noticed the room but the bed looked more than inviting so I stripped off my clothes on the hoof, flung back the duvet and collapsed into the bed. I don't remember falling asleep, nor did I dream. The hours of night were just one big blank.

At breakfast the next morning, I felt hung-over but a plateful of cholesterol soon made me feel better and a phone call on my mobile from David, who was on his way to London, cheered me too. 'I'll keep in touch,' he said, 'but I shall want a good meal as a reward when I get back.'

I thought I could manage the meal as long as that was all he had in mind.

In ICU, we were too early to visit, so we were directed to the visitors' room outside the unit. Much to my surprise, Vince sat there. 'I thought you were the two to ten shift,' I said.

'I'm a volunteer,' he said. 'I can't resist nurses.' At that moment a rather hawk-faced middle-aged nurse peered around the door to say we could go in in ten minutes. Vince managed a wry grin, 'Well, young ones anyway.' I told Vince he could disappear to the canteen if he wanted to and he didn't argue.

Megan, looking tired and wan, smiled as we trooped in. After all the usual *How are you? Did you sleep well?* There didn't seem a lot to say. I did tell her that David Todman was checking out the Georgiana Hotel and she smiled tiredly, but I sensed she was either so weary or so full of painkillers that she couldn't care less. Her lips were still dry and cracked and now she had a black eye that was just about open.

'When can I leave?' she asked.

'I'm not sure. You might be on the main ward today or tomorrow.'

'No, I mean, when can I leave the hospital?'

I hedged that question. 'Not for a while,' I said, guessing it would be weeks rather than days.

Hubert looked uncomfortable as a hospital visitor. He squeezed Megan's hand, asked her if there was anything she wanted and then opened his newspaper and began reading, as if trying to block out his surroundings. I knew he couldn't be away from his business for long and that, although Jasper was being looked after by Betty, he wouldn't want to be stuck like glue to my side for any length of time.

We'd been there half an hour and it seemed like for ever. Megan's eyes kept closing and, all around, monitors bleeped, machines ticked and patients breathed noisily. There were five patients in the unit — Megan was the only one conscious. Although now she'd fallen asleep, so she'd joined the ranks of the silent.

Another half an hour passed slowly, punctuated by a visit from the consultant surgeon. Mr Blenkinsop wore a grey pinstripe and, although he was probably only in his late thirties, he sported half glasses and a small moustache that made him look as though he were masquerading as an older man. He woke Megan easily enough by whispering in her ear. He lifted the folded-back sheet at the end of her bed and asked her to wiggle her toes. He smiled with satisfaction, felt both her feet and proclaimed that the circulation to her leg was good and all her vital signs were fine. 'This is good news, Megan,' he said. 'You can be transferred to the main orthopaedic ward in the morning or later during the day if the bed is needed.' He didn't wait for her to respond but merely said, 'Well done, Megan,' as he breezed on to the next bed. He meant, of course, well done to himself. Megan was merely his surgical canvas but he did seem to have done a good job, so I easily forgave him his air of detached grandeur.

Megan's eyes closed again and I whispered to her that Hubert and I were leaving her for a short time in Vince's capable hands. Vince, having returned from his breakfast, seemed more interested in the nurses who flitted between the machines and the patients like demented bumble bees. He preferred to stand at the nurses' station and catch them mid-flight for a quick flirtatious glance or the odd bit of banter. Jacky had thought him up to the job but I was a bit doubtful. At least the misery with a broken nose had an air of gravitas.

Hubert, growing more uncomfortable by the minute with his passive role, was already on his feet and, with a brisk Cheerio, was heading towards the door. Megan stirred and murmured. 'I'm sorry I'm so tired. I can't keep awake.'

'You just sleep,' I said. 'I'll be back soon.' As I stood up to go, her hand grabbed mine and, still with her eyes closed, she whispered, 'I lied, Kate. I lied.'

I thought I'd misheard her. 'Say that again, Megan.'

I bent down to her hear her better. This time I heard only too clearly as she murmured again, 'I lied.'

CHAPTER SEVENTEEN

I stood beside Megan's bed utterly bewildered. What did she mean? What had she lied about?

I couldn't just stand there like a prune wondering. So, I sat down again, moving my chair closer to her bed, and was just about to shake her arm to wake her up, so she could explain what she meant, when the charge nurse approached. She looked at me as severely as if I had been about to smother her with a pillow. 'Let her sleep,' she said. 'The anaesthetic hasn't left her system and she needs all the rest she can get.'

I left then, reluctant and uneasy. It would have to wait and I hoped that, when I next saw Megan, she'd come clean, because, if I was working on a false premise, I wanted to know about it.

Hubert's escape had only been as far as the car park, where he sat waiting for me. 'This isn't my scene, Kate.'

'I know that,' I said. 'You go back to Longborough. I'll do my best here.'

'Is anything wrong?' he asked, giving me a sidelong glance.

'Nothing other than the situation.'

Until I knew exactly what Megan meant, I didn't want Hubert to know.

As we drove to the guest house, my mobile rang. It was Jacky offering to collect me to pick up my car. She had a day off and did I want to go back to Tree Tops and see if I could glean any more information?

'That would be great,' I said, but I was doubtful that I'd learn much more there. Megan had thrown an unidentified spanner into my toolbox and it wouldn't stop rattling about until she told me which one. But she needed to sleep and I didn't know what to do next, so Jacky's offer was, at the very least, a way of removing me from the brain-stifling delights of morning television.

Hubert left with exhortations for me to be careful and to ring him every day. I knew he was relieved to be going back to dealing with the dead and the bereaved. He was at home, literally, in that environment. I supposed that was because it threw up no surprises and he was undisputed king in his own domain.

* * *

At the camp, Jacky flashed her warrant card and the guard waved us through. Instead of going straight to the medical centre, we wandered around. Young men wandered about too. Some smiled at us but many of them paced backwards and forwards, aimless and depressed. 'There'll be trouble here one day,' said Jacky. She looked much younger out of uniform, with her slim legs encased in blue jeans and her breasts pertly lurking beneath a tight black tee shirt. 'That's why the bosses like the police coming in. If there were a riot or a fire, we would at least know something about the layout of the camp.'

In the camp kitchens women detainees did most of the cooking under the supervision of a local cook. We watched them stirring huge cauldrons that produced such a variety of smells that they merged into one — boiled cabbage. We stood and watched and no one came to ask what we were doing, but the supervisor did manage to wave to Jacky. 'We'd better wait a while till they've got lunch under way. There would be a riot if lunch were late. There's always trouble over the food. They have to cook for so many different ethnic groups, plus vegans, vegetarians and diabetics, that the local cooks can't hack it for long.'

Outside, the fresh air and spring sunshine were a welcome relief from the smell of boiled cabbage. In the alleyway, alongside overflowing bins, two women from the kitchen were talking to Finbar. They were so engrossed that they didn't see us. 'That's Finbar,' she said. I was about to say that I'd met him yesterday, but she added in a low voice, 'I've heard he's bent. I don't think he's on the make, as such, but he's not very bright and he's as soft as soap where the women are concerned.'

'But if he's suspected of being bent, why do they keep him on?'

She shrugged. 'Who knows? This place is a law unto itself. He's not the only one. And, half the time, the authorities turn a blind eye. They do random drugs tests but, if it's only spliff, uppers or downers, they ignore that entirely and try to find the source of the crack cocaine or heroin. It's difficult. If they're found to be using the hard stuff and they didn't come in with it and they weren't users before they arrived, they must get it on the inside and the Home Office would rather not know.'

'But how do they pay for it?'

She looked towards Finbar, who was now offering the women cigarettes from his packet.

'Some of the asylum seekers have valuables,' she said. 'Jewellery, gold watches that sort of thing, and I think some of the more desperate women sell sexual favours.'

Finbar eventually lumbered away in the opposite direction and the two women slipped back to their kitchen duties. Now, I thought, was the time to tell Jacky. 'Megan's rapist . . .' I said. She looked at me questioningly. 'He's a cop. Worse, he's an inspector in the vice squad.'

'Oh shit!'

'I agree. Any suggestions?'

'Most bent cops do get caught,' she said, looking unconvinced. 'But if he's not working alone . . .'

'Then it's up to me to do something,' I said. 'I've got to get evidence that he is in on the baby racket. But if his cage is rattled he'll get rid of the evidence, won't he?'

'What evidence? What do you mean?'

'The baby.'

'What baby?'

I'd told Jacky about the drugged rape but not the consequences. I told her everything Megan had told me and that I still hoped our evidence, the mattress cover and the nappy tab, might prove something. 'I thought at one point,' I said, 'that if they had enough suspicion about Whitby, they might arrest him. But even if he was arrested, he's not working alone and, if they kill or manage to get the baby abroad, it's Megan's double loss and her word against his. And I think, if she was in court, a good defence lawyer could run rings around her.'

'Do you know where he lives?'

'No, but a policeman friend is in London doing what he can.'

We continued to walk around the camp in thoughtful silence. 'There is Special Operations, they investigate internally,' said Jacky. 'Or the Police Complaints Board.'

'We can only do that when we've found the baby. DNA tests could prove Whitby impregnated Megan.'

'How long can you wait?' asked Jacky.

It was a fair point but I had to give David a chance.

'Have you got a photograph of this Whitby?'

'No, but I've got a drawing.'

She stared at the image for a while. 'Can I keep this for a few minutes?'

'Yeah. What do you want it for?'

'If anyone knows him here, it'll be Finbar.'

Eventually we found him talking to a young girl outside one of the chalets on the women's side of the camp, which was separated from the male side by flimsy fencing. On seeing us, she hurried away.

'Finbar,' said Jacky. 'We'd like a word.'

A slightly worried look settled on his face.

'Is that chalet open?'

He nodded.

'In there, then.'

Once inside the drably decorated cabin, Finbar tried on the charm. 'Two beautiful women,' he said, 'vying for my body.'

'Cut the crap, Finbar,' snapped Jacky. 'This is serious.'

'Shall we sit down, then?' he asked. In the chalet were two single beds covered with threadbare green candlewick bedspreads, two wooden chairs and a small table, on which had been placed a silver crucifix. On the wall was a small painting of the Madonna and child. 'You sit there,' said Jacky, pointing to the chair opposite the crucifix and the painting.

I sat down on one of the frail beds and knew from Jacky's determined attitude that I was going to learn something from her approach, even if it didn't get a result.

'Are you a good Catholic, Finbar?' she asked, sweetly.

'I am indeed. I go to mass every week, and confession.'

'I'm glad to hear it. I'm a Catholic too. So, we'll be telling the truth, won't we?'

'Jacky, I wouldn't tell you a lie.'

Though outwardly bluff, I caught the slight loss of confidence in his voice. Big as he was, he was in the presence of Mother Superior and he'd become a small boy again.

'I'm going to show you a drawing and I want you to tell me who it is.'

He nodded, eager to please. He took the drawing and glanced at it briefly. 'That's Inspector Whitby from London.'

'Good,' she said smiling. 'Full marks, Finbar.'

He relaxed back slightly in his chair, as if it was all over. But Jacky hadn't even started yet.

'So, he's your supplier?'

Looking like a fish gasping for air, Finbar's answer came out as a mere grunt.

'Look at the crucifix, Finbar. God is watching you.'

'I only take a few sleeping pills from him,' he said in a rush. 'I don't pay him. The poor women don't get a wink of sleep. They're homesick. They need help.'

'Very Christian of you, Finbar. If he doesn't want money, what *does* he want in return?'

'He's just trying to help them too.'

'In what way?'

Finbar glanced nervously towards the Madonna.

'Why are you looking at our Holy Mother? Just answer the question.'

'He helped them get out of here.'

'By giving them sleeping tablets?'

'No. He found them jobs and somewhere to live and helped them with the paperwork.'

'And why would he do that? And don't tell me he was doing it as a work of charity.'

'He was working undercover, trying to get to the big drug runners.'

'So, that was why he only helped the young, pretty or pregnant ones?'

Obviously the thought had only just occurred to Finbar. Jacky carried on relentlessly.

'So, Finbar, you were never suspicious when the girls who left having been *helped* by Whitby were never heard of again?'

'Jaysus. I didn't give it a thought.'

'You don't think much at all, do you?'

'It doesn't seem like it.'

'I've found out that over the past year,' said Jacky, staring at him fixedly, 'several asylum seekers have managed to abscond. Turned your back, did you, Finbar?'

'I'm not the only . . .' He hesitated.

'I see. You're not the only one who acted blind and deaf.'

His face was suffused by a red blotch and he loosened his tie slightly.

'Have you been to confession recently?'

'I went last week.'

'With the amount you should have confessed,' she snapped, 'you should *still* be on your knees.'

Finbar hung his head. 'I only tried to help,' he muttered.

'Well, we're trying to help someone now and it's a matter of life and death.'

He looked up slowly. 'Is there something I can do?'

'Yes. You can tell us about Whitby. How often does he come here?'

'Every month or so. He was due this week but he didn't show.'

'What exactly do you know about him?'

'In what way are you meaning?'

'His address. His phone number. Anything?' Jacky was getting irritated but, if he did know anything, she was going to find out.

'He didn't say.'

Jacky pointed a finger at him. It could have been a gun the way Finbar cringed. 'Don't bullshit me,' she said between gritted teeth. 'You've got a choice. You can tell me everything you know, or we go straight to the office and I tell them all about your activities.'

'Please, don't do that. I'll never get another job. I'll stop giving the women sleeping tablets. I will. So I will.'

'I'm waiting for you to tell me something about Whitby, so stop bleating and think!'

'He told me he had an attic flat in London and a place in Scotland.'

'What sort of place? Where in Scotland?'

Finbar shook his head. 'I don't know,' he said, miserably.

'This flat, did he say where in London that was?'

'I'm trying to think . . .'

'Well try a bit harder.'

There was a long pause and observing Finbar's strained facial expressions was just like watching the cogs in his brain grind very slowly. 'I'm remembering he mentioned George something or other.'

'The Georgiana Hotel?' I interrupted.

'Sure. That was it.'

'Right,' said Jacky, leaning towards him. 'And if he comes here again, what are you going to tell him?' He hesitated.

'Look, you plonker,' she said, jabbing her index finger into his chest. 'You tell him nothing. We haven't seen you. Do you understand?'

'I do. I do.'

'It's not only eternal damnation you have to worry about. He'll kill you if he knows you've talked to us. Have you got that?'

'I have. I said nothing before.'

'When?'

'Two blokes came asking questions about Whitby. I said I didn't know him but they knew he came here. But I said nothing.'

'Good. But remember this — God is watching your every move. You've sinned big time. If Whitby comes here again — act normally, but remember to mention his place in Scotland. Ask him if he rents it out. But act casual. If he doesn't want to tell you — leave it! Then you ring Kate. Do you understand?'

I hesitated before handing him my business card. The last stranger to have been given my card had died, but there was no way he could commit my telephone number to memory.

'Be careful,' I said, as I handed him my card. 'Keep it safe.'

'There's the door,' said Jacky, pointing an imperious finger. 'Go before I change my mind about reporting you.'

Readjusting his tie, he lumbered to his feet and, with a nod to the both of us, he was gone.

It was a full three seconds before we both burst out laughing. 'I don't know how I kept a straight face,' she said. 'I always thought big feet were a good sign in a man but I think his brain is only dick-sized and, even if it's a big one it's still very small for a brain.' And so we carried on laughing and eventually, having brushed the tears from our faces, we made a hasty exit from the camp.

As we stood by our respective cars, I said, 'You were very good on the religious approach.'

'I had a convent education — well, half of one. I was expelled. There was far too much fear and superstition for me.'

'Well, it came in handy,' I said. 'You were a star.'

'Yeah. It works sometimes for the naıve Finbars of the world.'

She paused as she unlocked her car. 'Kate, I'm sorry but I can't help you any more at the moment. I've got my sergeant's exam in a couple of days. I need to study.'

I felt disappointed but she'd been a real help and I couldn't expect any more. 'I understand,' I said. 'And I'm sure you'll pass.'

'It is important to me. In the future I want to be in CID.'

'You will be.'

'Pray for me, then,' she said with a grin. 'And good luck. Let me know what happens.'

'I will,' I said. And I meant it.

I felt very alone driving back to the hospital. Hubert was gone, now Jacky. David was doing his bit but it still left me to worry, not only about Megan's condition, but also about what to do next. One thing I could do was ring David and get him to check out the attic flat. But first, I supposed, I had to find out what Megan had lied about. I still felt very uneasy about that. She had seemed so honest. Had I been misled? Was I the naıve one?

CHAPTER EIGHTEEN

In the hospital car park I rang David's mobile. It was switched off. I didn't leave a message, text or otherwise, just in case the phone fell into the wrong hands.

At the entrance to the ICU I took a deep breath and a sharper intake when I saw an unconscious man lying in the bed that had been Megan's. The staff soon directed me to the orthopaedic ward, which was situated along a dark, almost subterranean, corridor. My footfalls on the tiled floor slapped along, followed by the sound of porters behind trundling a heavy patient to the same ward.

There was no one around to ask, so I looked on the white board in the nurses' station to find Megan. She was in bay four, the furthest bay from the nurses' station, and, although there may have been nurses by curtained beds, I couldn't actually see one.

Megan was sitting up, looking better but miserable, *sans* tubes and drips, but there was no sign of Vince, and the other three patients were white-haired and either asleep or comatose. There was certainly no one to protect her here from an intruder.

She burst into tears when she saw me. 'I thought you wouldn't find me,' she said. 'And I hate it here. Take me home, Kate.'

'I can't take you home — you're not fit enough yet.'

* * *

I couldn't fail to notice that she now talked of Humberstone's as *home*, which, in itself, was more than a little worrying. There was nowhere else for her to go but it was still yet another dilemma.

I drew up a chair and sat beside her. She wiped her eyes with a tissue and sniffed loudly. 'You're feeling worse because you're getting better,' I said. She managed to smile disbelievingly at that. 'It's true,' I said. 'Once the shock is over and the worst of the pain goes, it gives you a chance to realize just how bad you do feel.'

'I can't stay here for weeks, Kate. I'll go mad.'

'We'll work something out,' I said. 'But first things first. This morning, before you drifted off to sleep, you told me you had lied about something. I want to know what you lied about.'

She hung her head. 'I lied because I was ashamed.'

'Of what?'

She was about to answer when a young nurse wheeled in the observation machine and started recording the obs of the patient in the bed opposite. 'Ignore that,' I said. 'And tell all about it.'

Megan looked warily across at the nurse, as if she had suprasensory hearing, and then whispered. 'I lied about the money.'

'What money?'

'The money in the bag.'

'You said you'd got it from the sale of the house.'

'That was a lie.'

'So, where did you get the money from?'

'It was in Alice's old wardrobe.'

'And you took it?'

'Well, it wasn't quite like that. I'd decided to run away but I couldn't go without saying something to Alice. She only managed a few words but she understood what was going on. So, I crept into her room and she was awake. I told her I had to leave, that my baby had died. She got upset and kept trying to tell me something. In the end she pointed to a wardrobe. It was one that was never used, because it was the old-fashioned type that could be locked. She kept pointing to the bottom of the wardrobe and she managed to say *Key*. I felt underneath the wardrobe and found the key. When I unlocked the wardrobe, there, under a pile of clothes, was all the money. I had loads of money in the bank and I told her that but she kept nodding and then she pointed to my bag and I stuffed it all in there. She smiled then and she sort of croaked, *Go, go*. I shouldn't have left her, should I . . . ?' She broke off, choked with tears.

'You did the right thing.'

'Did I? It was stealing, wasn't it? I've never stolen anything before.'

'Alice *did* want you to have the money and you wouldn't be alive now if you'd stayed.'

'I don't call this living,' she said, miserably staring at the ward. 'You will get me out of here, won't you?'

'Of course. But I can't stay with you every minute of the day.'

We fell silent as the nurse approached to do Megan's obs. 'You do know it's visiting only after two p.m.?' she said.

'I'd like to see the nurse in charge, if that's possible.' She nodded. 'He should be at the nurses' station.'

It wasn't just the charge nurse I needed to see. If police protection was being withheld, then I needed support on the visiting front. I couldn't sit by Megan's side for twenty-four hours a day. I'd go loopy in no time. 'I won't be long, Megan,' I said.

Megan looked imploringly at me, as if she knew I was up to something or planning not to come back.

The charge nurse, Richard Wayman, was as burly as a bouncer but, in contrast to his tough appearance, he was quietly spoken and very reassuring on Megan's condition and the prognosis for her future mobility.

'You do realize,' I said, 'someone tried to kill Megan. It wasn't just a hit-and-run. I don't know why the police protection has been removed but I'm going to find out. In the meantime, Megan won't be expecting any visitors except me, so I'd be grateful if you could brief your staff on that.'

'I'll do my best. But I can't guarantee that a determined person couldn't get to see her.'

'I'll talk to the local police,' I said. 'Maybe I can get them to change their minds.'

'That's the best idea,' he said. 'But Megan might be in for a few more weeks. Let's hope they catch him.'

A few more weeks! I had guessed it might be some time but having it confirmed was a different matter. There was no way I could sit for weeks at her bedside. If I was to find out what had happened to Megan's baby, I wasn't going to make any headway sitting on my backside. There was only one person I could think of. I walked outside and dialled my own number on my mobile.

'Hello pet,' said my mother. 'I thought you'd get round to calling me in the end.'

'How are you?'

'Fine. A bit bored.'

'Would you like a job?'

'How much?'

'Hundred a week.'

'You must be joking.'

'OK. One fifty.'

'Doing what?' she asked suspiciously.

'Hospital visiting. A young woman.'

'Pity it's not a young man.'

I ignored that. 'She's had a rough time,' I explained. 'And she needs someone to sit with her and encourage her. We're at the Royal Hospital, Lettering-on-Sea.'

'Never heard of it.'

'Not many people have. It's a backwater not far from Brighton. If you come on the train, I'll collect you.'

'When?'

'Today or tomorrow.'

'I'll be there tomorrow,' she said. 'I'll phone you from the train.'

'Thanks,' I said, surprised she'd given in so easily. But then my mother always was broke and a fraction desperate. 'And don't wear a short skirt,' I added.

'You're a real killjoy, Kate.'

I supposed where Marilyn was concerned, I was. She wasn't the home-baking, knitting sort of mother who could blend nicely into my existence. She was flighty, unreliable for the most part, dressed like a tart and was man-mad. But if she turned up and did the job, I might find it in my heart one day to examine her good points.

Back at the bedside, Megan smiled with relief at seeing me. 'I had bad dreams again last night, Kate.'

'About the baby?'

'Yes. My mother was holding it, singing to it. She was acting as if it were hers. When I asked her to hand it to me, she refused. The baby started crying and I snatched it away and then, when I looked again, it wasn't a baby at all — it was a doll. And my mother starting laughing and, as I stood there, the doll dissolved into ashes.'

Now seemed as good a time as any to mention my mother but I was wary. Megan was still disturbed and I just felt that even the mention that I might not be around every day was bound to upset her. But she wasn't a child and she had to be told.

I explained the situation and was met with a blank stare and a horrified 'But I haven't even met her.'

'I know it's difficult,' I said, 'but I need to be outside this place working for you.'

She didn't reply but she closed her eyes and lay back pale and exhausted against the pillows. She looked awful and I realized that she was still in pain and recovering not only from the trauma of being run down but from childbirth too. She needed all the rest she could get.

'Megan,' I said softly, knowing she was not asleep. 'I'm going outside to make some phone calls and then I'll have some lunch and see you later.'

* * *

By the next day, I'd spoken to Hubert, who was impressed that my mother had *volunteered* for patient-sitting, but neither of us had had any luck rousing David on his mobile. I was getting a little edgy about that but going to the local police station made me feel even edgier. I asked to see someone in CID and, after an hour's wait, a detective constable with greying hair, a wide face and an equally wide body came down to the front office. He'd obviously only made the first rung of the ladder in his police career but he was cheerful enough, introduced himself and told me he had some good news. There had been a positive identification of the driver of the stolen Fiat, he told me, and he fitted the description of a man wanted for the murder of Dr Lewis in Wales. He was now on his way to Wales in a police van. 'Who is he?' I asked the DC. He obviously didn't have time to sit down but he leaned towards me.

'All I know,' he said, 'is he's Romanian, possibly an illegal immigrant, and he won't admit to speaking English.'

'Thank God he's been caught,' I said.

'What's it all about, love?' asked the fat DC. 'Why was he out to get you?'

'It's too complicated,' I said. 'But my stepsister *is* from Wales.'

He gave me a knowing look. 'Some sort of love tryst, was it?' One plus one obviously made a threesome to him.

'You're very quick,' I said. 'Thanks for your help.' My exit too was quick. At least one of Whitby's little helpers was in custody, but how many more were there?

By late afternoon I was still waiting for my mother's call. Mobile phones weren't allowed in the hospital, so, for some time, I sat outside waiting. I tried my mother's mobile number but the unobtainable tone suggested she'd acquired a new one, because, broke or not, she'd have the newest and the flashiest.

Finally at five p.m. she rang to say she was due at the station at five thirty. By five fifteen I was waiting on the platform for her. The train was two minutes late and, as it disgorged the commuters who, I assumed, worked in Brighton or London, I scoured the groups of passengers, looking for my middle-aged slapper of a mother. There was no sign of her and, despondently, I decided she was probably on the wrong train. Then, out of the corner of my eye, I saw someone vaguely familiar. At least, as I looked closely at her, I realized I *did* know that face, even though it was scrubbed. She wore a red and white spotted headscarf tied behind her head, a long skirt to the ankles and a poncho that looked more like an old grey blanket. On her feet she wore flat brown sandals. On her back was a backpacker's bulging knapsack. Plus she carried two large holdalls.

'You look like a vegetarian bag lady,' I said, once I'd gathered my wits.

'There's no pleasing some people,' she said, giving me a peck on the cheek.

'You're in disguise,' I said.

'No pet. This is my new image.'

'Why?'

'Why not? I've realized there's more to life at my age than high heels and clubbing and chasing men.'

'Like what?'

'Spiritual things. A healthy mind and a healthy body.'

'Well, you'll need all that in the next few weeks.'

'What *have* you got me into, Kate?'

'I'll tell you all about it on the way.'

'Don't you want to hear about my travels?'

'Later,' I said, as I picked up the two holdalls and found myself staggering under the weight.

'You're looking well, pet,' she said. It was a convenience that I was well, because I needed to be to carry the weight of her luggage.

I began telling her about Megan and, by the time we got to the Royal, I'd briefed her on the situation. It was short and to the point, because I didn't want her to know quite as much as I did.

In the ward, Megan looked up expectantly as we approached. I hadn't told her anything about my mother's appearance. Either way would have been a surprise.

'Hello, pet. You're looking peaky,' she said, patting Megan's hand. 'Never mind, you'll soon feel better. How about a bottle of orange juice and some nuts and raisins?' She didn't wait for an answer but began removing her arms from the backpack and rooting around in its contents.

Megan looked at me imploringly, as if I'd just introduced her to a member of a satanic cult. 'I have to get on with the job, Megan,' I explained. 'I'm going to London for a couple of days. Marilyn is going to have my room at the hotel and she'll stay with you during the day.'

Tears sprang to her eyes and I hurriedly slipped my mother money for a taxi to the hotel and half her first week's wages. 'Off you go, pet,' she said. 'Megan will be fine with me.' I wasn't so sure but I left while I had a chance and couldn't help breathing a sigh of relief as I drove away from the hospital and made my way back to the hotel. The relief was tinged with guilt and I hoped Megan was not going to suffer any setbacks while I was away. My mother had been a carer in New Zealand but she was the type who'd offer a diabetic a cream cake and a bottle of lager. This remodelled mother was not someone I recognized.

During the evening, I lazed around, had a long hot soak in the bath, lazed on the bed and enjoyed a three-course dinner, even though I'd been placed for dinner next to a computer salesman who bored me rigid with his sales figures. My bag was packed by nine p.m. and British Rail had given me the times of the trains. My luck on the phone ran out after BR — there was still no reply from David. I toyed with the idea of ringing reception at the Georgiana but I dismissed that in case he was using an assumed name. The absence of any threatening calls on my mobile should have been reassuring but it wasn't. I kept my mobile well charged up and the battery was new, but when it fell totally silent I grew anxious. He'd made one major attempt at killing Megan and I felt that this was the silence before he tried again. I simply had to get to him before he got to her. And then what? Make a citizen's arrest single-handed? Or try a different approach? An approach like Jacky's only worked with someone as plank-thick as Finbar. It was likely that any verbal coercion would be as effective as sieved water. But if David was with me, we might have a chance.

At just after ten I went down to the bar for a nightcap. The bar itself was empty and the barman surly, so I took my drink through to the lounge, where a few souls sat in silence watching the news, as if *that* was their nightcap.

I was about to leave when the newscaster said: *The unidentified body of a woman was found yesterday in Camden Lock. A post-mortem will be carried out today but a police spokesman said today that foul play had not been ruled out. It is thought a drugs overdose contributed to her death in the canal. The victim had long black hair and was aged between twenty-five and thirty-five. Police are searching the canal for any form of identification other than a distinctive crescent-shaped necklace thought to be Romanian in origin. The police are appealing for witnesses to the incident, or anyone who might be able to name the victim, to come forward.*

Don't jump to any conclusions, I told myself. But ten minutes later, as I still sat there, I became convinced it was Teresa. When my mobile rang, I literally jumped. I expected it to be Hubert or David. It was neither. It was my mother.

'Are you still at the hospital?'

'We've just watched the news—'

I didn't let her finish. 'You don't mean Megan's still awake?'

'I pushed her bed into the day room to watch the telly and get away from the wrinklies and she says a woman found in Camden Lock is Teresa. She says she wore a necklace like that.'

'She didn't tell me before.'

'Well, she's telling you now.'

I didn't know what to say. I felt my three-course meal start to rise. 'Is she OK?'

'I'm staying the night here. If I can dance all night, I can also doze in a chair by the bed.'

'I'm really grateful.'

'So you should be. Take care of yourself, pet.'

'And you.'

I clicked off my phone. I felt a mass of contradictions; nauseated, anxious and full of amazement that my mother was being such a diamond.

I went to the bar and ordered a large brandy and drank it on the spot. Whitby was a face in pencil to me and until I saw him in the flesh I knew he had assumed an unrealistic power. And the trouble was, he was winning. The bastard had already arranged the murder of two women and had planned for Megan to die. He wasn't going to stop now. I also wondered if the death of his *midwife* meant that he had curtailed his operation, either because she was expendable or because he'd been sussed internally. Megan's baby, I assumed, was still valuable to him and easily hidden. But where? And how to find out? Even if I found out where, someone was passing off that baby as their own. Maybe in a camp somewhere with a refugee mother, an unregistered birth and a very uncertain future.

CHAPTER NINETEEN

It was raining in London, fine rain in a warmish atmosphere that mixed with car fumes and other noxious substances to form a miasma that wasn't fog or mist. It was what weathermen termed *claggy*.

In the reception area of the Georgiana, a few people were gathered at the desk to check in or out. The ones checking in smelt of damp. The receptionist I'd never seen before, so I signed in as Alison Fordyce, simply because that was the first name that came to mind. As I signed the book, I checked for David's name and it was there — room sixty-three, which was on the top floor. Mine was fifty-eight, also on the top floor. I considered it would soon be showdown time. He was here. Why the hell hadn't he rung?

On the way to my room, as I passed by his, I listened at the door. All was silent, so I assumed he was out pursuing our quarry.

I unpacked, took a shower and changed into a halfway decent blouse and skirt, applied some make-up and was fairly pleased with the result. I wondered if I might meet Whitby in the hotel. If so, would he recognize me? Had at least a description been relayed to him? I resolved to be careful, but if I did pass him in the corridor, I'd pretend I didn't recognize him.

I rang Hubert on the land line and left him a message saying all was well and not to worry about me or Megan, but I didn't tell him where I was, simply because he might want to come charging down to London when it wasn't necessary. For all I knew, Whitby could, by now, be in South America. If his great-aunt had left him the house, with all his extra money-making activities, no doubt someone was laundering his money and placing it in the safety of some foreign bank. If he was still working as normal, maybe he no longer considered Megan to be a threat. After all, she hadn't laid any charges against him and he could just have been furious when he'd found out she'd nicked his great-aunt's cash. He'd calmed down now, I thought, which was why the phone calls had stopped. Perhaps the driver who'd mown down Megan had been told just to injure, not kill.

I felt better now that I'd developed a positive approach. I couldn't let myself succumb to fear of a man I'd never even seen. Everything was going to be just fine. David and I would win through. It was just a case of time and perseverance.

Dinner was at seven, so at six fifteen I was knocking on David's door. I knocked several times and called his name and I was thinking of slipping a note under his door when I heard a muffled sound from inside. I tried the door handle, opened the door and found myself in total darkness. The heavy curtains were drawn. The room was stuffy and, as my eyes grew accustomed to the dark, I could make out the bed and that someone was in it, but I couldn't recognize the face.

'David? Is that you?'

His mumbled reply was lost on me.

'Let me turn the lamp on.' I moved to the bedside and switched on the lamp. 'Oh my God! What happened to you?' My hand had gone to my mouth in shock. Both his eyes were black and closed and his mouth was twice its normal size. Dried blood had formed at the corners of his mouth and he had a huge bruise on his forehead. 'Why aren't you in hospital?'

'Don't keep asking me questions,' he said, between swollen lips. 'Get me a drink of water.'

I filled a cup from the sink in the bathroom, hoping it was drinking water, but in his condition it was the least of his worries. I handed him the cup but as he tried to move he cried out in pain. I held him up so that he could drink. Even so, he winced at the smallest touch or movement. I refilled the cup twice more and then finally, his thirst quenched, he lay back exhausted. 'You should be in hospital,' I said as a variation on my previous question.

'I have been,' he said. His voice wasn't normal but the water had obviously helped and now I could at least understand him. 'I was on a trolley for hours. I discharged myself and got a taxi back here.'

'You *have* reported it to the police?'

'Yeah,' he said grimly. 'I know how it feels to be mugged now.'

'It was a mugging?'

'For my mobile and my wallet.'

'Why didn't you get one of the staff to ring me and let me know?'

'I thought you'd got enough to contend with.'

'Maybe, but Hubert would have come. What about money?'

'I haven't got any. The chambermaid gave me extra milk and biscuits but I haven't been up to eating meals.'

I sat down beside his bed. 'You're going to have to let me help you. Calling a doctor might be a good start.'

'No. There's no point. In a few days I'll be fine.'

'When did this happen?'

'Two days ago. My first evening in here. I was following Whitby and I lost him, so I went into a rough-as-hell pub near King's Cross. I had one drink and came out to phone you. Three yobs came from nowhere and attacked me. I didn't have a chance.'

'Did you describe them to the police?'

'I wasn't in a condition to say much but I got the idea that, unless they'd been picked up on a CCTV camera somewhere, there wasn't much hope.'

We both fell silent. But after a few moments I decided that he didn't need questions, rather, he needed nursing. I sorted him out two painkillers from the stock in my handbag, fetched him more water and just said, 'Swallow these.' He didn't argue — patients don't when they feel as weak as a soufflé on the point of collapse. 'I'm going down to the dining room now to organize you something light to eat.'

Again he didn't argue.

In the dining room I explained the position to one of the waitresses and asked if he could have soup, omelette and ice cream. That was no problem. For myself, I ordered steak, chips, salad and apple pie and cream. I needed all the strength I could muster.

Back in David's room I helped him to sit up on the side of the bed. He was still wearing a bloodstained shirt. I undid the one button that was still fastened and looked in horror at the bruises on his chest and especially those over his ribs. I didn't say a word and I managed to slip off the shirt without him screaming. I found a thin tee shirt in his drawer and carefully put that on him. 'Try to stand up,' I said.

'I can walk,' he said. 'I managed to have a pee yesterday.'

'Was there any blood in it?'

He made a slight sound that might have been a brief chuckle. It was hard to tell. 'I don't know,' he said. 'I can't see properly, can I?'

Eventually I had him sitting in the chair. I combed blood from his hair, bathed his eyes and put some lip salve on his lips. I can't say he looked any better but he did say the painkillers were kicking in.

'That's an unfortunate phrase, David.'

'Yeah. What a bloody disaster this has been.'

A knock at the door signalled the arrival of our meals. The waitress nearly dropped her trays when she saw David sitting there like a bruised and bloodied Buddha. I took the trays from her and asked if clean sheets and at least four more pillows would be possible in about half an hour or so. She nodded distractedly and almost ran from the room.

David coped with the soup quite well, and with the rest of the meal. It was obvious he hadn't eaten anything since the attack. We'd both just finished eating when there was a knock at the door and the hotel manager entered, followed by a porter and a woman member of staff laden with sheets and pillows. The manager, whose badge named him as Gary Hobbs, was in his early thirties, tall and slightly stooped. He took one look at David and said, 'Christ almighty. You've had a going-over.'

'I know. I was there.'

'Is there anything we can do?'

David shook his head.

'Could you send up meals to his room?' I said. 'And arrange for a doctor to visit.'

'There's no need,' said David irritably.

'I think she's right, old son,' said Gary. 'But you'll have to pay for the doc.'

'That's fine,' I said. 'As soon as possible, please.'

'No problem, madam. Do you want the bed changed?'

'No thanks. I'll do it.'

When they'd gone I set about stripping and making up the bed and, once the pillows were piled up, I helped David back into it. 'That's better,' he sighed, as he sank back against the pillows, then fell silent. I presumed he'd fallen asleep, because his breathing grew deeper and slower. His eyes were mere slits in a mass of swelling and bruising but, even if he was feigning sleep, I didn't plan to disturb him by asking him about Whitby. That would have to wait.

I sat and watched him for a while, then switched on the TV with the volume off and tried to guess what was going on. That of course was the problem with Whitby. We were trying to nail him but with both sound and vision off. It was no wonder we weren't getting very far.

If he was still living in the attic flat it was definitely worth a stealthy look round. Once the idea formed in my mind I couldn't sit still. It had to be now. I opened David's door quietly and looked out into the corridor. There was no one about, so I made my way to the small staircase that would lead to the attic flat. At the top of the staircase to the right was a door with no number but, to my surprise, there was yet another staircase beyond. This time it was narrow and winding and I nervously trod the boards, hoping they wouldn't creak. There was a slight creak on two of them but when no one challenged me I carried on. At the top was a closed door and next to it a small alcove with a window that looked out on to a flat rooftop. I huddled there for a while listening, hearing nothing but as jumpy as a cat flea. Then I emerged to listen at the door. There was no sound at all from inside. Timidly I tried the door handle and was faintly relieved to find it was locked. Now I could leave. I'd started to go back down the windy stairs when I heard footsteps and voices. I crept backwards up the stairs and into the alcove. The voices became a bit clearer. There was a man and a woman. 'How much?' he was saying.

'I told you, fifty pounds. It's up to you.' She sounded young, a Londoner. That was all I heard. They disappeared into the room below. I made a hasty exit as fast and as quietly as I could.

Back in David's room he was just beginning to stir. 'I thought you'd gone,' he said.

I pulled up a chair and sat down. 'I've been nosing around. There's either a knocking shop below that attic flat or it's being used to sell drugs.'

'Nothing surprises me here,' said David. 'I thought getting mugged happened to other people.'

'What are we going to do about Whitby?'

'There's not much I can do in my condition.'

'If I could get hold of the master key—' I began.

David raised a hand to interrupt me. 'That's if the attic flat has the same locks as the rooms.'

'If I could get the keys from the chambermaids, I could at least try.'

'How are you going to do that?'

'I'll think of something.'

'Just make sure,' he said, 'he's not in the room if you do by chance find a key that fits.'

He closed his eyes again, or at least they appeared to be closed, which I found quite disconcerting. I was never sure if he could see me through those slits. I was also worried that he'd develop an eye infection. He needed a doctor to check his eyes with an ophthalmoscope. It was now ten p.m. and there was no sign of him or her. So, I watched the news, this time with the volume turned up. The very last item was to say that the woman's body found in Camden Lock was thought to be Magda Ionescu, a Romanian asylum seeker, and a known drug addict. Foul play was not now suspected.

I should have felt relieved that it wasn't Teresa but I didn't. I felt uneasy and suspicious. The move from being unidentified to identified had happened very quickly. I couldn't help wondering if the death of a refugee drug addict was treated more casually than that of a British national. Did someone pop into the morgue and say, *Ah yes, that's Magda?* End of story. How much proof could there be if she had no papers or passport? What if, maybe, she'd escaped from Sangatte?

My musing was interrupted by the phone. It was an internal call to announce the arrival of Dr Singh.

Dr Singh was middle-aged, wore a startlingly white turban and spoke with a London accent in a very quiet voice. 'Were you mugged, squire?' he asked.

'Yes, Doc,' answered David, as he struggled to sit higher up in bed.

Dr Singh opened his black bag and, starting with David's head, he began examining him from top to toe. He spent some time listening to his chest and feeling his abdomen. He made little clicking noises with his tongue occasionally, then asked, 'How's your plumbing?'

David didn't cotton on for a moment. 'Oh yeah, I'm peeing OK.'

'Any blood?'

'No, Doc.'

'Very good. You're a very lucky chap. Your eyes will be fine once the swelling has gone down. You've probably got some broken ribs but they haven't perforated your lung, so that's very good too. I'll take your temperature and your blood pressure now.'

We waited for the final verdict as keenly as a defendant in the dock would have done. Dr Singh smiled broadly at me. 'I'm pleased to tell you, Mrs Todman, your husband is not seriously damaged.'

I tried to keep a straight face but he made David sound like a post-office parcel that had burst open in transit.

Dr Singh sat down and began writing out a prescription. 'You need ointment for your eyes, painkillers to be taken every four hours, no more than eight a day, and some antibiotics prophylactically. Please finish the course.' He handed me the prescription and told me where the nearest all-night chemists were.

At the door, he handed me his bill. 'I have to ask for payment now,' he said. 'Some people do a moonlight.' Luckily I had the cash on me, as part of a bundle Megan had given me.

'Any problems with his breathing or his kidneys,' said Dr Singh, 'please take him to the nearest hospital.' I sensed a reproving inflection in his voice.

When he'd gone David said anxiously, 'What's this prophylactically stuff. It doesn't go up my arse, does it?'

I laughed, slightly hysterically. 'Oh well,' he said. 'Obviously I got that one wrong.'

When I'd stopped laughing I explained that prophylaxis was a medical word for prevention of disease. 'Well, why didn't he bloody well say that? I nearly passed out with shock. I had this horrible vision of you advancing on me wearing rubber gloves.'

'Relax, David,' I said. 'There are worse nightmares.'

'Not in my book.'

I left then to find the all-night chemist but, although the night receptionist rang a minicab firm for me, it would be a half-hour wait. So, I walked into the near-empty bar and ordered a drink. Danny the barman was just getting my drink when a man walked upside me.

'Hiyah, Mick,' said the barman.

'Hi, Danny. Busy?'

'Quiet as the grave, mate.'

Danny handed me my drink and it was all I could do not to spill it. My hand trembled so much. 'Steady on,' said Mick. I had to look at his face then and it *was* Whitby. I smiled, or tried to. 'Only my first,' I said.

'Will you join me to drink that?' he asked, indicating a table by the window.

'OK. But I'm waiting for a taxi.'

'You're leaving?'

'No. I'd like to say I was going to an all-night party but I'm not. I'm going to the all-night chemist.'

He took me by the elbow and led me to the table. Inwardly I shuddered at his touch. At least I thought it was inward. 'You're nervous,' he said. 'I don't bite.'

I smiled feebly and sat down. 'So, tell me what's wrong.' he said.

'Nothing's wrong with me . . . It's my stepbrother. He's been mugged.'

'That's terrible. Is he OK?'

'The doctor thinks he'll live.'

'Have the police caught the bastards?'

'No. They don't seem to think there's much chance.'

'So, how long are you staying?'

'A few days at least — until he's well enough to travel.'

'Are you on holiday?'

'Here? No. No. I just took a few days off from my job to look after him.'

'What do you do?'

'I'm a nursery nurse.'

Where that lie came from I'll never know, but it was a non-technical job and I guessed I could bluff my way through if he asked me any questions. And at the moment he was the one asking all the questions. 'What about you?' I asked. 'Are you on holiday?'

'No. I've got a flat here. Broken marriage, cheapest place I could find and all my meals thrown in.'

Now that my insides had stopped churning I looked at him closely. He was attractive in a gold-medallion sort of way. Sexy eyes. He stared but not for too long. Megan's drawing had captured him perfectly. 'What about you?' he asked.

'What about me?'

'Have you got a broken marriage behind you?'

'No, nor in front of me, I hope.'

'You don't like men?'

'I didn't say that. I just haven't met one whose socks I was desperate to wash.'

'You haven't met any *new* men, then?' he asked, flashing me a smile.

I shook my head. 'I've met some men who think that being able to dish up a bowl of pasta makes them god's gift to womankind. But they don't feel the same way about washing up or cleaning the loo.'

'So, there's no special man in your life at the moment?'

'Since you ask . . . no.'

He leaned further towards me. 'I'm Michael, by the way. Although some people call me Mick. And you are . . . ?'

I hesitated. What the hell had I signed the register as? The name got dredged slowly from brain to lips. 'Alison, but I'm called Ali.' He stretched out his hand to shake mine and I was aware my palms were clammy and his were dry. I had to admit that, if he hadn't been Whitby, I might have been attracted to him in a twisted sort of way. He was far too confident.

'Well, Ali. It's lovely to meet you. Are you doing any sightseeing while you're here?'

'Depends how my stepbrother is.'

'What about your parents?'

'They're both dead — we're orphans.' God forgive me, mother, I thought.

'I'm sorry.'

'It was a long time ago.'

He sat back in his chair and watched me. 'I think you're going to need a break from looking after your stepbrother. How about if we do some sightseeing tomorrow afternoon? I'm on a rest day tomorrow.'

'Rest day?' I enquired.

'I'm a cop.'

'Oh, I see.'

'Nothing against the police, have you?'

'No, I like a man in uniform.'

'Never mind. I'm in CID. Which room are you in?'

I was about to tell him when there was a call over the tannoy saying there was a minicab for Ms Fordyce.

'Don't move,' said Whitby. 'Give me the prescription. I'll get the taxi driver to fetch it.'

'No, really, there's no need.'

'London late at night is a dangerous place,' he said, wagging a finger at me. 'Especially the all-night chemists. They're full of junkies. It's not safe.'

I handed him the prescription and was busy rummaging in my purse for money when he said, 'Don't worry about it — my treat.'

He had a few words with the taxi driver, then came back to me. 'Three items,' I said, 'is at least eighteen pounds, plus the car fare must make nearly thirty.'

'Forget it.'

'No.'

'I'm a Londoner and a cop. Call it a small recompense for your stepbrother's brush with our criminal element.'

'It's not your fault.'

'True. Now let me buy you a drink. Same again?'

Weakly I nodded. I could see how Megan had been swept along by his assertive personality. I watched him waiting at the bar to be served. Was this where he slipped something in Megan's drink, I wondered? If I watched him closely enough, would I see him do it? Or was Danny doctoring drinks on his say-so? Even though I had these misgivings, when he came back with a gin and tonic, I began drinking as if such thoughts had never entered my head.

'Where do you live, Ali?' he asked.

'You're off duty,' I said with a bright smile. 'Why is it you make me feel like a suspect?'

'Do I? Sorry about that. I'm not good at chat-up lines.'

Lying bastard!

I began glancing at the clock in the bar, willing the cab driver to return. 'You've got time for one more drink,' he said. 'He'll be at least another ten to fifteen minutes.'

'Just a Coke, then, thanks.'

When he returned with my Coke he said, 'Now then, what do you most want to see in London?'

'I can't really make any plans,' I said. 'It depends how David is.'

'I'll give you a knock anyway. Maybe we could go to the Tower. What's your room number?'

He only had to look in the hotel register anyway, so I told him to save him the trouble, then fixed a time.

Thankfully the minicab driver arrived a couple of minutes later with the prescription. I again tried to pay but Whitby remained adamant.

'I must go now,' I said, as I stood up. He stood up too and grasped my free hand and raised it to his lips. The smile was fixed on my face like a nervous tic. 'See you tomorrow,' he said. *Not if I see you first.*

Back in David's room I breathed several sighs of relief. 'I thought you'd been kidnapped,' he said. It was only after I'd bathed and creamed his eyes and given him the painkillers and antibiotics that I told him what had happened.

'You mean you let him buy you drinks?'

'I didn't want to make him suspicious. I told him you were my stepbrother.'

'You silly bitch!'

I was shocked at the words and his tone. 'Just because I told him you were my stepbrother?'

'No. You accepted drinks from him.'

'I feel all right.'

'Rohypnol isn't bloody cyanide, it doesn't work instantly. It has to get into your system.'

'I feel fine,' I said. I was peeved because it had crossed my mind the drinks could have been tampered with but I'd drunk them anyway. 'I'm going to bed. I'm sure he'd wait a while before trying to drug me.'

'Keep your door locked and put something against it.'

'Barricade myself in?'

'Yes. Don't be a silly bitch twice in one evening.'

'Do you want a new nurse?'

'No, you'll do. Good night, Kate, and thanks.'

In my room I locked the door and slipped the bucket-style chair beneath the doorknob, got undressed, cleaned my teeth and got into bed. I felt fine, a bit tired but not drunk or woozy. David had overreacted, I decided. I seemed to start falling asleep sooner than usual but there was nothing I could do about that.

Something woke me. It took me a few seconds to remember where I was. I looked at my alarm clock. It was two a.m. I peered into the darkness. I couldn't see anything but even in the dark I recognized the sound. Someone was trying my door handle.

CHAPTER TWENTY

I listened but didn't move. It could be a drunk trying the wrong door, I decided, because the effort to get into my room was none too subtle. After all, the noise had woken me. Whoever it was hadn't moved away, so I shouted, 'Piss off!' loudly and I heard the sound of dropped keys and then a door slamming. It *was* a drunk, I decided, and I tried to get back to sleep, only now I was wide-awake and worried that I hadn't phoned either the hospital or Hubert. But, of course, they hadn't phoned me either and, since I had no news to give them, other than that David was out of action, it was probably just as well.

I dozed on and off and by seven thirty I was ministering to David. I was surprised at the improvement one night could bring. His eyes were still black and swollen but they were at least half-open. He could now get out of bed more easily on his own and he winced far less. I decided that he was fit enough to be left for the afternoon and he might be able to get into Whitby's flat.

'How do you suggest I might do that? I haven't got the strength to kick the door in.'

'Could you make the stairs, do you think?'

'I could try,' he said, sounding less than convinced that he'd succeed. 'But I'm not up to any heroics.'

'I thought I could tell one of the chambermaids you're an undercover cop and you need to have a look around the flat — she could keep the door open and watch you.'

'Why should she do that?'

'For fifty quid.'

'Will she keep her mouth shut?'

'That's a chance we'll have to take.'

'You'll have to give me the fifty quid.'

'And, David, you need to let Longborough Police know what's happened to you.'

'Yeah, yeah. How embarrassing.'

'You're lucky you're not dead.'

'I don't feel lucky.'

When breakfast arrived he ate heartily, mainly, I think, because he could see what he was eating and his lips were almost back to normal.

Later on in the morning, I spoke to my mother. Megan was progressing. I need worry about nothing. Hubert said more or less the same. I had the feeling they didn't *want* to talk to me and I was more worried after speaking to them than before. Something was going on there and it bugged me, but until we found a lead on where Megan's baby might be, there was nothing I could do.

I stopped one of the chambermaids as she was wheeling her trolley outside my room and asked her if Rosa still worked at the hotel. She shrugged her shoulders and said nothing. Not a chatty type, I thought, which was a good thing. She was in her twenties, thin, with straggly hair and hollow eyes. The sort who lives on fags and cider. Fifty pounds might be more than welcome. I directed her to David's room and hung around in the corridor to catch her on the way out.

When she did come out she managed a wry smile, so I took that to mean she was up for it.

'Well — is she going to do it?' I asked him.

'Says she will. Did you pick her for her looks?'

'Very funny . . .' I paused. He looked worried. 'What's up?'

'I rang Longborough. I had to speak to the super. He went ballistic because I hadn't told him. A private ambulance is coming to collect me and I have to go the police convalescence home.'

'Where's that?'

'The south coast. He wants me thoroughly checked out.'

'When?'

'Early evening — well, about three p.m. to be precise. One good thing — police funds are paying both our hotel bills.'

That wasn't much consolation to me. If I left with Whitby for my jaunt to the Tower, it would give David an hour to search the flat, leaving no trace. It would probably be long enough, but then I was on my own again and I wasn't that happy about the prospect.

David looked at me solemnly. 'It's working out badly,' he said. 'There's only one thing we can do.'

'What?'

'Abort the plan.'

'No. No way. I haven't come this far to give up now. If Whitby has a place in Scotland, there's a chance we could find out where and that's where the baby might be.'

'That's the point, isn't it, Kate? Might. You don't even know if the baby's alive. If it ever lived at all.'

'I have to believe that it is alive, because, if it is, Megan is the mother and she hasn't got much else in life. She deserves to have her baby returned to her.'

'Have you ever thought,' he said, 'that it might be you who wants the baby more than her.'

'What are you talking about?'

'Think about it. The baby was born as a result of rape by a man who is involved in murder, drugs and vice. Would you want a baby by a man like that?'

I had to admit he did have a point. Had I bamboozled Megan into doing what I thought was best? Was it best for her? He had to be stopped but she was the one to pay the price. If the baby was found, was it too late now for mother and child to bond? And if the baby had already gone abroad, would Megan wonder for the rest of her life what had happened to him or her?

'You may be right,' I said, 'but Megan has the right to make her own decisions and, if she has the baby officially adopted, at least the baby has been spared a ghastly fate. After all, the baby too deserves a chance.'

'I rest my case,' said David with a shrug. 'But if you found a baby and you were convinced it was hers — then what are you going to do? Snatch it? Or ring the police? Will they believe you anyway, especially if the woman's convincing? Either way, I don't want to see you upset when Megan's not overjoyed at the outcome. Or when, having raised her hopes, you fail.'

I didn't want to think about failure but it remained a strong possibility and I'd never be able to live with myself if Whitby got away.

It was that thought that steeled me as the time approached for our date. I'd said goodbye to David and he had promised me he'd do what he could the moment he was released from the convalescent home. He'd leave me a note with details — if he found anything in Whitby's flat.

On the dot of two p.m. Whitby knocked on my door. 'You look nice,' he said. *Nice!* What sort of word was that? I'd made an effort too, so that I felt more confident. He took my arm as we went down the stairs and I tried to think of this excursion as a date. A date with an ordinary Joe, not some bent cop with as many rackets going as a Mafia Don, although even the Mafia didn't stoop to selling babies.

At the Tower, we followed a guided tour of mainly American and Japanese tourists. The sun shone and, for a while, I tried to immerse myself in the history of the place, except Whitby was either holding my hand or hugging me to him. One day in the not too distant future, mate, I thought, I'm going to make you sing soprano.

On the way home we had tea and cakes in a café and he told me how both his ex-wives had let him down. One had been too young and immature. The other had cheated on him. Although he'd forgiven her once, he hadn't been able to forgive her twice. He was now looking for the faithful type who wanted children. I nearly choked on my Chelsea bun.

'What about you, Ali? What ambitions do you have?'

I tried being a little coy, because part of me wanted to lead him on to see what would happen and the other half wanted to run a mile. 'The nursery I work in is due to close soon, so at the moment my only ambition is for another job.'

'Perhaps I could help you,' he said. 'I know people who want nannies. It's well paid these days.'

'I wouldn't want to live in London *or* live in,' I said swiftly.

'Not even if I was around to take you out and about?'

I could feel a sickly smile cross my face. 'I might consider it.'

'Let me take you out to dinner tonight and we can talk about it some more. And, by the way, how's your stepbrother?'

This was something I couldn't totally lie about. Someone in the hotel was bound to see him taken off in a private ambulance.

'He's got lucky,' I said. 'A friend of his who runs a private ambulance firm is picking him up today and whisking him off to a family friend by the seaside.'

'So, I'm the lucky one too,' said the smooth bastard.

'How do you mean?'

'I'll have you all to myself.'

'With my brother gone, I'll be going home tomorrow.'

'Where is home?'

I didn't hesitate. 'Just outside Birmingham.'

'Surely you could stay a few more days. I could find you a job in no time, then we could really get to know each other.'

His arm slipped around my shoulders and it was as if a giant python had me in its grasp, poised and ready to choke the life out of me. I glanced at my watch. 'Is that the time already? I really must go. I've got phone calls to make.'

His arm dropped from me and he feigned disappointment. 'I am going to see you tonight, though?'

'Unless I have to get back to work for tomorrow.'

'I don't want you to slip away from me, Ali.'

He was so slippery himself he'd have made sandpaper slither, but once more I smiled and told him I'd got some thinking to do.

He delivered me to my hotel room and I blew him a kiss and closed the door abruptly in a moment of inattention on his part. There was no way I was letting him into my room. I felt released once my bedroom door was closed. I knew now how celebrities felt when their bodyguards finally left them for the day.

David had left me an envelope on the bed. It read:

Thanks for everything. Nothing incriminating in his room re vice and drugs, but he does have half shares in Canadian Cabins in Scotland, based near Dunoon — office at Sea Front Villas, Macken. It might be worth investigating — don't attempt anything on your own.

Keep in touch.

Love, David.

I tore the letter up into the smallest of shreds, flushed it down the loo and then began to pack in haste. I wanted out of the Georgiana and its ever-changing staff, out of noisy, grimy London, but most of all I wanted to be away from Whitby. I used my mobile to ring BR and find out the times of the trains to Glasgow. There was one at six thirty. I debated with myself whether I should or should not leave a note for Whitby. In the end I thought, sod it, I don't have the time. At reception I told them there was a family emergency and I had to leave immediately.

It was Friday evening, Euston was heaving, the train was packed and the only seat I could find was with a mother and two excitable children with snotty noses and voices as loud as the more moronic football supporters. I prayed they weren't going all the way to Glasgow. In the end I asked the mother. She was young and fat in a lumpy way and her voice could only be described as megaphonic. 'Preston, we're getting off. If I don't throw the little buggers off before then. Kylie! Eat them crisps properly. Brad, if you don't stop kicking your sister, I'll cut your bleedin' legs off.' And so it continued until Preston.

As their stopping-off point, I'll always remember Preston with gratitude — it was a town very welcome to the family from hell. I luxuriated in having the seat next to me empty and the seats opposite now taken by two men who were asleep by the time we were five miles north of Preston. I slept too. It was dark when I woke up, and we'd stopped. We were not at a station and my heart sank. The train manager, in a flurry of words which I think was an apology, mentioned something about technical problems. It was two hours before we moved again.

I arrived in Glasgow very late, very stiff, hungry and exhausted. And still I had to get to Gourock and then catch the Ferry across to Dunoon. It was raining, with chill winds. I should have remembered spring arrives late in Scotland. I needed waterproofs, long johns and thick Aran jumpers, not a thin jacket and skirt.

By the time I arrived in Macken, it was late morning. By now deep cold, damp and depression had been added to my list of complaints.

The manageress of Canadian Cabins, Patricia Stewart, a smartly dressed woman in her forties, with blood-red fingernails and smelling of Chanel, seemed surprised I wanted a cabin. 'They're very isolated. Have you got a car?'

I shook my head.

'It's a wee way by taxi,' she said. She glanced at my jacket. 'And it's cold this time of year. There's no shops nearby.'

'I need to be on my own completely,' I explained. 'Just for a week or so. I've been under considerable stress. I just need a really quiet break.'

'Aye, well, you'll get peace and quiet all right. It's such short notice, I'm afraid it will have to be cash.'

I nearly fell off my chair when she told me it would cost five hundred pounds for the week. 'It's a wee bargain. At peak times it's a thousand.' For that sort of money, I would have expected Canada itself but I was obviously out of touch. Did I even have the money? I counted out my cash. I did have enough — just. I handed it over and was handed the keys, a brochure and a map. 'Any problems, give me a ring. Now, there's a wee grocery shop two doors up. Take this docket and you'll be given a complimentary basket. There could be snow,' she said. 'So, make sure you get a good fire going. There's plenty of logs.'

'How many cabins are there?' I asked.

'There's six. But they're well separated. You'll not be overlooked. Only two occupied at the moment, on six month lets. Some people like to spend all spring and summer here.'

'Families?'

'No, not on the long-term lets. There's a woman in one, whose husband works away, and two women — artists, I think.'

My heart sank. After my nightmare journey, which would take me two days to recover from, there was, at the moment, only the prospect of rain, the threat of snow and total isolation. I'd spent several hundred pounds and for what? Now it seemed this idea too was doomed to failure. And this was plan A, there was no plan B.

I went along to the grocery shop with my docket and the sour-faced owner began filling a quaint woven basket with bread, butter, cheese, bacon, eggs, tea bags, instant coffee, milk, sugar and shortbread biscuits. 'Anything else you'll have to pay for,' she said. I felt in my pocket for some loose change and chose two packets of crisps and four bars of chocolate.

'Is there a bank nearby?' I asked.

'Aye, but it's closed.'

'Is there a hole in the wall?'

'Aye, but it's not working.'

'Is there a taxi rank or a minicab firm near here?'

'Aye. I'll ring Duncan Cars for you.'

She disappeared into a back room just as another customer came in. When she returned, she smiled broadly.

'Hello, Mrs Macdonald. You're looking well.' How on earth she could tell, I didn't know, as Mrs M. wore a plastic hood, a black padded coat, boots and gloves and her face was a reddish blue.

'Aye. I'm fine,' she said. 'Weather's worsening though. They say there'll be a wee fall of snow tonight.'

'That'll be twenty pence for the phone call,' the shopkeeper said to me. I grovelled in my handbag and eventually found one. 'Taxi's outside waiting for you.'

A minicab was indeed already outside the door. Very odd. Perhaps she had yelled to him over the back gate.

We drove out of Macken and along twisting, winding roads, the rain drumming relentlessly. 'Hae ye stayed here before, hen?' he said, or words to that effect. 'I'm Jimmy. Macken's best taxi driver. I hear you're going up to Clacken Forest to the cabins.'

He smelt of whisky and damp and he watched me in the mirror. He wore a tartan cap and a tartan jacket and he had a face as big as the moon. 'How much will it cost to get me to the cabins?' I asked.

'Nine pounds should do it.'

Fortuitously I had just ten pounds left. If I used him again, he'd have to take me to the bank and wait for me. He drove on into the Scottish hinterland and I caught a glimpse of a loch but in the rain it held no charm, just an expanse of the black and dismal. Eventually the car began to climb and the road became a single track. Pine trees filled my view, with the occasional clearing. We climbed higher and then he turned to a clearing on the right. 'I'll go as far as I can but I cannae go all the way. I've been stuck up here in the mud a wee while, I can tell you.'

The car ground to a halt. 'Here ye are, hen.' I couldn't see anything but trees and grass and rain. He wound down the window as I opened the door. He had no intention of helping me with my luggage or the basket. 'You'll be needing a brolly,' he said. I scanned the trees. 'A wee way to your right,' he said, directing me with his index finger. I could just see a wooden construction peeking through the trees. 'Where are the other cabins?'

'Higher up. Nearest one is about half a mile.'

I paid up, giving him the last of my money. He handed me his business card, saying, 'I can get you any messages you want, hen.' It took me a moment to remember that, for the Scots, *messages* was shopping. At the rate I'd been spending money, the basket would have to last the week, if I was here that long. And at the moment it seemed this was yet another general cock-up on my part.

I struggled in the rain and mud to the cabin and, had the sun shone, I would have been quite impressed. It nestled between pines in a forest glade, it had decking and windows without external shutters and it could indeed have been a Canadian log cabin. Not only was it made of logs, there was also a huge pile on the stoop. I flicked on the lights and was relieved that it seemed relatively warm and cosy. There were rag mats and tartan throws on the armchairs, and logs waiting to be lit in the fireplace. I quickly checked out the two bedrooms. One had a double bed, the other a single. Both were covered in patchwork quilts.

I decided my first priority should be to light the log fire. I had no matches with me and it took me ages to work out that my only method of lighting it would be by making a spill, lighting it on the electric cooker in the kitchen, then walking to the logs in the sitting room. I decided against that for the moment and put the electric kettle on instead and began unpacking my basket. I hoped that somehow there was a box of matches in my supplies. There wasn't and I thought that was a major oversight, but to get some warmth, at least in the kitchen, I switched on the oven and opened the oven door. If I sat close enough at least I wouldn't freeze to death.

I made a pot of tea and toasted two slices of bread, then pulled up a kitchen chair and sat by the oven. Outside, it was darkening and the rain was changing to sleet. It was only then that I noticed there was no lighting outside. All I could see was the looming pine trees and in that moment I felt very alone. I switched on the television and felt quite reassured that out in the real world everything was still going on as normal.

The telephone, one of those replica early models, black with a separate earpiece, was on a table next to the sofa, beside a lamp with a red shade and pink beaded frill. The lamp reminded me of a bordello in an old Western. I picked up the earpiece and dialled Hubert's number. There was no sound at all. I replaced it and tried again. Nothing. I checked the phone was plugged in — it was. In my handbag I found my mobile. I stared at it. It was a pay-as-you-go phone but I'd used it often lately. I rang to check the balance on my phonecard. 'You have twenty pence in your account.'

No problem, I thought, I've a phonecard in my purse. Wrong! The orange that I'd glimpsed in my purse was a book of stamps, not a new phonecard.

Tomorrow is another day, I told myself. I pulled the curtains against the dark night that was now being flecked with white, checked that the front and back doors were locked, washed up my cup and plate and put my small supply of groceries away. Then as if something had to happen to lighten my sense of gloom and doom, I found in one of the cupboards a hot-water bottle. I hadn't used one since I was a child. I'd never needed one. Now I did, so I boiled the kettle again, let it stand for a few minutes and then filled it carefully and carried the hottie, as if it were some fragile furry animal, to the haven of my single bed. Among the drawbacks of this cabin in the wilds there was the lack of matches, the phone that didn't work and there was no bath — only a shower. Presumably in the Rockies only showers are popular. Like it or lump it, I thought, so I decided the shower would invigorate me too much, had a wash instead and, shivering, jumped into bed to clutch my hot-water bottle to my bosom.

I was fast asleep when I heard my mobile ring. It was on charge near me on the floor and I nearly fell out of bed in my haste to answer it. 'Hubert, what time do you call this?'

There was no reply.

CHAPTER TWENTY-ONE

I looked at my watch. It was eleven p.m. I'd been asleep exactly an hour. I flicked on my bedside lamp and gazed at the number showing on my mobile. It wasn't one I recognized and I tried to convince myself it was merely a wrong number. I tried ringing Hubert but he was switched off. The call had disturbed me and, suddenly, I was wide-awake. The air in the bedroom now seemed as cold as a fridge. Surely, I thought, there was some subsidiary heating. I began searching and, finding nothing in the cabin itself, I opened the back door, with the patchwork quilt from my bed around my shoulders, to be shocked at the amount of snow that had already fallen. It was nearly May but here time had moved backwards to January. The snow, I supposed, was just a dusting to the Scots, but to me it seemed a major fall, especially in spring. On the back porch there was a door to what I presumed was a storage cupboard. The key was on the key ring and on opening the door I was delighted to find two oil-filled radiators. Shedding the quilt, I fetched them both inside and plugged one in at the sitting-room socket and one in my bedroom. Frostbite receded from my mind. Even the silent phone call receded a little. But my wakefulness continued. I had writing paper, so I wrote three fairly brief letters to

Hubert, Megan and David. I told them my address — cabin number one etcetera — and that everything was fine and I would start investigating tomorrow. Except that I should have written that I was in the middle of nowhere in blizzard conditions, with no ready cash, a non-working land line, no matches, no phonecard and, all in all, there seemed as much likelihood of finding Megan's baby as there was of finding a Yeti. But I didn't want them to worry and Megan needed a bit of hope. Also, with my mother looking after her, she'd probably need counselling to get her over the experience. David too didn't need or deserve to feel any anxiety on my part, so I reassured him that I was indeed on a wild goose chase and I would be back in Longborough in a couple of days at most.

I lay awake most of the night listening to the wind and, perhaps in my imagination, the snow falling on the sloping roof and slap-slapping at the windows. I obviously slept, because it was light when I woke up. In fact it was too bright. I pulled back the curtains to see that snow had decorated the whole of my field of vision. It looked truly beautiful but, rather like a Fabergé egg, was of no use at all.

The moment of appreciation passed in a flash when I realized I had no boots, no warm coat, and the shoes I did have were utterly flimsy for the purpose of trekking through two or three inches of snow. I switched on the TV for the weather report and then set about cooking myself a hearty breakfast. If I was to go calling on my neighbours, then I needed plenty of fuel. Today the cabin, even with the radiators on, felt far colder than yesterday.

Eventually the weather forecast came on. The day would worsen and by late afternoon there could be real blizzard conditions. A thaw with sunshine was on its way midweek.

What was left of the morning seemed like the best time to visit my neighbours and, of course, to ferret for information. Even news of a mere visit at some time by Whitby might reveal something new. At least that's what I had to believe to make my tramp through snow worthwhile.

I put on a long-sleeved jumper over a tee shirt, as well as donning two pairs of knickers, two pairs of tights and my pair of best black trousers. My thin jacket wouldn't be warm enough without something else, so I utilized one of the tartan throws from an armchair as a shawl. As an afterthought I put a few paper tissues inside the cups of my bra. Frostbitten toes I felt I could cope with, but frostbitten nipples were another matter entirely.

Initially I felt warmer than I expected to but it didn't last. First I walked downwards towards the lane where I'd seen a postbox. I posted my letters and began the walk back to my cabin and beyond, where the incline grew steeper. As I continued to walk upwards the soft snow crept into my shoes and after a few hundred yards my feet felt as if they were encased in cold, wet face flannels. I couldn't see any other cabins but I knew they were there somewhere. Half a mile between each one, Jimmy the taxi man had told me. I supposed the distance between cabins was a delight for the unsociable. But was that a country half-mile or a Scottish half-mile? Either way it was bound to be longer than my townie's perception of half a mile. I tried to enjoy the walk. The sun was bright but without any warmth and the snow was dazzling and a little disorientating. There were no paths, no footprints to follow, no landmarks, just pine trees and snow.

I trekked on, still moving upwards and, although it wasn't particularly steep, I began to feel tired, as if the air were thinner — or was it that fresh air itself, after London, came as a shock to my brain and vital organs?

Eventually, though, I spied another cabin. It looked identical to mine but there was no sign of life in or around it, neither was there any smoke coming from the chimney stack. When I did reach it and knock on the door, the only sound was melted snow dripping from the trees, but I wasn't too surprised, just disappointed, because my feet were now squelching and painfully cold. Still, I reminded myself of Shackleton and other explorers who'd suffered so much crossing the polar wastes. My mere mile or so in light snow would have seemed a relaxed stroll to them.

The second cabin seemed even further than half a mile but smoke was drifting from the chimney and, squinting in the sunlight, I could see a figure sweeping the snow from the decking. As I got nearer I could see it was a woman. 'Hello there,' she called out. I was a little out of breath but I managed to say I was from the first cabin. 'Come on in and get warm,' she said. 'I'm Sandra Gilmore.'

Inside, a log fire flamed energetically. Purple tulips in a purple vase on the pine dining table added a certain degree of sophistication to the interior, which was almost identical to mine. 'How about coffee with some Scottish sugar?' she said. 'You look as if you need it.' She'd made me an offer I couldn't refuse. 'Take your shoes off if you want and warm your feet.' I took my shoes off and stared at my toes to check that they were still there.

Sandra wasn't a Scot, judging by her accent, and she either used a sun lamp or she'd spent time abroad. Her silver hair was short and framed gamine features.

Judging by her beautifully kept hands, she was not one of the artists I was told was staying here, for there were no tell-tale spots of paint on her hands, or easels or brushes or any sign of artistic endeavour.

When she came back with the coffee she saw my feet were steaming in the heat of the fire. 'Take those tights off,' she said. 'I've got some socks I can give you.'

In the bathroom, I noticed there were two toothbrushes and two tubes of toothpaste, plus assorted washbags. As I left the bathroom, I noticed the larger of the bedrooms had its door closed, whereas the door to the smaller room remained open. Even I could deduce there was someone else staying with Sandra Gilmore.

I drank the well-laced coffee and we both had two pieces of shortbread and, with warm, dry feet, I felt quite cheerful. 'Your colour is back,' she observed. I already felt as if my cheeks were burning, so I moved back a little from the fire. 'Are you on holiday?' she asked.

'Yes. Just a week's break. I thought it would be spring. I prefer warm weather.'

She nodded in agreement. 'I live in Spain,' she explained. 'I took early retirement from my teaching job and now I sell time-share holidays.'

'So, what brings you here?'

'My god-daughter, Sophie. She's having a lie-in at the moment.'

I waited for her to tell me more but she didn't elaborate and I certainly preferred not to tell her my real reason for being here.

'The weather should slowly improve,' she said. 'You might get some sunshine.'

'I've trekked up here,' I said, 'hoping you might have some spare matches.'

'You're in luck. We've got two boxes. We probably had your share.' She walked into the kitchen and returned with a giant box. 'Do stay for lunch,' she said. 'We could do with the company.'

'I'd love to but there's someone I have to see.'

'You have friends here?'

'No, not exactly. An acquaintance who might be staying in one of the cabins.'

'Sophie's seen a young woman walking about but she wasn't friendly. I've only been here a week and you're the first to visit.'

'Is your phone working, by the way?' I asked.

'No. It isn't,' she said. 'In a day or so I'll go down to Macken and report it. Sophie's lost her mobile or had it stolen and I foolishly left mine in Spain.'

I wanted to stay longer but, outside, I could hear the wind whipping up and see that the sky was full of dark sodden clouds. 'I'll have to go,' I said. 'Before the blizzard starts. But I'll return your socks as soon as I can.'

'I've got a waterproof coat you could borrow,' she said, but as Sandra was a size ten at most, I declined her kind offer. 'Well, just make sure you stay to lunch next time.'

My shoes were still soaked but I felt a whole lot stronger after the coffee and biscuits. Sandra stood on the porch to wave me on upwards. She seemed a nice woman and I hoped that next time we met I'd have something sorted, but I wasn't sure what or how. After all, I was only here on a hunch.

The snow seemed crisper as I walked on. Perhaps it was the increased altitude or the temperature had dropped, but at least I walked *on* snow rather than in it. By the time I saw the other occupied cabin I was breathless and exhausted. I'd passed two that were empty but ahead I could see a tell-tale curl of grey smoke that was hardly distinguishable from the greying sky. I had to pause to get my breath before knocking on the door. All the curtains were drawn and it took some time for the door to be opened a fraction. The woman who half hid behind the door was about twenty, pale, with her dark hair scraped back and dark circles under her eyes. I knew from the tone in which she said, 'Yes?' that she wasn't going to invite me in.

'I've come to find out if your phone is working,' I said with a broad smile.

'My phone does not work. Sorry.' With that she closed the door in my face. She had a foreign accent, was perhaps from Romania or Bosnia, but that was as much as I was going to find out at that moment.

I left the porch and stood outside by one of the windows, trying to will a baby to cry, but there was only the sound of the wind whining through the pine trees. I had no choice but to wend my way downwards. The walk back to my cabin seemed shorter, and easier, but it was now much colder and the wind itself was snatching at my breath.

My cabin seemed a haven from the elements, but even before I changed my clothes I was at the fireplace lighting the fire, or at least trying to. In the end I sacrificed my writing paper and used twists of that to wedge between the logs. And eventually, with much blowing and swearing, the fire took hold. I felt as elated at the sight of it as any barmy arsonist setting their first fire. I watched it roar into respectable flames, then changed my clothes and made lunch. Looking at my supplies, there didn't seem much variety, so a cheese sandwich and a packet of crisps would have to do. It was while I was eating that I remembered that Sandra Gilmore had told me she'd been at the cabin for a week — she hadn't said *we* she'd said *I*. That seemed odd. She'd also told me nothing at all about Sophie. I wondered idly if Sophie's sojourn in the hills was due to drugs, mental illness — or was she suffering from a broken heart after young love had gone awry? Several months in a log cabin seemed excessive. When I was eighteen and crossed in love, my mother merely told me to *Pull myself together. There were plenty more fish in the sea*. But then my mother never did lay claim to being an original thinker.

The warmth of the fire caused me to doze and I told myself I was too young to nod off after lunch. But I did, and I woke up to the sound of roaring winds and the sight of heavy snow and the sky as dark as night even though it was only three o'clock. My nap had lasted for one and a half hours.

It was then that I went to check my mobile phone, because it was very odd that Hubert hadn't phoned. It wasn't just odd, it was very worrying. But a mobile phone does need to be recharged and mine was not plugged in. I rectified that but, as the hours passed, the mobile showed no sign of life. The bloody thing had died on me. I supposed that the signal itself could be weak. But why now, in my moment of greatest need? Sod's law, I thought. And you, Hubert, I rambled on to myself, couldn't manage to ring me before my mobile decided to call it a day, so I am here alone risking frostbite and death from dietary boredom and you don't even know how worried you should be.

Once I'd stopped mentally whinging I started to read the one novel I had with me, which consisted of thirty-ish women talking about job angst, childhood angst and man angst. I'd been more engrossed in conversations at bus stops but it passed the time, although it didn't pass it quickly enough. Putting logs on the fire and watching the snow in between chasing the TV channels for something other than football or crime passed even more time.

Outside, the wind alternated between whining and loud rumbling. It was then that I caught another sound, a human moan or a cry. I wasn't sure which. I peered out into the night but I could see nothing but the white of the snow and the bowing trees. I'd just decided that I was either having aural hallucinations or it was merely the gale-force winds when I heard it again. This time I was sure it was a groan. I opened the cabin door to a face full of snow but, as I squinted and looked to one side of the cabin, I could see two dark figures approaching. One seemed to be supporting the other.

CHAPTER TWENTY-TWO

As the couple moved closer I could now make out the slight frame and face of Sandra Gilmore beneath a hooded coat. She was supporting a girl with a frightened face, who was of much bigger proportions and was walking with a waddling gait. The sort of walk pregnant women have to perfect when they are near to term. It took me a few moments for the fact to register that she was indeed heavily pregnant. What the hell was she doing here in that state?

As I helped them both in, Sandra was saying breathlessly, 'I didn't know what else to do. I've no children. The only time I've seen a baby born is on TV. I couldn't just stay up there with her on my own.'

'Let's just get her inside,' I said, as we helped her up the two steps to the porch. We were then hefted in by one big gust that even blew the snow in with us. I took Sophie's coat and scarf off. She looked terrified and began to whimper. 'I'm so scared,' she said. 'Well, there's no need,' I said briskly. 'I know what to do.' My confident approach was well acted. I had delivered about ten babies but that was under the supervision of a qualified midwife. I presumed it was like swimming or riding a bike, something you never forgot and, after all, the mother did the work.

'What shall I do?' asked Sandra.

'Tea would be great.'

'Oh yes,' she said abstractly, as if somehow childbirth precluded making tea.

I eased Sophie into a chair. 'How many weeks are you?' I asked.

'I'm not sure,' she said, miserably. Her scrubbed face was pale and childlike. She had luminous green eyes and long blonde hair.

'When did you last see your doctor or a midwife?'

'My boyfriend called the doctor about a month ago. I had a urinary-tract infection.'

I needed to establish an estimated delivery date from her, or EDD. For most mums it's the most important date in their calendar. I could make a guess by laying her down and assessing her girth but I hadn't examined a pregnant woman in years. And although I was trying to give the impression that I knew exactly what I was doing, in reality I was trying to dredge back some of the things I'd learnt. 'Have you got your progress chart?' I asked. Her answering expression suggested that I'd asked her if she could speak Swahili. 'So, you haven't had any antenatal care?' I tried to sound casual about it but casual was the last thing I was feeling. 'Have you had any swelling of your fingers or toes?' I asked. She shook her head. I'd remembered that pre-eclamptic toxaemia was *the* serious medical emergency of pregnancy and oedema or swelling in the tissues was one of its main characteristics.

I relaxed a little. She seemed like a healthy young girl, so there was no reason why there should be a problem. For the few minutes she'd been sitting down, I'd noticed she'd only grimaced once slightly. There was a chance that the contractions she'd been feeling were merely practice ones known as Braxton Hicks in the trade.

Sandra meanwhile had made the tea but, as she passed me my cup, her hand trembled. She was as agitated as Sophie was and I needed both of them to be calm, so getting Sandra on-side was very important. I needed to talk to her alone, so I sent Sophie off to lie down on my bed and told her I'd examine her tummy in a few minutes. 'And if you have a contraction,' I said, 'give me a shout.'

Once she'd gone and, thankfully, closed the bedroom door, I asked Sandra what had been going on. Sandra shook her head sadly. 'Just over a week ago,' she said, 'I had a letter from her telling me she was pregnant, living in a cabin on her own, expecting her boyfriend, and she was scared. I didn't ask too many questions. I got on a plane and came up here.'

'Where was she living before?'

'London. She was an art student, in her second year. She lived with a group of friends but then she met this chap at a party, older than her, but she won't say how old. In fact, I don't know anything about him at all. Just that he was the one who suggested she came up here. He seems to be one of these New-Age types and he wants her to have a home birth with a private midwife.'

'He is the father, isn't he?'

Sandra stared into the fire. 'To be honest, I'm not sure. I think Sophie must have been too drunk to remember the actual conception. She wasn't on the pill or anything. In fact, she'd never had a proper boyfriend. She'd been to a girls' boarding school and I think, prior to this, she was a virgin. She used to stay with me in school holidays and we had some very happy times together. I never married and Sophie's been just a joy . . .' She broke off. 'I feel that I've let her down badly by going off to Spain.'

'There was nothing you could do,' I said. It was all beginning to sound horribly familiar. I fell silent and then heard a slight murmuring from the bedroom. I walked in to find Sophie crying bitterly.

'I can't even let him know,' she sobbed. 'He'd come here straight away if he knew.'

'Michael Whitby?'

'Yes,' she said, the surprise causing her to stop crying. 'How did you know his name?'

'I'll tell you later, but you have a rest now and make sure that you time any contractions you get.'

'They seem to have gone,' she said. She sounded disappointed.

'Let me feel your tummy,' I said. 'You tell the baby to kick me.' She managed a half smile. 'Have you chosen a name yet?' I asked, as I placed my hands on her abdomen. She shook her head and watched me intently as I examined her. Judging by her size, I guessed she was at least thirty-eight weeks. I felt the baby's head well down in the pelvis but not yet engaged, which wasn't unusual. If the baby was born this night, at least it wasn't a breech presentation and, at thirty-eight weeks or so, it would have a good chance of survival.

Whitby would be the one to know the exact time of conception, I thought, but I said, as casually as I could, 'Does he know Sandra is here?'

'No, I haven't told him.' In those few words, I knew she was a little afraid of him, that somewhere her intuition had told her he wouldn't approve.

'So, when's he coming?' I asked cheerfully.

'That's the point, isn't it? I don't know. He last came a fortnight ago for the weekend. It was just before he came that I wrote to Sandra. I was so lonely but I didn't think she'd come straight away.'

'She's been like a mother to you, hasn't she? And you trust her?'

She looked a little shocked at the question. 'Of course I trust her. How could you ask such a thing?'

'Whatever happens in the future, I want you to remember that.' Her face screwed up in puzzlement, but I didn't pursue it. 'What else did Michael say?' I asked.

She was still watching me with slight suspicion. 'He told me a midwife would stay with me for the last week or so and he'd come on her say-so, because he doesn't want to miss being with me for the birth.'

I bet he doesn't, the slimy git, I thought.

'I wanted to have a scan,' she continued in a rush. 'But he doesn't approve of scans. He says, me being young and fit, it's totally unnecessary.'

I neither agreed nor disagreed. She watched me carefully as though waiting for me to express an opinion.

'You're a midwife, aren't you?' she said excitedly. 'Are you the one? Why didn't you say straight away? That's how you know Michael, isn't it? I'm so relieved.'

'I'm only a last-minute stand-in. When I found out you had Sandra staying with you, I thought it best to say nothing. But you came to me anyway, didn't you?'

'I'm so relieved,' she said again. 'Has Michael told you when he'll be here? We're going to get married, you know.'

'No, but tomorrow I'll get a new phonecard and you can ring him.' I added quickly, 'Best not to tell him I'm here, though, or he won't rush, will he? You tell him you're on your own and he'll be up here by tomorrow evening.'

'That's a good idea. Thanks, Kate. I'm so glad you're here.'

'You get some rest, Sophie. I don't think you're in labour at the moment. But trust me too, everything will be just fine.'

I went into the main bedroom, sat on the bed and tried to think rationally. David had given me the Macken address. He must have guessed where I was by now and, since I hadn't phoned him, he was probably getting worried. Hubert too. Although it felt as if I'd been here for ever, it had after all, been only one complete night. Scotland's road and rail system was in chaos, so any hope of the cavalry arriving was pretty remote. If Sophie was in labour, which I very much doubted now, the truth about Whitby might have a detrimental effect. She'd be devastated, however we told her, and keeping her calm and persuading her to go into hospital might prove very difficult. She'd been brainwashed and kept in ignorance. I needed Sandra as an ally and she did, after all, know Sophie well. She might be able to help me explain the situation to her god-daughter.

Who was I kidding? She wasn't going to believe a word of it. Whitby was her knight in shining armour. Believing he was a baby trader and murderer would be like telling her Picasso was not an artist but a serial killer.

Sandra sat staring into the fire. She turned anxiously as I entered the room. 'How is she? Is she in labour?'

'I don't think so. But I need to talk to you urgently about the situation.'

'The baby is all right, isn't it? I mean, she won't lose it?'

'It's nothing to do with the baby, at least not directly.'

She frowned. 'Who are you?' she asked. 'What are you doing here?'

'I'm a private investigator,' I admitted. 'But Sophie thinks I'm the midwife sent by Whitby. I do have some midwifery experience, so it's not a total lie.'

'But what has a private investigator got to do with Sophie?' Sandra's voice was getting higher with agitation.

'I've been employed by a young woman,' I explained, 'not much older than Sophie, to try to stop the activities of Michael Whitby.'

'I don't understand.'

'Michael Whitby, in his thirties, twice divorced and with a history of violence.'

'Oh my God!' she said. 'I thought he was a student.'

'No. I'm afraid it gets worse, much worse. He's a police inspector working in the vice squad.'

Sandra stared at me, not knowing quite if his being in the police was a point in his favour or not. 'But if he genuinely cares for Sophie . . .'

'It's not Sophie he wants.'

'What do you mean?' Sandra was now wide-eyed.

'I mean, he targeted Sophie as a healthy young virgin and deliberately got her pregnant so that he could steal her baby.'

'Why? What for?'

'To sell for very large amounts of money.'

Sandra's hand went to her mouth in shock. 'You mean, desperate infertile couples would buy stolen babies?'

'Not knowingly perhaps. Couples have bought babies from China and Romania, but this is worse. At least those children were orphans. They were being offered a better life. There is a suggestion that Whitby's babies go either to rich paedophiles or are used for medical research purposes.'

I could see Sandra's face changing colour to greenish ashen. She ran from the room and I could hear her vomiting in the bathroom. She came back a few minutes later in tears. 'We must call the police.'

I shook my head. 'We have to forewarn Sophie as gently as we can. She'll swear they are a couple in love and that their only crime is in wanting to have a home birth, which, with a qualified, licensed midwife, is perfectly legal.'

Sandra still didn't look convinced.

'I've got some forensic evidence,' I said. 'But if that doesn't hold up, one pregnant girl, even two, willing to be a witnesses may not be enough. He'll be seen as a misguided Jack-the-Lad with the right barrister. Proving he raped girls under the influence of Rohypnol will be hard if he had no complaint laid against him at the time. Especially if, throughout their pregnancies, the women saw him, shared his bed and presumably trusted him.'

'You're telling me she was raped?'

'Yes. Then, when the pregnancy comes as a terrible shock because she remembers so little, he's around to offer emotional and financial support. In Sophie's case it seems he's now offered to marry her.'

Sandra's hands trembled and she began tapping her knee with anxiety. 'This is too much for me to take in.'

'If Sophie is told all this,' I asked, 'how do you think she'll react?'

Sandra looked me straight in the eye. 'She'll have a breakdown. I know she will.'

'How can you be so sure?'

'She tried to kill herself when she was sixteen. She'd met this boy. She decided she was in love with him but he'd only taken her out a couple of times. She declared her love and he ran so fast that his heels nearly caught fire. She took an overdose of paracetamol, only about twelve tablets, but she would have died if I hadn't found her.'

'OK,' I said, reluctantly. 'We'll keep quiet for the moment. I'll just drop in little bits of information about him to sow the seeds of doubt in her mind. She might begin to wonder how much she really does know about him.'

'But he's coming here,' she said. 'Sophie told me the plan was that a week before the birth he'd send for the midwife and she'd ring him when necessary.'

'Yes,' I said, thoughtfully.

'What are we going to do?'

'I really don't know.' I didn't want to tell her yet that I intended to lure him out of his lair. Once out in the open, perhaps he'd show his true colours. If he suspected there was an entourage waiting, he might well go to ground.

As if to compound my own general feeling of nervous indecision, Sophie came out of the bedroom then, saying, 'Can we go back to our place now? I'm starving.'

'Have you seen the blizzard?' asked Sandra sharply. 'It's worse now than when we came down here. Weather permitting, we'll go back in the morning.'

I volunteered to make some toasted sandwiches and I was grateful for the time alone in the kitchen. I stood watching two hard-boiled eggs bob beside each other for nearly ten minutes. My theory, over the egg-watching, was that if she said she was in labour, Whitby would catch the next train or he'd drive. Either way, he could be here by tomorrow evening. In the morning, whatever the weather, I was walking into Macken to buy a new phonecard. I needed Hubert and he needed to know that I needed him. In the meantime, we had to stay put and hope that Sophie didn't go into labour.

Thankfully, after my toasted sandwiches, Sophie decided to go to bed. She'd taken a liking to mine, so off she went.

'We're sharing the double, then, Sandra.'

'I won't sleep a wink. I'm worried sick. Is there anything else you're not telling me?'

I hesitated. Sandra seemed to have aged in hours. She frowned often and when Sophie was around she avoided looking at her. She also seemed near to tears. If it was having this effect on her, it was anybody's guess how Sophie would react. The one person who could perhaps help her was Megan, someone of her own age who'd had a similar experience.

We watched the weather forecast on TV in silence. Blizzard conditions would last overnight but the gale-force winds should have eased by morning. There would be snow flurries for a day or so but temperatures were expected to rise slowly as the week progressed.

Sandra had more than the weather on her mind. 'This history of violence you mentioned . . .'

'Yes?'

'Forget it,' she said hurriedly. 'I don't want to know.'

I banked up the fire with more logs and hoped they would last until morning. Then we sat by the fire trying to ignore the howling winds outside and I tried to get Sandra to talk about her life in Spain. She made an attempt but every so often she couldn't help but mention Sophie. 'I should have insisted she came to Spain with me,' she said. 'I really wanted her to live with me but she thought the art college in London would be superior to anything in Spain. I suppose she wanted a bit of freedom . . . If I hadn't been so selfish . . .'

'It's not your fault. Do you know where she met him?'

'She said it was at a party. She didn't give me any details.'

We watched TV without speaking for some time but, every so often, Sandra sighed. I hadn't yet told her about my suspicions that the woman in the cabin above theirs was guilty of harbouring a stolen baby. With too much information, Sandra was likely to go into overload. With all that had gone on, Sandra had forgotten that I'd mentioned my *acquaintance*. There was no doubt that she would eventually remember but I decided to wait for her to ask first.

In the lull between loud gusts, I heard a different sound. At first I thought it was on TV, so I turned down the volume, but then I heard it again. A soft squelchy swish. The sound of tyres on snow.

CHAPTER TWENTY-THREE

Sandra stood up abruptly. 'It's him, isn't it?'

'I don't know,' I said. 'It might be, but for God's sake don't go near the windows. Don't let him see you.' I was also on my feet now, activated by fear, revved up as if someone had just switched me on. 'Stay still,' I said. 'Don't move.' We waited for the knock at the door but none came. We could hear the car's engine start up, the tyres whirring and then, apart from the low moaning of the wind through the trees, there was silence. I went to the window and pulled aside the curtain just a fraction. The car had stopped not far from the porch and, although I couldn't see anyone, there were footprints, visible black patches on white. 'Sandra — I have to go. I can't explain but I need to know where that driver is going and what he's planning to do.'

'I'll come with you,' she said.

'No — you must stay with Sophie. She might need you. I'll be OK. I'll need a torch though.'

'There was one in our cleaning cupboard. You should have one too.'

I rushed into the kitchen and found a heavy-duty torch and a spade next to a floor brush in the cupboard. I handed Sandra the spade. 'Use this if you have to.' She looked at me as if I'd gone mad but took it without a word. I threw on as many clothes as I could and draped myself in a throw. With her *Be careful* ringing in my ears, I emerged into the blizzard. I'd slipped a sharp carving knife into my pocket, not for protection, but to slash the car's tyres. I'd never done such a thing before but if someone was planning to take the baby away I wasn't going to make it easy for them. I looked up once as I worked and could see Sandra's horrified face as she glimpsed the knife in my hand. Was she wondering if I was kosher? Would she turn against me when I returned?

I finished my first act of vandalism feeling relieved that I had at least been proactive. As I walked I tried to ignore my cold wet feet but the effort of breathing in the sharp air really sapped my energy. The wind destabilized me and I fell over twice and even as I scrabbled to my feet the thought was there — *What are you going to do when you get to the cabin*?

As I approached Sophie's cabin I stopped, wondering if they had bothered to lock the door. They hadn't and I walked in to shelter for a few minutes. It took me a while in the warmth of the room to breathe normally again and I was surprised at how exhausted I felt. The fire was still smouldering and I slipped off the wet throw and my damp jacket. At least I could borrow one of their throws.

I still had no plan and I could only guess that the man, whoever he was, had come to either take the woman and baby away or just the baby. The latter seemed the least likely scenario, so, if I did have to make a stand, it was going to be two against one — plus the fact that I wouldn't be able to risk harm to the baby. Whilst I fretted about my non-existent plan of action, I began looking around. Sophie could have letters or a diary and, although it seemed underhand, all was fair, I reasoned, where a baby's life hung in the balance. I began rooting through drawers and cupboards. There was no sign of a diary until I remembered where I kept mine when I was young, because if I hadn't made my own bed my mother certainly wouldn't, so it would be perfectly safe either under my pillow or under the mattress. I searched Sophie's bed and found not a diary but a mobile phone. There it sat, under her pillow alive and well. The stupid little . . . I stopped. She was misguided but, more to the point, at the first twinge she would have rung Whitby. I clutched the mobile to me as fervently as if it was a religious icon and then pulled back the curtains so that I could see if anyone passed by. Surely, I thought, no one but a total maniac would attempt to walk a baby through this sort of weather. But who was this man I'd followed? Sandra had immediately assumed it was Whitby. But was it perhaps an underling, sent merely to transport the surrogate mother and Megan's baby to another location? Or could it be Whitby himself, intent on moving mother and baby, then returning to cope with Sophie.

I rang Hubert immediately. 'Why didn't you ring?' he asked. I hadn't got time for explanations so I started to give him my address.

'I know where you are,' he said. 'I've been in touch with David and I got your letter. He was worried when you didn't phone. He's on his way to you now.'

'Is he fit to drive?'

'No. He's just keen on you.'

I ignored Hubert's blatant attempt to make me think David Todman was the answer to my life's problems. 'How's Megan?' I asked.

'She's fine. Now, don't move from there, Kate. Stay exactly where you are. Lock the door. Barricade yourself in. I'll drive up. I should be there by morning.'

I didn't say that the morning could be too late. I was grateful to them both but, when the cavalry arrive, you need them in time for battle, not when the enemy has fled the scene.

There was no point in my hanging around in the comfort of Sophie's cabin, so I donned my jacket, a dry throw and a scarf that I found in Sophie's room. Then I braved the elements again. The snow still fell but it was much lighter and the gale-force winds had dropped to occasional gusts. My torch guided me ahead into the blackness and it was only when I stopped with a stitch in my side that I lowered my torch and saw, there in the snow, footprints, two sets going downwards together. Whilst I'd been sheltering they had sneaked past the cabin.

I started to run downwards but I fell over twice. The second time, I fell badly, twisting my ankle. I dropped my torch and swore loudly as I flailed around trying to find it. Losing the torch almost eclipsed the pain in my ankle. When I did find it, in deep snow, it no longer worked. Dragging my ankle like some foreign appendage, I carried on hobbling downwards. But there was no relief when I did see my cabin.

Outside were parked a police car and a minicab. I hung back. By the light of the open door, Sandra stood with two huge uniformed policemen, one of whom was guiding the couple, *not* to the police car, but to the minicab. The woman was carrying a well-wrapped bundle and a small suitcase. I could now see that the man was not Whitby. He was much younger. The policeman settled them into the cab, then got into the driver's seat of the police car. It didn't take great powers of deduction on my part to recognize he was providing a police escort. I wanted to run out from my hiding place and shout and scream but I knew that would be pointless. When both cars were out of sight I still hesitated. Sandra had probably told the cops I'd slashed the tyres and now he was waiting for me to appear.

I had two options — either try to hobble back to Sophie's cabin or try to convince the cop that the couple were bogus parents. Convincing the cop would, I decided, be the less painful option. I staggered towards the cabin, deciding that bravado and bluff would carry me through. I wasn't going to be arrested for vandalism in a good cause.

The uniformed constable stood easily six foot five and was of proportionate width. It was impossible to guess his age but he looked like a contender for the World's Strongest Man competition and had a face so square it looked as if it had been constructed from a DIY flat-pack. I started on the offensive. 'Why did you let them go?' I demanded. 'That's not her baby. And he's not the father.'

'Aye,' he said. 'And I suppose you didn't slash his tyres.'

'Yes, but only to stop him leaving with a baby that isn't his.'

'You'd better sit down,' he said. I realized by his tone he thought I was a madwoman.

'Officer. I'm a private investigator—'

'Aye. And I'm the High Sheriff.'

'Here's my business card,' I said, as I ferreted in my jacket pocket to no avail. 'I'll find one in the bedroom.' I started to stand up.

'Just stay where you are, lass,' he said. 'As soon as my colleague has escorted them to the hospital, he'll be back and we can sort all this out at the station.'

'Sandra,' I said. 'Tell this Scottish dork what I told you.'

Sandra looked embarrassed. 'It's all so confusing.'

'Well, let's ask Sophie to explain to the officer what she's doing up here, in the middle of nowhere, waiting for a man old enough to be her father.'

'She's asleep.'

'Did you know she lied to you about not having a mobile phone? I found it in your cabin. Which is why help from South of the border is now on its way.' Neither of them knew what I was talking about but my comment was obviously a slur on Scotland.

I could see I'd riled PC 142. His brown eyes were bulging but I was past caring.

'The wee baby is very poorly,' he said gruffly. 'I think you should keep quiet. You can say your piece at the station.'

I wasn't getting very far. I could see that, so I stayed silent and slipped off my wet shoes and rubbed my fast-swelling ankle. No one spoke for a few minutes, then Sandra asked nervously, 'Anyone like a cup of tea?'

We both nodded and, at that moment, Sophie walked in clutching her belly. The eyes of the PC bulged even more. 'What's happened?' she asked, looking at all three of us.

'Nothing for you to worry about,' said Sandra. 'A young mum from one of the cabins has had to take her baby to hospital under police escort . . .' She tailed off as Sophie looked questioningly at the policeman.

Sophie seemed about to query his continuing presence when her face contorted. 'I'm all right,' she said. 'It's nothing. Kate told me it was only practice contractions — they're nothing. Nothing at all.'

The big cop stood up and, taking her arm, moved her towards the armchair. 'You sit down by the fire, lassie. When my partner comes back we'll take you to the hospital.'

She looked up at him defiantly. 'I'm not going to hospital. My fiancé is on his way here now. And Kate is my midwife.'

His answering glance at me made me want to crawl under a stone. I was saved from further questions by his phone handset ringing. He listened intently for some time. 'Do your best, Dougie. Get Control to send a car up here.' He switched off and stared at me. 'Well,' he said. 'Perhaps I should be listening to what you have to say. The minicab drove straight past the hospital and the minicab firm has lost radio contact with the driver. My friend Dougie is in hot pursuit.'

'Is he a good driver?'

'Aye, he's the best.'

'I do hope you're right.'

'What is going on?' asked Sophie. 'It's making me feel sick.'

I was beginning to feel sick too, thinking about them making a getaway.

Sandra walked over and took Sophie's hands. 'Darling, I know you're in love with Michael, but he's not what you think he is.'

'I know he's been married before,' she said, calmly, 'and I know he works in the vice squad. He's been totally honest.'

'Did you ever go to his flat at the Georgiana Hotel?' I asked.

She looked at me sharply, unbelieving.

'I've been there,' I said in a rush. 'I've drunk with him, been sightseeing with him. And so has my client, Megan

Thomas. He found her a job looking after his elderly aunt. He found her a private midwife. She had the baby and she thought she heard it cry but they told her the baby was still-born. Megan managed to run away and, if I'm right, the couple who just left here have Megan's baby with them.'

'That's rubbish,' snapped Sophie. 'You're a liar. You just fancy him yourself. I suppose he took you out once and you thought he was madly in love with you.'

'No. But I did think he wanted to use me as an incubator.'

'What are you talking about?'

'I'm saying he deliberately gets young, healthy women pregnant so he can sell their babies.'

Sophie smiled nastily. 'You might be healthy, but you're not young. You're just jealous because you can't get pregnant. He'll be here in a few hours and then he can put you right. I've read about women like you — stalkers. They get obsessed with a man and they just can't leave him alone.'

'I'll ask you one more question, Sophie,' I said calmly. 'And I want you to be honest. Nearly nine months ago, on the night you lost your virginity, do you remember anything about it?'

She paled almost immediately and tears seemed imminent. Sandra put an arm around her.

'It wasn't Michael — it wasn't him! It wasn't.'

Sophie began to sob quietly but, at the sound of a car drawing up outside, she stopped immediately. We all turned expectantly to the door and in walked another police officer, a sergeant this time. He removed his cap to reveal pure white hair. Without acknowledging us he said to the big cop, 'Well, Hamish — Dougie caught them. The lad had put a knife to the driver's throat but they had to stop at a train crossing and Dougie was right behind them. They left the wee baby in the car and made a run for it. They're in custody now at Dunoon.'

'And the baby's all right?' I asked. He gave me a brisk glance. 'Aye, seems so. She's in hospital being checked out.' He nodded at Hamish. 'A wee word outside.'

Sophie, no doubt feeling that everyone was ganging up against her, said, 'Those people have nothing to do with Michael. It makes no difference. I'm not leaving here.'

The sergeant and Hamish stood outside with the door closed and, although we tried to listen, we couldn't hear a word. When they did come back in, the sergeant surprised us by saying that Sandra should stay in my cabin and Sophie and I should be together in hers. Big Hamish would also be with us until the morning. Sandra would use the mobile to alert us that he was on his way.

'But can't you stay with Sandra?' I asked the sergeant.

'We haven't got the manpower, lass. Hamish will be all you need. I've seen him take three men at once.'

'What do you think, Sandra?'

She shrugged. 'It's OK with me, as long as Sophie doesn't mind.'

'Nobody cares what I think,' she said, petulantly. She turned to me, her expression positively venomous. 'And you,' she said. 'Please don't speak to me again.'

'I'll away then,' said the sergeant, 'and take you three up the top.'

The four-wheel-drive police car drove us easily to Sophie's cabin and, once there, she tried to flounce into her room but it was still a waddle and I had to try to keep a straight face. Any hint of hysterical, backs-to-the-wall bravado soon faded when I looked at Hamish. He wasn't a man for small talk and after checking the windows and doors he said, 'I'll be having a wee nap. Get to your bed, lass.'

In the bedroom I pulled back the curtains. The snow had been replaced by rain and already the white carpet was beginning to dissolve. I kept the curtains open and watched the rain from the bed. It was two a.m. and I knew I wasn't going to sleep. My hearing seemed hypersensitive and, although I heard distinctly every moan of the wind and the drumming of the rain on roof and decking, it was the sounds I didn't hear that worried me. My ears and brain were trying to decipher sounds beyond the immediate noise. In the end

I could stand no more and I pulled the duvet over my head and put my hands over my ears. It was childish, I knew, but it worked and I fell asleep.

What noise did wake me I don't know, but I emerged from the duvet once more hyper-alert. I'd imagined it, I decided, and lay back and waited for sleep to take me. But then I did hear a noise. Sophie was moving around in her room. A drawer closed, then a cupboard door opened. I moved fast, swung open her door. She was dressed, carrying a holdall and with her mobile in her hand. 'Sandra should have that,' I said, as I snatched it from her to read a text message — *I'm outside. Come out.*

I put out a restraining hand but what came next I didn't expect. She socked me straight in the jaw. I reeled backwards and couldn't save myself. I scrambled to my feet as she made for the door, then, just as she was opening the door, she pulled it back and slammed the door full in my face. It caught me between the eyes and I felt blood fill my mouth. I staggered but I managed to open the door to see Hamish and her grappling together. She was biting and kicking and he was reduced to grabbing on to her legs.

Then she screamed loudly, 'Michael! Help!' Seemingly in slow motion, the door opened and a man dressed in black wearing a black balaclava stood outside wielding a gun.

'Let her go, mate, or you'll be singing soprano for the rest of your life.' In the moment of fear for his private parts, Hamish loosened his grip around her legs and she then kicked him hard. As if by divine intervention, or maybe it was the physical activity, Sophie was suddenly bent double with pain. Whitby, whose voice was easily recognizable, grabbed her arm and muttered, 'For Christ's sake, move.' I'd been rooted to the spot but Whitby suddenly looked me full in the face, as if only then realizing I was there. Hamish was by now getting to his feet. The sheer size of him seemed to unnerve Whitby. There was no warning, no *Get back or I'll shoot.* The shot rang out and Hamish was felled like a giant tree. The sheer horror of the moment paralysed me. He raised his gun again but

Sophie's arm flailed out, knocking his aim off-course. 'You stupid bitch,' he shouted, trying to push her out of the door. I dropped to the floor, not knowing if it was a conscious decision or if my legs had just given way. I slithered behind the sofa as another shot rang out.

Sophie then found her voice. 'No, Michael,' she was screaming hysterically. 'No!' I couldn't see what was going on but I heard a slap and then the door slammed shut.

I stayed where I was for what seemed a long time, but probably only a minute or two, and then I crawled over to the unconscious Hamish. Blood was pouring from high in his chest. It took all my strength to turn him into the recovery position. Then I ran into the kitchen for a clean tea towel to stem the flow of blood. I snatched one from the drawer and ran back to kneel down and press hard with one hand and with the other freed his phone from his belt. I rang 999. A woman's reassuring voice answered me. Once she'd taken the address she told me she'd stay on the line until help arrived. I tried to rouse Hamish by talking loudly to him but I wasn't getting any response. 'They're on their way, sweetheart,' the voice said. 'You just hang on.'

It was Hamish who needed to hang on. His pulse was fast and thready. His face ashen, his lips blue-tinged. The bleeding had slowed down and the tea towel was soaked through but my fist was firmly pressed above his right breast and I couldn't let up the pressure. Time stood still. And in that time, Hamish's life seemed to be ebbing away and there was nothing I could do.

CHAPTER TWENTY-FOUR

The operator was still talking to me when the police and paramedics arrived. I felt I shouldn't leave Hamish's side but my hand was removed and, although I struggled to stay put, I was gently moved away as Hamish was intubated and a IV infusion was put up. I recognized the sergeant and he took my arm and began guiding me to the door. It was then that I realized that he was leading me towards the ambulance. 'There's nothing wrong with me,' I was saying.

'You need checking over, lass,' he said. 'You've got a few bruises.'

As I was sat down and strapped into my seat in the ambulance, he said, 'You'll be glad to know they didn't get far. They were clocked for speeding and the lads did a great job — they barely got out of Macken.'

'He didn't try shooting his way out?'

'The bastard fired a couple of shots but the wee girl put up a fight and he lost control of the car and ploughed into a row of parked cars.'

'Is she all right?'

'Aye. A few cuts and bruises but she's on her way to hospital.'

'And him?'

'He'll live.'

'Pity.'

By the time we arrived at the hospital in Dunoon, Hamish looked a little better, but the paramedics were making no forecasts. They wheeled him away and all I could do was cross my fingers.

I was whisked down to X-ray for my skull to be examined for fractures. It seemed to me totally unnecessary but when the young A&E doctor told me I had to stay in at least for one night I was outraged. 'There's nothing wrong with me,' I said. 'I'm fine.'

And I felt fine until I was given a mirror. My forehead was a living bruise, my eyes were turning black and my jaw was swollen. My lips looked somewhat enhanced, as if I'd just had cosmetic surgery but, until then, I'd felt no pain or soreness. Having seen the state I was in, I felt ill and queasy and I stopped arguing.

Once in bed on a ward, I closed my eyes and prayed for all nurses, doctors, carers and catering staff to leave me in peace. But peace is something denied to hospital patients, so I feigned sleep, which made no difference. I was still woken for observations, woken up to ask if I needed painkillers and woken by noisy trolleys with squeaky wheels.

Just as lunch was being placed on my bedside table, Hubert and David, wearing dark glasses, turned up. When he slipped off his glasses to look at me, I could see his face had much improved in two days but he still looked exhausted. They were both surprised at the sight of my face. 'Did that bastard do this to you?' asked David.

'No — I walked into a door and a pregnant eighteen year old socked me one.'

Hubert sat down by my bed and held my hand. 'We'd have been here sooner, only we decided to come by train — there were track problems, snow on the lines, the buffet car ran out of food and the heating failed.'

'No change, then, on British Rail.'

Hubert smiled sympathetically. 'You *are* all right?'

'I won't always look like this,' I said, finding his solicitude worrying. 'I'm fine. How's Megan coping with my mum?'

David had by now settled on the other side of my bed. He was looking at my face as if it were a specimen pickled in formaldehyde. I managed to force a smile. Hubert was hesitating long enough to arouse my suspicions. 'Please tell me my mother hasn't done a bunk?'

'No. She and Megan are getting on really well—'

'Sorry to interrupt,' said David. 'I'll be back.' He'd tried to sound like Arnold Schwarzenegger but his impersonation had failed miserably. Hubert and I exchanged a glance, which only showed how well we tuned into each other's thoughts. 'David's a nice guy,' said Hubert.

'Yes,' I said. 'And one day he'll look great in a pinny, but it won't be at my kitchen sink.'

'As we're talking of kitchen sinks, Marilyn—'

'What's she planning?' I knew by the nervous expression on Hubert's face that he was about to impart delicate news.

'She's so impressed the staff on the ward that they've offered her a job as a care assistant . . . but she's asked if she can look after Megan at home — your home.'

'My place in Farley Wood?' I was stunned, but I wasn't sure if it was caused by the fact that my mother had been offered a job or that she wanted to use my little cottage as a nursing home. 'I'm not being churlish,' I said. 'Well, all right, I am — but Megan won't be on her feet for weeks and I can't see my mother coping.'

'She has so far.'

'Yes. For a few days, but I know she's got as much staying power as frayed knicker elastic.'

David returned to the bedside then, carrying a bouquet of flowers. As he handed them to me, he leant down and kissed my cheek. I was touched and suddenly tearful. 'While you're here,' I said, 'I'd like to see the baby.'

Hubert and David exchanged non-plussed *I'm-male-I-don't-understand* glances. 'The baby they tried to abduct — Megan's baby.'

'You don't know that for sure, Kate,' said David, in tones reserved for wayward five year olds.

So, I responded in character. 'I shall have a tantrum,' I said. 'A really big scream.' I knew this was likely to work. They would do anything to avoid a scene.

No one saw me leave the ward but outside in the corridor was a wheelchair and David insisted I be whisked to the children's ward in it. I had felt dizzy out of bed, so I made no more threats and settled back to be pushed along the corridors.

It was a small hospital, a mere hamlet compared to other hospitals that are as big as a village or a town. The children's ward had only six beds, three of which were empty. Megan's baby had a room of her own. David flashed his warrant card at the young ward sister and she said, 'We've heard all about it. It'll be the talk of Dunoon for years to come.' I stood staring at the sleeping cherub dressed in a pink Babygro. I wanted to say that she was the image of Megan but I couldn't see the likeness. All babies have roundish faces, so, although Megan had a round face, that wasn't conclusive. The baby's eyes opened and the ward sister handed her to me, saying, 'She's a lovely wee girl.' I was surprised and wondered if Megan had misheard or if she would have preferred a boy. If this baby was indeed Megan's. But at that moment it didn't matter. I held her close and murmured to her that she was beautiful. I kissed her soft cheek and smelt her baby smell and nuzzled her wisps of fair hair. I could feel myself getting choked. 'Do you want to hold her?' I asked Hubert and David. They both backed away as if I was offering them some form of alien life. So I held on to her a little longer.

Reluctantly, after a few minutes more snuggling and cooing, I handed her back to the ward sister, who was perhaps beginning to wonder what my connection was with the baby. 'Have the police mentioned DNA testing?' I asked her.

'It's all in hand,' she said, smiling. 'They've been in touch with a hospital in Longborough. I believe a woman there says she is the mother.'

I looked questioningly at David. 'I've explained some of the details to Megan's consultant,' he said. 'The results, he says, will take two weeks.'

Two weeks! I took a last look at the baby, sighed inwardly, thanked the ward sister and was then trundled back towards my ward. As we passed ICU I asked David to work his charm and ask if I could see Hamish.

Hubert and I waited outside in the corridor for some time, watching the various comings and goings of staff and watching the walking wounded slip outside to a designated smoking area for a reviving nicotine fix. I was still people-watching, so I didn't hear when the ICU's door swished open. I just felt David's hand on my shoulder. 'I'm sorry, Kate,' he said. 'They couldn't save him.' Somehow I was shocked that he hadn't pulled through. 'No . . . no . . .' I blurted out. 'He couldn't be — he was so big and strong . . .' I broke off in tears. I found it hard to speak but I managed to ask if he was on his own. Somehow it didn't seem right that he should be alone.

'No,' said David. 'He's not alone. His wife is with him. She's taken it very badly.'

We made a sad pilgrimage back to the ward. His death had really shaken me, for, although Hamish had been a stranger, from the moment he'd been shot, he had ceased to be that. He'd become someone I'd met on life's path, who I would never forget, because, although I'd failed to save his life, I'd been there as it neared its end. Somehow that forged a bridge between us. He was on the river Styx being ferried to the afterlife and I was on the bank waving . . .

'Are you OK?' asked Hubert, anxiously.

'I just want to go home now.'

Hubert, surprisingly, didn't argue but went off to find a nurse. About fifteen minutes later a doctor came to see me and, with a caution about headaches, vomiting etcetera, told me I could go.

David managed to arrange a hire car in an hour, no doubt on the strength of his warrant card and, because I couldn't face going back to the cabin, I agreed to wait whilst Hubert packed my things.

I was sitting feeling desolate by my bed when Sandra walked in. 'I've just heard about the policeman,' she said. 'I'm so sorry — and sorry I half doubted you.'

'Not to worry. None of it was your fault. How's Sophie?'

She sat by my bed and I noticed how jaded she looked. 'She's fine physically,' she said. 'Still getting twinges but they seem to think it could be another week or so before the event. She sends her sincere apologies. She's distraught about hitting you and she's both angry and heartbroken, if you know what I mean.'

'She might need some professional counselling,' I said. 'Especially after the baby's born.'

'She's planning to keep it. I've suggested she comes to live with me in Spain.'

'Will she do that?'

Sandra smiled wistfully. 'I do hope so. I always wanted children but it wasn't to be. I'd love to be involved.'

'She'll need all the help she can get,' I said. 'In fact, I don't think she'll manage without you.'

Sandra stared at me thoughtfully. 'I'm looking forward to it, although in the circumstances I feel guilty about that.'

'Well, don't,' I said. 'A new baby is a gift. A clean slate. You'll forget about . . . all this.'

That probably wasn't true but a new life in a new country was as good a beginning as any.

* * *

On the journey back to Longborough I slept most of the way and, although I was keen to see Megan, Hubert insisted I wait until morning. Being home was wonderful but I felt strangely disorientated and all I wanted was more sleep.

Hubert brought me breakfast in bed and, later on in the morning, he drove me to Longborough General. As I walked into the ward, I noticed there was a change in the atmosphere. Everyone seemed busy. Megan looked up and called out, 'Kate!' Then, noticing that I wasn't looking exactly my best, her voice fell to its usual melodic tone. 'What happened?' Before I could reply, Marilyn suddenly appeared from under a bed.

'Well, pet, you do look a sight,' she said.

'Why were you under the bed?' I asked, noting that she was back in tarty mode, although I had to admit the tight leather trousers and silver spangled tee shirt were more her style than gypsy bag lady. Having said that, the gear she was wearing was more suited to a nightclub. It could one day be her epitaph — *Marilyn Kinsella — Never Quite Appropriate.*

'I was hiding from a porter,' she explained cheerfully. 'He's taken a fancy to me.'

I looked at the elderly ladies in the ward. They were all smiles. One of them, who, the last time I'd seen her, had been comatose, was now grinning wickedly and pointing to my mother. 'She's a real tonic, your mum. She's had us making cards for Bingo today and last night we had a sing-song. Mind you, we got told off.' The others smiled and giggled.

I had to admit grudgingly that the high spirits were infectious. 'If you want a word in private with Megan,' said Marilyn, 'we can wheel her bed to the day room.'

I waved goodbye to the patients and we wheeled Megan out through the ward doors and along the corridor to the day room. Two nurses saw us but merely smiled. Megan going backwards and forwards was obviously not unusual.

The TV was on in the corner of the day room, being *watched* by a sleeping old man. Marilyn winked at me and left.

'Your mum has been great,' said Megan, in the most animated tone I'd ever heard her use. 'She's made us all laugh. Tonight she's—'

'Megan — has anyone taken a mouth swab from you?'

Brought rudely down to earth, she couldn't look me in the eye. 'Yes, they have,' she answered tightly. Then, after a short pause, she murmured, 'You found a baby, didn't you?'

'Yes.'

'I'm so scared,' she said in a whisper. 'If I hope too much and it's not mine, it'll be as bad as if my baby had died again.'

'I know. There should be results in two weeks.'

'That's such a long time to wait,' she said. 'Your mum is trying to get me out of here quickly. She says my bones will heal better away from hospital. She says hospitals are dangerous places that cause malnutrition and infection.'

'Did she tell you that her culinary skills peaked with beans on toast? And her idea of cleaning is to spray polish in the air to give the *impression* of it being clean.'

'I think your mum is a lot more capable than you give her credit for.'

'Maybe,' I agreed reluctantly.

I wanted Megan to show a little more interest in the baby. She'd asked nothing about her. I didn't think that now was the right time to tell her she had a daughter and not a son. But I could understand that, if the baby I'd seen wasn't hers, then she was only trying to spare herself more heartache. Strangely too, she'd not asked about Whitby. I waited for a while but she still didn't ask. Eventually I said, 'Whitby has been charged with murder.'

'My doctor?'

'No, a policeman.'

'I'm sorry about that. What happened?'

'He was shot.'

Her lower lip trembled. 'I don't want to talk about this anymore, Kate. Thank you for all you have done but could you wheel me back to the ward now, please?'

* * *

The first week passed slowly. I walked Jasper and read and ate too much and visited Megan every day. But my visits grew shorter and shorter. My presence seemed to remind her of unpleasantness. With Marilyn she seemed happy and chatty. They did crosswords, played bingo with coloured table-tennis balls in a bucket and with bingo cards made from old

Christmas cards, watched TV and ate chocolate together. I felt excluded and a bit jealous. Marilyn had never given me so much attention. In fact, during my childhood, I'd had more attention from her small army of friends whom she used as babysitters. When I grouched about it to Hubert he wasn't that sympathetic. 'Was she ever cruel to you?' he asked. When I shook my head he asked, 'And did she feed you?' I nodded to that. 'Well, stop moaning. You've turned out OK. You're not Brain of Britain but you've got a career of sorts and, apart from not having a man — which you could have if you glammed yourself up a bit — you should think yourself lucky.'

During the second week, which seemed to pass even more slowly, I spoke to Megan's consultant. He agreed that I could be present when the results came through. He also informed me that it would be possible for Megan to return home if she could be nursed downstairs.

The next day Hubert helped me bring my bed downstairs and I had to admit that I felt a pang as I rearranged my home for Megan. I still worried that my mother would leave the moment she tired of being jolly and caring. I was also concerned that Hubert's torch would be reignited. Once, when she was wearing high-heeled boots, I'd seen the pupils of his eyes nearly explode. They were both at dangerous ages. My mother's life had been one long mid-life crisis but I didn't think Hubert had had his yet. In gloomy moments I saw Hubert selling up, buying an expensive camper van and whisking Marilyn off to a life touring the Mediterranean and buying her expensive Italian shoes and very short leather skirts.

I was, of course, getting edgy about the results of the DNA test. Not that Megan seemed to share my anxiety. She was the happiest I'd seen her. I was the one with disappearing fingernails and a rising desire for cream cakes and chocolate.

And then, on the thirteenth day, the hospital called to say Mr Blenkinsop would like to see me on the ward. Hubert had a large funeral to conduct, so I drove alone to the hospital, sat in the car park until the appointed time and then made my way to the ward. Megan had been wheeled into the day room and I met Mr Blenkinsop in the ward office before we went to join Megan. His expression gave nothing away. Megan, though, was pale and couldn't keep her hands still. 'Well, Megan,' he said. She looked up from her hands only briefly and, in that moment, she looked about fifteen and scared to death. 'I won't bore you with the technicalities. The baby found in Scotland *is*, and I repeat *is* yours.'

She stared at him wide-eyed. 'You're absolutely sure?' she said. 'My baby didn't die?'

'Your baby, a daughter, is alive and well.' He was smiling broadly and I expected Megan to smile back but she didn't — she burst into tears. The consultant looked somewhat confused. I hugged Megan and she cried for some time.

Finally, after much gulping and wiping away of tears, she said, 'That's the first time I've had a good cry since . . . she . . . was taken away from me.'

Mr Blenkinsop, looking increasingly uncomfortable, said, 'I do have some other information, which may or may not be welcome news. The baby's father is not Michael Whitby. He has proved to be infertile. From his medical records it seems he had an operation for prostatic cancer three years ago.'

I heard the words but it took me a few moments to take it in. I didn't know if it was good news or bad. Megan smiled. She obviously thought it was good news. 'Who is the father, then?' she asked.

'We don't know yet,' he said. 'Someone from the Metropolitan Police will be here today to see you both. But, in the meantime, perhaps you'd like to see your daughter.'

Megan's mouth dropped momentarily. 'She? It's a girl? She's here? I can see her?'

'Yes.' He picked up the phone. I didn't hear what he said. I was far too excited. Five minutes later a nurse brought in the baby.

As she handed the baby to Megan, the look of sheer wonderment on Megan's face even caused Mr Blenkinsop's eyes to turn glassy. Megan gently stroked her baby's face with one finger, then the downy hair. Megan's daughter opened her eyes and fixed them on her mother. And in that moment it seemed to me that the baby recognized her. I supposed I was being fanciful, but when their eyes locked and the baby continued to stare at Megan, I knew that a bond was being formed that would never be broken. Finally Megan spoke. 'My hair was that colour when I was a baby. She's so beautiful, isn't she?' Megan didn't need an answer and Mr Blenkinsop indicated that we should leave mother and baby alone.

Outside in the corridor he said, 'I believe you're a trained nurse and you're willing to look after Megan at home.'

'Well, my mother—'

'Ah yes. Quite a character, your mother.'

'Well, social services are quite happy with the idea of the two of you caring for Megan and the baby. Megan should be on her feet in a few weeks and I'm sure she'll be a very competent mother. On that basis she can leave here whenever she likes.'

He shook me by the hand and walked away, leaving me in a state of shock. My mind was reeling: nappies, baby clothes, a cot, bottles, teats — the list seemed endless. How would we cope?

I walked back in to Megan. 'Kate,' she said. 'Would you mind very much if I called the baby Kate — Katie while she's small?'

'I'd be honoured,' I managed to say, trying to keep the tears at bay.

* * *

Hubert, as usual, was a tower of strength. He rang Mothercare and organized all the essentials. 'You'll have to pull yourself together, Kate,' he said, as we took delivery of baby supplies that would last for at least a year. 'And try to get on better with Marilyn. You two arguing and squabbling won't be good for little Katie.'

Megan and the baby were delivered to my house the next day, much to the surprise of the neighbours, who were promptly invited in for drinks by Marilyn. I felt like an onlooker in my own home and I suppose I was jealous it wasn't my baby. Megan's happiness illuminated my small front room and baby slept through the homecoming celebrations.

It was two days later that two male officers of an outfit called SO7 turned up. Thankfully my mother was out shopping at the time. Megan was feeding the baby and their grim faces did soften somewhat at the sight of the bed-bound young mum doting on her new-found baby.

'Whitby is gradually helping us with our enquiries,' said the taller of the two men, who'd introduced himself and partner merely as Harris and King. 'He has been under investigation for some time, although mainly as a drug-running suspect. He's got nothing to lose now, so he's admitted using Rohypnol on several young women — solely for the purpose of impregnating them. However, this was done by artificial means.'

'Could you explain that to me?' I asked. Megan, meanwhile, absorbed in the process of bottle-feeding, seemed oblivious to what they were saying.

'A debt-ridden medical student,' explained Harris, 'was paid a hundred quid for each *contribution*. It seems he didn't ask too many questions and he turned up on request.'

'You're telling me Whitby used a syringe?'

'Yes.'

'But how would he know when these women were at their most fertile? Surely it could take several attempts.'

'More than three, he'd give up. His baby racket had been going on for some time. The women, some of them just girls, would never have come forward. Now he's on a murder charge, everything will come out in the open. And, since he's going inside for life for one murder and two conspiracy-to-murder charges, with the additional charges, he'll never be released.'

'He asked me,' said Megan. We turned towards her in surprise, as she suddenly joined in the conversation now that Katie had finished her bottle and was being burped.

'What do you mean, he asked you?' I queried.

'I was a bit quiet one day and he asked me if it was the time of the month and I said no, I was in the middle of the month.'

Sometimes, I thought, explanations can be that simple. I waited for Megan to ask more questions about the donor but she didn't seem to want to know. It was only after Harris and King had left that she said, 'I'm so glad she's not Whitby's child.'

'A hard-up medical student is definitely a better bet.'

'Yeah,' she said with a huge grin. 'Much better.'

* * *

Two weeks on, Marilyn and I are sharing the workload. Every other night, I sleep at Humberstone's and it seems to be working. All four of us are besotted. How long Megan will want us fussing round I don't know.

One night over a nightcap I confessed to Hubert I was getting so broody I could imagine my ovaries bulging like overripe peas in a pod.

'You're going yampy,' said Hubert. 'Get a grip.'

I knew I wasn't quite normal, because, suddenly, David Todman did seem like a regular guy — honest, reliable, decent and not bad looking. But . . . There was always a but.

'Why are you looking at me like that, Kate?'

'No reason really,' I said. 'I'm just trying to imagine you twenty years ago.'

Hubert stood up. 'I'm off to bed. Your hormones are frightening me. Come on, Jasper, old boy — we males must stick together.'

Jasper stirred slightly from my lap but obviously preferred to stay where he was.

'Still just you and me, then,' I said with a sigh. I couldn't be sure, but I think Jasper sighed too.

THE END

THE JOFFE BOOKS STORY

We began in 2014 when Jasper agreed to publish his mum's much-rejected romance novel and it became a bestseller.

Since then we've grown into the largest independent publisher in the UK. We're extremely proud to publish some of the very best writers in the world, including Joy Ellis, Faith Martin, Caro Ramsay, Helen Forrester, Simon Brett and Robert Goddard. Everyone at Joffe Books loves reading and we never forget that it all begins with the magic of an author telling a story.

We are proud to publish talented first-time authors, as well as established writers whose books we love introducing to a new generation of readers.

We won Trade Publisher of the Year at the Independent Publishing Awards in 2023. We have been shortlisted for Independent Publisher of the Year at the British Book Awards for the last four years, and were shortlisted for the Diversity and Inclusivity Award at the 2022 Independent Publishing Awards. In 2023 we were shortlisted for Publisher of the Year at the RNA Industry Awards.

We built this company with your help, and we love to hear from you, so please email us about absolutely anything bookish at feedback@joffebooks.com.

If you want to receive free books every Friday and hear about all our new releases, join our mailing list: www.joffebooks.com/contact

And when you tell your friends about us, just remember: it's pronounced Joffe as in coffee or toffee!

ALSO BY CHRISTINE GREEN

KATE KINSELLA MYSTERIES

Book 1: DEADLY ERRAND
Book 2: DEADLY ADMIRER
Book 3: DEADLY PRACTICE
Book 4: DEADLY PARTNERS
Book 5: DEADLY BOND
Book 6: DEADLY ECHO

Printed in Great Britain
by Amazon

37055929R00148